I've travelled the world twice over,
Met the famous: saints and sinners,
Poets and artists, kings and queens,
Old stars and hopeful beginners,
I've been where no-one's been before,
Learned secrets from writers and cooks
All with one library ticket
To the wonderful world of books.

© JANICE JAMES.

DEAD MAN'S CANYON

Sundance made a deal with a Baron from the Austrian Court that for $35,000 he would take the nobleman into deadly Apache territory to search for Emperor Maximilian of Mexico's priceless treasure of lost jewels. But before it was over Sundance would face his own death and a score of men's bones would bleach in Dead Man's Canyon.

BRING ME HIS SCALP

Someone wanted Sundance dead, enough to pay eight men to tail him into the hell-hot Texas desert, to risk their lives for one yellow scalp. There was only one way for Sundance to save himself—kill them all!

JOHN BENTEEN

SUNDANCE:

DEAD MAN'S CANYON

and

BRING ME HIS SCALP

Complete and Unabridged

ULVERSCROFT
Leicester

First Large Print Edition
published July 1984

British Library CIP Data

Benteen, John
  Sundance: Dead Man's Canyon; and,
    Sundance: Bring me his scalp
    —Large print ed.
  (Ulverscroft large print series: western)
  I. Title   II. Benteen, John.
              Sundance: Bring me his scalp
  823'.914[F]   PR6052.E/

  ISBN 0-7089-1153-6

Published by
F. A. Thorpe (Publishing) Ltd.
Anstey, Leicestershire
Printed and Bound in Great Britain by
T. J. Press (Padstow) Ltd., Padstow, Cornwall

DEAD MAN'S CANYON

1

ALL day long, he had seen the smokes—Apache sign. This far north, he figured, they were probably made by Tontos, Delt-che's band. But maybe by Chiricahuas or Yavapais, possibly even by Mescaleros from farther east. Right now, every Indian in Arizona Territory was on the warpath, and even though he had lived among the Apaches and spoke their dialects, he kept to cover, taking advantage of every bit of broken ground the desert offered, careful never to expose or skyline himself. Nowadays, whites and Indians alike shot first at strangers and asked questions later.

He was a big man, on a tall appaloosa stallion that he had got in Nez Percé country. He wore a battered sombrero, a red neckerchief, a shirt of fringed buckskin decorated with colorful Sioux beadwork, denim pants, and moccasins. His weapons were the most modern available: an 1866 Winchester rifle across his saddle, a Colt Army revolver converted from cap and ball to metallic cartridges—the same loads as the Winchester—on his hip. Behind it, in a beaded sheath, rode a Bowie with a fourteen-inch blade, especially made by a master craftsman in New Orleans for fighting. Looped to the horn of the big Mexican saddle was a short-handled hatchet, made for throwing. It was a lot of armament, but he had use for all of it and more in his trade; he was a professional fighting man. He called himself Jim Sundance.

The afternoon sun was like a sledge-hammer. Its heat pounded at man and horse alike, so Sundance reined in, swung down, allowed the stallion to rest awhile in the shade of an enormous boulder. Crawling to the crest of a ridge ahead, he reconnoitered. Below, the desert was like the grate of an enormous furnace, clumped with cacti and littered with rock. But, not too far away, shimmering in the heat, there was a mist of green: trees, water, the Agua Fria and Duppa's Station.

Sundance lay motionless, scanning the space between with eyes trained to read the country as a scholar might read a book. His eyes, jet black, did not move as he turned his head slowly from side to side—the Indian way of observing, which would catch any flicker

4

of motion immediately. His face was the color of an old penny, the deep bronze hue of an Indian. His features were Indian, too: high cheekbones, strong beak of a nose, wide thin mouth, hard, solid chin. In startling contrast, the hair that spilled from beneath his hat down to his shoulders was as yellow as freshly smelted gold. The features were his legacy from his Cheyenne mother, the hair inherited from his white father. The combination had made him known from the Missouri to the Pacific coast, from Canada to deep Mexico, the territory he had ranged for more than thirty years.

Smokes still arose from the distant hills, but even he could not be sure of their meaning. They were prearranged signals, changed from time to time, like a military code. He was, however, fairly sure that the way was clear from here to Duppa's. He scrambled back down the ridge, returned to Eagle, the spotted stallion. He tightened cinches, checked the big buffalo-hide panniers behind the saddle in which were stored things of vast importance to him. Then he swung up, touched the horse with his heels. Eagle broke into a dead run from a standing

5

start. The way to cross the open country down there was fast.

Eagle understood that, too. Trained for both war and running buffalo, he stretched himself, hoofs pounding, long stride devouring ground with speed almost magical. Now that blot of green drew closer; a few meager cottonwoods and, beneath it, the outlines of a house. Sundance rode straight up, rifle at the ready, head swivelling constantly; every few seconds, he turned in the saddle to watch his back-trail.

But he made Duppa's station safely, pulled up the lathered appaloosa in the welcome shade. "Hello the house!" he yelled, but the sound of hoofbeats had already brought Duppa out, a Winchester in his hands. He stared, then grinned. "Jim Sundance!" he shouted. "Well, damn my eyes!"

Sundance swung down, and they shook hands. Darrel Duppa was tall and burnt by life in the desert to the tough lean thinness of a slat. He was not much older than Sundance and had shaggy hair, but his narrow, weathered face was clean-shaven. He wore a dirty flannel shirt and grimy denim pants and high black boots; in addition to the Winchester in his hands, he was armed with two

6

Remington pistols on his hips. "Jim, it's good to see you again. Come in the house. My man will take care of your mount." In contrast to the roughness of his appearance, Duppa's voice was cultivated, with a slight English accent.

House was far too grand a name for Duppa's dwelling. Its walls and roof were of branches laced with rawhide thongs to slats and posts of cottonwood, then plastered with adobe. Inside, the floor was of dirt, and tarpaulins and gunnysacks had been hung along the walls to break the wind and catch the sand that blew in through the chinks. Guns, saddles, ropes, and belts of ammunition hung everywhere. In the center of the room, there was a long pine table, unpainted, a couple of benches. Save for some pots and pans around the fireplace at the end, the place contained no other furnishings. Duppa and his two men slept on the floor. So did the dogs that swarmed around the place.

"You must be baked dry." Duppa put out an olla and a dipper, then produced a bottle and two tin cups. "Sit down and drink, Jim."

Sundance swallowed cool water thirstily. Lowering the dipper he grinned at the man. "They haven't run you off, I see."

"Hardly!" Duppa laughed. "Oh, they keep trying, the Apaches, but I'm a stubborn man. I won't let anybody dictate to me where I can live. That's why I settled here to begin with, you know. They hit me at this river crossing, I fought them off, then built this ranch just to show 'em they couldn't frighten me." He poured whiskey, sobering. "But it gets rougher every year. Jim, Arizona's a battle-ground."

"So I've heard. I've been up in Oregon, though, and . . . bring me up to date."

"Things were fairly quiet during the War. The California Column came in, chased out the Confederates, rounded up the Mescaleros and took them to Bosque Redondo over on the Pecos. Put them to farming there, and they seemed happy—until Kit Carson whipped the Navajos and brought them there, too. The Navajos and Mescaleros were old enemies—and the Navajos outnumbered them. So the Apaches left, went back to the mountains.

"The Chiricahuas used to be fairly peaceable. Tried to get along with the whites so they could raid in Mexico and have a place to come home to. Cochise even had a contract to cut wood for the Army."

8

Duppa laughed bitterly. "Then the Army arrested Cochise and his brother on some minor charge, killed the brother. Cochise barely managed to escape with his life. That put the Cherrycows on the warpath. And the Yavapais—they desperately tried to make peace, camped outside Camp Grant for months, while the Army shilly-shallied. Then a bunch of drunken whites and Mexicans hit them without warning, killed dozens, men, women, children—" He shrugged. "And so it's gone. The country's filling up with whites, especially toughs and hardcases run out of California by the vigilantes in the mining camps. The Indians are crowded, game running out; now they figure they have to fight or starve. They're damned good at fighting and not much at starving. So the whole Southwest's in flames. The Army's helpless, the redskins ride rings around them. I understand they've sent a new general in to command the Department in Arizona. But if he's like the rest, he'll do no good."

"George Crook? He ain't like the rest." Sundance sipped whiskey. "I knew him up in Oregon. He's learned Indian ways, taught himself to understand their problems, their

9

thinking. If anybody can quiet 'em down and make peace, he can."

"One hopes so," Duppa said. He took a long gulp of whiskey. Sundance, watching him, felt kinship with him, and not only because Duppa was a superb fighting man. Duppa came from a good English family; wild, a blacksheep, he had been sent away, paid to stay out of England. Sundance's father had been a remittance man, too. The difference was that Duppa had chosen the white man's road. Nicholas Sundance—as he had called himself after adoption into the Cheyenne tribe, giving up his real family name forever—had taken that of the Indians, living among them as a trader, marrying the daughter of a Cheyenne chief. Maybe, Sundance thought, Duppa had been the smarter of the two. At least he wasn't caught between two worlds, white and red.

"What brings you down to Arizona?" Duppa asked, setting down his cup. "Things too hot in Oregon or out on the Plains?"

"Things are hot everywhere," Sundance said. "Sioux and Cheyennes and all the other horse tribes on the warpath, crowded by the railroad, settlers. They've made peace half a

10

dozen times and the Army's broken every treaty."

Duppa nodded. "Jim, there's no doubt about it. The next ten years will decide the fate of the Indians. And between now and then, there'll be a full-scale war from Canada to Mexico."

"That's right," Sundance said. "And—" He broke off, set down his cup, shoved back the bench, sprang up, reaching for his rifle.

Duppa heard it at the same time, leaped to his feet, snatched up his own gun. The two men ran to the door, squinted out across the flats, which shimmered in the heat. Far out there, piling out of a deep draw, came fifteen riders, lashing their mounts—white men, twisting in their saddles to trigger shots. They made the flats, strung out, sending a great dust cloud boiling up behind. In it, Sundance saw more riders emerging from the draw—twenty, thirty of them, hard behind the others. And even at this distance he could see that the men of the second band were Apaches, Tontos.

Sundance whirled. "Duppa! Get your men! As soon as they're in range, we'll have to cover them!"

"Right!" Duppa yelled something; his two

hands came running. Sundance's mouth twisted: they would not be much help as fighting men—an old, lame, bearded cook and a wide-eyed young Mexican boy. The Englishman pointed. "Up there on the rise, Sundance. The stone barricades."

Sundance saw them, heaps of boulders piled up to make defensive firing positions. "Shoot for the horses!" he called out. "They make bigger targets!"

Legging it up the rise a few dozen yards in front of Duppa's house, he kneeled down behind the rocks, found a rest for the Winchester's barrel, dug some extra cartridges from the belt around his waist. The two streams of dust out on the flats were drawing closer together, even as they made straight for Duppa's station. The white men were firing as fast as they could work the levers of their weapons; the Indians were shooting back. Gunfire crackled like the sound of burning sticks, and powder smoke made white clouds like cotton tufts. Three minutes more, Sundance thought, two . . . Then the Apaches would be in range.

Nick Sundance, as a trader, had lived with every tribe of any consequence in the West, had been on good terms with all of them.

More than once as boy and young man, Sundance had spent a summer in a Tonto Apache *ranchería*. Some of those braves down there might have been his playmates, hunting partners, friends. Right now, that made no difference. This was Arizona, this was war, and he knew that if the Apaches took Duppa's station, his hair would go along with that of all the others. He did not intend to lose it. Notching front bead in rear sight, he judged that the Indians now were just within extreme reach of the Winchester. He selected his target: a brave on a white horse riding in the forefront. For a moment, the gunsight covered the man's head, then Sundance dropped it lower, squeezed the trigger.

The slug caught the horse in the chest, killed it instantly. It fell like a rock, its rider sprawling. The mounts of two more Tontos, pounding hard behind it, hit the carcass, went down in a plunging tangle.

Now Duppa and his men were firing, too. Another horse went down, another. Sundance worked the lever of the Winchester, sent slug after slug lancing across the flats. Some missed, but most connected. Men and animals fell; and the fusillade had its effect. Under that hail of lead, the Apaches checked,

13

sheered off, galloped hard out of range. Behind them, on the flats, the corpses of men and horses were dusty blots.

That was the slack the pursued whites needed. They quit shooting, bent low in the saddle, lashed their mounts. Sundance, Duppa and the others continued to lay down a covering fire. The Apaches spread out, galloped into it again, lost another man, turned back once more. They dismounted, knelt, fired at the fleeing riders. One white man threw up his arms, pitched from his saddle, was dragged foot-in-stirrup for a dozen yards, then came loose, lay motionless on the dun-colored sand. The others, riding hard, gained the safety of Duppa's station.

They pulled up in a cloud of dust, lather flying from their horses, swung down. Sundance saw a big man with a carbine in his hands snap orders. "Jimson! You and Bailey hold the horses! Rest of you, spread out, them bastards come in again, blow the hell out of 'em." He pitched down on the ground, lined his rifle. He was handsome, red-bearded, in black sombrero, blue shirt, leather shotgun chaps. A bandolier of rifle cartridges was slung across his barrel chest, and big Chihuahua spurs jingled on his heels.

14

The Indians mounted, came again. Now, though, nearly twenty rifles sent a sheet of lead across the flats. Beneath the roar of guns, Sundance heard the big man laugh with the sheer joy of battle. Two more Apaches went flying off their mounts, landed like sacks of meal; again the Tontos whirled, fell back out of range.

Out there, beyond gun-shot, they conferred. Sundance smiled coldly, side-loading more cartridges in the Winchester. As well as if he stood among them, he knew what they were saying, what would happen next. Apaches were different from the Plains Tribes. A warrior of the Plains Indians fought for glory, was happy to die in battle, become a hero. Not Apaches. They fought for loot, always counted the odds. To an Apache, a man who threw his life away for nothing was a fool; their heroes were the braves who brought in the most plunder with the least risk.

Right now, Sundance thought, they were tallying up the odds. Although they still out-numbered the men at Duppa's station, the defenders had the edge. They knew Duppa, too, knew what a demon he was in a fight, how cool and clever and ruthless he could be.

Sundance's eyes counted corpses. Six dead

15

men lay out there. He was not surprised when, suddenly, six warriors broke from the band and bent low in their saddles, suddenly charged back into gun-range. "Let 'em have it!" the red-bearded man roared; and his bunch resumed firing.

Sundance raised his head: "Hold it!" he bellowed. "They're only picking up their dead!" But his words were lost in the fusillade, and he could only hold his breath and watch admiringly, as those warriors rode into the teeth of that storm of lead, retrieved the bodies of their comrades, rode out again. One man was wounded in the foray, but he made it to safety, clinging to his mount's mane.

Then it was over. The Apaches whirled, galloped off, headed for the draw out of which they'd come. The dust cloud they raised swirled, obscuring them. When it faded, they were gone. Suddenly the desert was very still. Above, vultures were black specks, already gathering to feast on horse meat, and on the body of the white man which still lay sprawled out there.

Duppa arose, dusting off his shirt. "That does it," he said. "They're gone. They won't come back."

The red-bearded man got to his feet, spat into the dust, squinted out across the desert. "Wish to hell they would. I'd kill me some more redskins. All right, boys, on your feet. You're Duppa, huh?"

"I'm Duppa." Then Sundance came up. "This is Jim Sundance."

Red-beard frowned. "Sundance? An Injun name, and—halfbreed?"

"That's right," Sundance said thinly.

"Well, I'll be damned. Duppa, I thought you hated Injuns. And here you got one in camp!"

Duppa sucked in a long breath. "Sundance is my friend. He helped save your hide. Suppose you tell me who you are, what happened."

"Shore. My name's Gannon. They call me Red."

Sundance saw Duppa stiffen. "Gannon, I've heard of you."

White teeth gleamed in Gannon's dusty beard. "I reckon a lot of people have." He jerked his head. "These here are my boys."

"Gannon's Wolves," Duppa said. Sundance noticed that he still gripped his Winchester.

"They call my crowd that sometimes. But don't worry, Duppa, we won't give you no trouble. You got nothin' here we want, and even if you did, every man in Arizona would be on our tail if we did harm to Darrel Duppa; I got sense enough to know that."

Duppa let out a long breath. "I've always had the policy that any man could find sanctuary at this station. I'll hold with that for you, Gannon; but if there's any trouble, Indians or no, you ride on. Peaceable travelers are one thing, outlaws are another."

Gannon's grin faded. "Who says we're outlaws? Okay, maybe we're wanted in California. But there's no warrants out against us here in Arizona."

"At the rate you're going, there will be soon," Duppa snapped. "I've heard too many stories of stagecoaches robbed, wagon trains ambushed."

"Injuns, all Injuns, and people put the blame on us." Gannon's grin was sardonic; he spat again. Then his blue eyes went hard. "It works both ways, Duppa. We got you outnumbered. Don't you give us any bad time, neither, if you know what's good for you. We'll be peaceable as long as you are; come mornin', we ride out to Tucson. All we want tonight's water and a place to sleep. We've got our own grub."

"All right," said Duppa. "We'll leave it at that. Come in the house." He hesitated. "Don't you want to go out and bring in that body?"

Gannon snorted. "Charlie Jakes? To hell with him; he was never any account nohow. Let the buzzards have him."

"Then I'll send out my own men. He'll have a decent burial," Duppa said.

"Suit yourself," Gannon said. "Don't expect me to dig. Christ, I'm dry! Duppa, you got any whiskey?"

"Not enough to go around," Duppa said, and Sundance knew instantly that he was lying.

"Makes no difference. We got some of our own, but it's lousy rotgut. Come on, boys. Bailey, you and Jimson see to the animals. Rest of you, let's git out of this sun."

Duppa held back as they filed into the house, spurs jingling. Sundance stood beside him. "Jim," he said quietly, "we've got to watch that bunch. Gannon's a bad lot. Used to be a member of the Hounds, the waterfront gang in San Francisco. They ran him out of California, he came here, built up a bunch of drifters and gunmen. He's right, nobody's pinned anything on him here yet, but he's

19

dangerous as a rattlesnake, and he'd cut his own mother's throat for a 'dobe dollar. Don't turn your back on him."

Sundance laughed softly. "Didn't aim to."

Duppa sighed. "It's going to be a long night. I'd almost rather have the Indians."

2

OUTSIDE, coyote howls mixed with the mournful cry of a big lobo wolf. Occasionally, fights broke out among the scavengers feasting on the dead horses of the Indians, and even at this distance the snapping, snarling, barking was audible. Inside Duppa's house, a fire crackled against the desert chill, and Gannon's men, except for a few on guard, were ranged around it, while Gannon sat with Sundance and Duppa at the table.

The red-bearded man had been drinking steadily from a bottle of raw whiskey. The cartridges in his bandolier winked in the firelight and their brassy glitter matched the gleam in his pale eyes. "We was comin' down from Prescott," he said thickly. "Figured on makin' your station and Phoenix all in one haul. Seen the smokes, allowed we was strong enough to stand 'em off if they hit us. But even with all of us keepin' our eyes peeled, damned if they didn't hit us by surprise. One minute, nothin'. Next the whole damn

21

canyon full of them red bastards." He laughed hoarsely. "Well, there's six or eight ain't gonna pull a trigger again in this life. Wish I could wipe 'em all out!"

Sundance, at the table's end, said nothing. With a whetstone, he was carefully sharpening knife and hatchet. Gannon shoved the bottle across the table. "Here, halfbreed. I don't include you in that, because you helped save our skins. Have a drink."

Sundance looked up, lean face expressionless. The firelight struck gleams from his yellow hair. "No, thanks," he said tersely and the whetstone went on making its squeaking sound as it slid across steel.

Gannon's eyes changed, went cold. His mouth thinned. He sat up straight. "What's matter? You think you're too good to drink with me?"

"That might be it," Sundance said. He was a patient man, Indian upbringing had bred that into him. But there was a temper within him, too, fierce as a ravening wolf, and though he had taught himself to keep it chained, there were times when it took every ounce of will to hold it. When it finally went, he smashed, killed, the object of his anger. He did not like to kill except for a reason, an

22

urgent reason, and a quarrel with a drunk was not one. Still, Gannon rasped him, had all night long. He fought back anger. "But the main reason is that I can't take much whiskey. Two drinks are my limit, and I've had those. More, and I get mean."

"Like all Injuns." Gannon laughed again, but his handsome face had no mirth in it. "Okay, halfbreed, suit yourself."

Sundance laid down the knife, picked up the hatchet. "My name is Sundance," he said.

"I don't give a damn what your name is." Gannon drank again.

The wolf howled again, outside. Duppa had been cleaning his revolver in lantern light. Now he poked brass caps on the nipples of the cylinder, laid the gun on the table so its barrel pointed toward Gannon. "Gannon," he said, "ease off. You're getting out of line."

Gannon stared at him. "What?"

"So you don't know Jim Sundance, eh?" Duppa's voice was soft. "Maybe if you did, you'd pull in your horns." He laid one big hand over the Colt, still pointed at Gannon. "Jim won't talk about himself, but let me tell you—"

"Darrel," Sundance said.

"No. He ought to hear."

Sundance ran his hand over the ax's blade. "Suit yourself." He turned away, went to the fire. Gannon's men stared at him as he edged between them, poured himself a cup of coffee.

"His father came to America in the beaver days," he heard Duppa say as he straightened up. "A man of education, cultivation—one who had been a soldier, served with distinction in His Majesty's Army. He liked the way the Indians lived, the freedom, the simplicity. That's why he married a Cheyenne woman, was adopted into the tribe. He got the name Sundance because he was the first white man ever to participate in the ceremony. It's the big religious ritual of the Plains Indians."

Gannon spat on the dirt floor, took out a cigar, bit off its end. "He's just another halfbreed to me."

Duppa's grin was cold. "Old Sundance traveled among all the tribes, was known, respected, traded with them all. Jim's lived with all of them, speaks their languages, knows their ways. They respect him, too."

Gannon only rolled the cigar across his mouth.

24

"If you're smart, you won't tangle with him," Duppa said.

"That's enough, Darrel." Sundance came back to the table.

"No, let me go on." Duppa leaned forward. "One little instance, Gannon. It was a long time ago, outside Bent's old fort. Six men—three Pawnees, three white toughs . . . they caught Nick Sundance and his wife out on the plains; when Jim found his parents, they were dead."

"Darrel!" Sundance snapped.

Duppa went on, disregarding him. "Six men, Gannon. Jim struck their trails, alone. It took him a year to run down all of them. But he did it." Duppa gestured toward the bullhide bags from behind Sundance's saddles. "Their scalps are over there right now."

Gannon's eyes shuttled to the bags, then to Sundance's face. "White men's scalps?"

Sundance said, "Murderers' scalps. Darrel, hush." Duppa had been drinking a little, too; his tongue was loosened. He paid no attention to Sundance. "After that, Sundance drifted. The War came, he fought with the bushwhackers and Jayhawkers in Missouri and Kansas for the hell of it. A tough school, Gannon. Only the best gunmen came out of it alive. That's why I say, don't crowd Sundance. He can take you apart with rifle, pistol, knife, or any other weapon you might choose. Including bow, arrows, lance or tomahawk. So you've been warned, Gannon."

Sundance picked up the hatchet, sheathed it. "Darrel, you talk too much."

"Not in this case," Duppa said and shot Sundance a significant glance. Then Sundance understood. Duppa, himself, the old man and the Mexican boy against a man like Gannon and thirteen or fourteen hardcases. And Duppa had said Gannon was treacherous as a rattlesnake. Duppa was afraid that Gannon might turn against them; he was the sort, Sundance judged, who killed for the love of it, wouldn't hesitate—if he thought he could get away with it—to cut the throats of all of them for their gear, horses, and whatever money they might have. Duppa wanted him to know what kind of men he'd be up against if that notion struck him.

But everything that Duppa had said was having an opposite effect. Gannon ran his gaze over Sundance curiously, taking in the more than six feet of height, the wide, sloping shoulders beneath the buckskin shirt, the deep chest, the long, hard legs; and Gannon's eyes, muddy with drink now, also were lit with challenge. The knife Sundance had been sharpening still lay on the table. Now Sundance picked it up.

"Don't start with that damn whetstone again," Gannon rasped. "The sound of it gits on my nerves."

"I'm through," Sundance said. He was about to sheathe the knife when he saw the flicker of motion on the wall, ten feet away. A vinegaroon, a big scorpion, had crawled out from beneath the gunny sacking that covered the wattles. Sundance smiled faintly. His hand hardly seemed to move, but suddenly the thrown knife gleamed in the firelight. Its blade chunked into the wall. Split, impaled, the scorpion twisted frantically, lashing with its venomous tail. Then it died.

Sundance went to it, pulled the knife, and the creature dropped.

Duppa, understanding the gesture, smiled. "See what I mean, Gannon?"

Sundance kicked the dead scorpion aside, wiped the blade on the sacking, put it in its beaded sheath. Gannon's eyes followed the gesture. "You're fast with that. Good with it." He poured more whiskey, drank deeply. Then he leaned back on the bench, looked at

Sundance, and his mouth twisted beneath his beard. Then his own hand moved, a blur. Suddenly a knife whistled past Sundance's head, missing it by a fraction of an inch, thudded into the wall beyond. "But you ain't the only one," Gannon said.

Duppa jumped to his feet. "Gannon, that's enough!" His face was furious.

"Hell, if I'd meant to hit him, I would have." Gannon shoved back the bench, rose. He was nearly as tall as Sundance, perhaps even longer in the arms. His chest was bigger, a great barrel, but there was a softness in his paunch which Sundance lacked, and his legs were shorter. He stood there with hand dangling by his holster. "Bring me my knife, halfbreed."

Sundance stood motionless.

"Goddammit, *move* when a white man talks!"

That wolf within Sundance fought furiously to get loose. He exerted every ounce of will to check it. "Sure," he said quietly, and went to the wall, tugged the blade free, a Bowie like his own. Then the wolf got loose. Suddenly he threw the knife. It landed hard, point embedded in the wood, hilt quivering, in the table in front of Gannon's belly. Gannon jumped back.

"There," Sundance said quietly. But he'd had enough of Gannon now; the man seemed to shimmer in a red haze that danced before his eyes. Suddenly he went to the table, took Gannon's bottle, drank long and deeply from it, set it down. The raw whiskey seized him at once, heightened what was building in him.

Gannon's face twisted furiously, then smoothed itself in satisfaction. Gannon had finally found what he sought. He reached out slowly, took the bottle. Then, with great ostentation, he poured the whiskey on the floor. "I wouldn't put that to my mouth," he said, "now an Injun's drunk out of it."

Duppa made a sound in his throat. He swung to the wall, and when he whirled away, he held a double-barreled shotgun. "Gannon," he roared. "Stand hitched! This thing's loaded with nine buckshot to the barrel!"

Gannon did not move or speak. Duppa went on furiously: "Damn your eyes, Sundance was my guest before you came. He helped save your dirty skin from Indians. And all night long you've done your best to insult and taunt him." He broke off, breathing hard. "Take off your gun, Gannon!"

"I don't do that for nobody, Duppa."

"You'll do it for me, or you'll get blown to hell—and any of your men that makes a wrong move." Duppa's breath rasped in the silence of the room. "Jim, you disarm yourself, too. There's moonlight outside, plenty of it. You want a try at Sundance, Gannon, you'll get it. But not with guns or knives. Try him with your hands!"

Suddenly Gannon grinned. "Maybe I'll do that, Duppa. And when I'm through, I have business with you." His eyes fastened on Sundance's black ones. "What about it, halfbreed?"

Sundance felt a leap of exultation. The whiskey had him in its grip now; he wanted nothing more than to get his hands on Gannon. He unlatched his gunbelt. Gannon was doing likewise. His men got to their feet. Gannon said, "Stand fast, boys. This is between me and halfbreed here. I'm gonna chop him into cowbait. I don't want Duppa hurt. I'll deal with him myself, later, when I'm through with the redskin."

Sundance put down knife and hatchet. "Come on, Gannon." He strode outside. The night wind was cool on his face; as Duppa

30

had said, the moon rode high, and the sandy level ground before Duppa's house was flooded with silver light. Gannon came after him, and the others crowded out, too. Duppa, holding the shotgun ready, said: "All right. It's between the two of you, no holds barred. But any man that reaches for a gun gets blasted."

Gannon laughed. "Cold day in hell when I can't take a redskin with my fists." Then, with no warning, he came at Sundance.

Through the red mist of rage, his contorted face swam in Sundance's vision. Sundance had a half second to judge Gannon's style, back off. Then Gannon was after him ferociously, aggressively, full of killer instinct, hard fists flailing. Sundance got up his guard just in time to shunt fists off his arms and shoulders, weave his head aside so Gannon's whistling blow just passed his ear. Gannon was fast, savage, furious, and the force of his battering fists sent Sundance rocking back, though they did not hurt him. Gannon did not slow, kept coming in. At the same time, he jerked up a knee. Sundance saw it coming, caught it with the hard muscles of his thigh. Then he landed a blow on Gannon's jaw.

Gannon grunted, but with miraculous

speed seized the opening Sundance's swing gave him; his own fist smashed in, chopping Sundance's mouth. Sundance's head jerked back; and in that instant Gannon hit him in the belly and, before Sundance could recover, had crowded in, and now his thumbs were in Sundance's throat.

Sundance's head swam, but a wild joy rose in him. Even as Gannon tried to crush everything inside his neck, he swung his arms wide, brought both fists in like sledgehammers. The blows caught Gannon in the kidneys, and his choking hold on Sundance's throat relaxed; he tried to knee Sundance in the groin again. Sundance blocked that try as he had the first and hit Gannon in the kidneys once more, but Gannon butted and rammed with his head and caught Sundance beneath the chin. Sundance almost went out; his knees sagged. Off balance, he fell. He heard Gannon's grunt of triumph, and then he was on his back and Gannon was on top of him, this time trying to get thumbs in his eyes.

Sundance rolled, got slack, and it was his knee that came up now, and it caught Gannon unprotected. Gannon moaned with agony, but he raised his hands, clubbed his fists, struck down at Sundance. Sundance grabbed his wrists. The red-bearded man twisted, and they rolled over and over on the moonlit sand. Gannon's thighs came up to lock Sundance in a scissor-hold; Gannon squeezed, and Sundance snorted with pain. He butted his own head into Gannon's face, heard Gannon gasp. His hair was wet with blood from Gannon's smashed nose when he jerked his head back. Gannon wriggled away, brought up a booted foot, got it between them, planted it in Sundance's belly, shoved. That broke the halfbreed's hold on Gannon's wrists; the two men rolled apart, rebounded, were on their feet in the same instant. Both were insane with fighting fury, neither hesitated; they ran at each other, and then it was a slugging match.

Sundance took punishment and felt it. Fists on flesh filled the night with a sodden rhythm as he and Gannon slugged it out. Both men were powerful, both were tough. Gannon's blows rocked Sundance's head, exploded fireworks behind his eyes. But he dealt back the same, feeling his knuckles ache with their impact on Gannon's jaw.

Less than a minute of that was all flesh and blood could stand. Panting, Gannon and

Sundance backed off from each other. Gannon stood, barrel chest heaving, smashed nose pouring blood, eyes gleaming. His fists had opened an old scar on Sundance's cheek, and blood sluiced over coppery skin. But there was a difference between them, now, and Sundance caught it. Gannon was hurting and could not deal with hurt as Sundance did. Indian trained, Sundance was like an animal, ignored pain, refused to be frightened by it. But Gannon felt enough of it so that he was afraid of feeling more; he was distracted by it. And that, Sundance realized in triumph, was going to make the crucial difference. He summoned all his strength to go after Gannon again.

When he lunged, even though Gannon raised his hands, Sundance saw fear flicker in his blue eyes. Sundance laughed, went in hard and mercilessly, and scarcely felt a blow that should have knocked him sprawling. He took it to give Gannon two like it; his right came over and then his left came up. They made sounds like a butcher's chopping with a cleaver. Gannon's head snapped back, then rocked around. Sundance gave him not a second to recover, kneed him, slugged him in the belly. Gannon cried out, bent forward.

34

Sundance brought up a right upper-cut—again that butcher's cleaver sound. Gannon moaned softly and his knees buckled. Sundance was lost in the red mist of fury, caught up in savage triumph. He grabbed Gannon by the slack of a bloody shirt, jerked him upright with his left hand, hit him again with his right. And again, and again and again.

Then Duppa's fingers dug savagely into his shoulder.

"Sundance, for God's sake! The man's out, don't kill him. I'll not have him killed here at my station! Sundance!"

Sundance flung out an arm, making Duppa stagger back. Then Sundance hit Gannon again. Gannon was dead weight in his grasp. He laughed, let him drop, stared down at him, sprawled senseless on the sand. He was about to straddle him and choke him when he felt the cold barrels of Duppa's shotgun in the back of his neck. "Jim, that's enough. Up."

Duppa's voice was as much cold iron as the weapon. A shaft of reason pierced the red fog in Sundance's brain. "All right," he heard himself say, and his voice seemed to come from very far away. He got to his feet, stepped back, moccasins whispering in the sand. "All right, Darrel."

Duppa let out a long breath. "That's better, Jim." Sundance saw him swinging the shotgun to cover Gannon's men again. "Nobody moves, nobody takes up the quarrel. It's over, understand?"

There was silence. Then a man with a black mustache spat a stream of tobacco juice, stepped forward. His face was weathered; he wore a concho-silvered Mexican sombrero, a red shirt, greasy canvas pants, high boots and big silver spurs. Two Dragoon Colts were slung on his hips.

"I'm Jessup, Red's major-domo," he said. "He and I run together a long time, Duppa. All right, you kept the halfbreed from killin' him, that stands in your favor." He looked at Sundance. "But you . . . Once we leave here, you'd better not cross our trail again."

Sundance, chest heaving, shoved back blond hair that had fallen over his eyes. "Maybe you'd better not cross mine," he rasped.

"Enough!" Duppa snapped. "Jessup, take him inside, patch him up. Come daylight tomorrow, you ride. All of you, whether Gannon's fit or not."

Jessup nodded coolly. "That's what we'll do. We got business in Tucson." His eyes went to Sundance again. "A place you'd do damned well to stay out of, 'breed."

Sundance looked at him and laughed. "As a matter of fact," he said, "that was where I was going, too." Then he turned away and staggered into Duppa's house where he washed his face in cold water and buckled on his gun again, as Gannon's men lugged his limp body in and laid it by the fire.

The sound of a crowing rooster—one of Duppa's game chickens—awakened Sundance. He came bolt upright, not used to sleeping past sun-up, but the cabin was flooded with daylight. Like an animal, the moment his eyes were open, he was fully awake. Remembering Gannon, his hand went to the holstered Colt by the saddle he used as a pillow. Then, looking around, he relaxed. Duppa's house was empty; Gannon and his men were gone.

Sundance arose, wincing inwardly at the pain it cost him. His face was cut and swollen; cold water would take care of that, and of the bruises on his body. But he knew he'd been in a fight. He slipped into his moccasins, buckled on gun belt, knife and hatchet. As he latched the belt's tongue, Duppa entered, carrying a wooden pail of water in one hand, a rifle in the other. At Duppa's station, nobody ever went outdoors without a gun.

Duppa set the bucket on the table. "Morning, Jim."

"Darrel. Where's Gannon and his gang?"

"Rode on at dawn. *They* rode, that is; Gannon was tied to the saddle. That was a terrible beating you gave him. Henry? Henry! Some breakfast for Mr. Sundance."

The gimpy oldster scurried in, crouched before the fireplace. "Right away, Mr. Duppa." He rattled pans.

"Any Indian sign outside?" Sundance asked.

"None. The Apaches have gone off to look for easier pickings. Everything's calm."

"Good. While breakfast's cooking, I'll take a wash in the river."

"Not a bad idea," Duppa said. "I'll join you."

There was not much water in the Agua Fria, but enough to bathe in. Sundance, brought up in a Cheyenne camp, had acquired the Cheyenne habit of washing every

38

day, summer or winter, if there were a stream around to do it in. Duppa looked at him keenly as he stripped off his clothes. The Mexican boy stood guard beneath the cotton-woods with a rifle.

"Damn, Jim, I wish I had your muscle. All those scars, though."

Sundance said, "A man fights for a living, he accumulates some scars."

Duppa shed clothes from his own lean body, which was pale as a fish's belly. "You've done a lot of fighting, then. What about those two on your chest? They don't look like bullet or arrow wounds."

"They aren't. Those are from the Sun Dance ceremony."

"Oh," Duppa said. "I've heard of that. How old were you?"

"Fourteen," Sundance said. "But I had already done my dreaming, had my medicine. I wanted to prove myself. They cut the skin, slipped rawhide ropes through the cuts, tied buffalo skulls to the trailing ends. I danced until the ropes pulled through the flesh. Then I went on my first war party."

Duppa waded out into the stream, shivered. Sundance followed; the cool water felt good on his bruised flesh. "You're a full-fledged

Cheyenne Dog Soldier, aren't you?" Duppa asked.

Sundance nodded, immersed himself, began to swim.

"I know more about Apaches than Cheyennes," Duppa said. "The Dog Soldiers are the chief fighting society of the Cheyennes, right?"

"One of 'em. There are several." Sundance floated on his back. "It depends on how well they distinguish themselves. Sometimes the Dog Soldiers rank highest, sometimes the Red Shields, sometimes the Kit Fox Men . . . or one of the other societies."

"Still, you're a big man with the Cheyennes." Duppa submerged himself, paddled around. "And I've heard the Apaches talk about you and your father. They haven't forgotten you. But for that matter neither have the other tribes around here." He stood up, dripping, and Sundance saw that he had scars of his own, remembered that Duppa had taken at least three wounds from Apaches, and yet did not hate the Indians who wanted to kill him and whom he'd had to kill so often himself. Darrel Duppa, Sundance thought, was a remarkable man.

They climbed out, rubbed themselves down with clean sacks. The sun felt good on their naked flesh. "And so," Duppa said, "maybe you're the last man in the West with yellow hair who can walk into any Indian camp anywhere and still be welcomed—and trusted. I've known you for a long time; I don't see how you do it. You can think like a white man, then you can shift over and think like an Indian. And bridge the gap between the two races. I wish . . . I wish to the devil there were more like you. Maybe if there were, there'd be some peace."

Sundance's face was grave. "There won't be peace anymore, Darrel. It's like you said; for the next ten years, it's war."

"The Indians can't win." Duppa began to draw on dirty socks.

"No," Sundance shrugged into his shirt. "They don't see that yet, but I do."

"Then it must be hell," Duppa said quietly. "Where does that leave you, half red, half white?"

"Not much of anywhere," Sundance said. He pulled on his pants. "Not much of anywhere at all, Darrel." He reached for the revolver, buckled it around his waist, looked out across the river at the desert shimmering beyond. "There ought to be room," he said. "There ought to be room in a country as big as this for both peoples, red and white. Maybe, somehow, somewhere, there's an answer, a way of making people see that. Anyhow, I keep on trying. I've made friends with the Army, a lot of generals. Sherman, Crook—the important ones. And I've kept my friendship with the chiefs, the tribes."

He would have liked to talk to Duppa; Darrel was an intelligent, a cultivated, sensitive man. He himself had had the best education Nicholas Sundance could give him, and that had not been insignificant. Sometimes he hungered for association with people like Duppa. But this was not the time. Then Sundance said, "I'm tired of talking. Let's go eat. I've got to strike out for Tucson."

Duppa stared at him. "Not yet. That's where Gannon and his bunch headed. You run into them, next time you might not get off so easy."

"I can't help that," Sundance said.

"Why?"

"Because I've got a job there."

Duppa stood silent for a moment. Then he spat into the river. "Okay, Jim, it's your affair. Breakfast ought to be on the table."

3

THE ride to Tucson was a long one, and Sundance did not hurry. Traveling south, he entered the country of the Chiricahuas, and they were far more dangerous than the Tontos. He sacrificed speed to safety, using desert craft learned from the Apaches themselves to mask his passage. Besides, he had no desire to run into Gannon and his band, whose sign he read on the trail ahead of him, two days old.

Occasionally, he saw smokes. Once he passed a deserted ranch, its inhabitants fled to town and the safety of the Army. Presently, he reached the valley of the Santa Cruz, and the city that lay within it.

City, though, was perhaps an overly impressive designation for the Territorial Capital of Arizona. It was a sprawling mass of adobe huts and older stuccoed Spanish houses, with a population of about three thousand, its narrow streets littered with trash and swarming with burros, dogs, and rooting pigs, as well as the traffic of men and wagons from the High

43

Plains, or come north from Sonora. Soldiers, gunmen, bullwhackers, gamblers, traders, settlers driven in by Indians: all thronged the place, along with its impassive original Mexican population. The men looked at the tall rider in buckskins on the magnificent spotted stallion with curiosity; there was something more than that in the eyes of the women, the Mexican girls swathed in *rebozos* and *velos*, the brassy American honky-tonk harridans who called from the doorways of the numerous saloons and gambling halls. Despite the Apaches, Tucson was booming, Sundance thought. He rode through it with his rifle across the saddle horn, his hand dangling near his pistol, his eyes searching the street for any sign of Gannon or his men.

He saw none, and he passed on through the town, took the trail to nearby Camp Lowell. It was less a fort than Tucson was a city, only a cluster of mud-plastered buildings outside town. An American flag dangled listlessly in the middle of its dusty parade. Nobody challenged him as he rode in. He turned Eagle toward the biggest building: that had to be headquarters, and that was where he would find General Crook.

He reined the appaloosa up, swung down,

44

hitched the stallion. A guard on the building's porch spat tobacco juice and shifted his carbine to his right hand. "General Crook here?" Sundance asked.

"This is where he hangs out," the soldier said. He spat again. "See the adjutant."

Sundance entered the building. A captain, sharp in heavy woolen blues, sat sweating behind a desk. He looked at Sundance with dubious eyes, taking in the red skin, the Indian features, and the blond hair. There was hostility in his voice as he asked, "Something you want?"

"Yes. To see General Crook."

The captain frowned. "General Crook's busy. Far too busy to see a —"

"Halfbreed," Sundance said, smiling faintly.

"Well, yes. He's just arrived, is organizing the Department for combat."

"That I don't doubt," Sundance said. "All the same, you tell him Jim Sundance is here."

The captain's eyes changed. "Wait a minute. Sundance?" Suddenly his manner was respectful, almost obsequious. "Just a moment, sir." He sprang up, whirled, went quickly through a door behind his desk. Almost immediately, he reappeared. "Mr.

Sundance, I'm sorry I didn't recognize you. General Crook will see you now."

"Thanks," Sundance said dryly, and he went in.

General George Crook hadn't changed a bit. As Sundance entered he arose from behind his desk, a man about six feet tall, bearded, with a hawk's beak of a nose and piercing eyes. His face was deeply tanned, weathered; as usual, he wore no blouse, was in shirt sleeves, and they were cuffed back. "Jim!" he exclaimed, grinning, and thrust out a big, hard hand.

"General." Sundance shook that hand vigorously. He had known a lot of Generals. He admired Sherman for his cold common sense and practicality; he despised Custer for his stupidity and arrogance; but he loved George Crook. He had seen Crook in action against the Northern Indians, the Rogues and Pit Rivers, had seen how quickly the man comprehended Indian psychology and turned it against the Indians themselves to minimize bloodshed. He had hunted with Crook; the man was a superb outdoorsman, totally fearless, with a keen, incisive mind and great powers of observation. In fact, except for

Nicholas Sundance, Crook was the closest thing to a white Indian Sundance had ever known; and he stood out like a giant among the mediocre pigmies who commanded most of the Western forces. He and Crook had shared too many campfires, too many canteens, for there to be less than total regard between them.

Crook gestured Sundance to a chair. "Sit down, Jim, sit down. Will you have one drink? I won't offer you any more, knowing your propensities."

"One would be fine, General."

Crook took a bottle and two glasses from a desk drawer, poured, shoved the glass to Sundance. He leaned back, sipping his own whiskey, strong face glowing with the pleasure of reunion. "By Jove, Jim, it's good to see you again. So you got the letter I sent to Laramie."

"We reached there on the same day," Sundance said.

"Good. Laramie is the place, of course; everybody in the West touches there sooner or later. It was a shot in the dark, but lucky things broke right. Well, Jim, shall we reminisce, or shall we get down to business?"

"Maybe business would be better."

"Sure. Well, you know I'm Commander of this Department now."

"Yeah," Sundance said. "And I'm glad of it. If anybody can make headway with the Apaches, you're the one."

"I appreciate that compliment. I hope to. The former Commandant made his headquarters in Los Angeles; me, I like to be on the scene. You know my theory, Jim; the Indians are like everyone else. Give them full stomachs, something constructive to do, work they can see is in their own interest, and they would rather prosper than fight. I hope, eventually, to put those policies into effect in this Department. Of course, there will be some fighting first.

"Maybe you can scout for me eventually. I would like to enlist some Apaches as scouts, once I can convince them that it's in the best interests of their people. But that's not why I sent for you. Scout's pay wouldn't interest you right now."

"No," Sundance said, "it wouldn't."

Crook was suddenly serious. "You're not having much luck with your lawyer in Washington, are you?"

Sundance arose, went to the window of the office, looked out on the parade. "No," he said, "but I keep trying. He does the best he can. He's a good lobbyist."

Crook sighed. "But not good enough. Not with all the other people who have influence in Congress and want to see the Indians wiped out. The railroads, the land speculators, the banks—"

He arose, too, came to stand beside Sundance, put a hand on his shoulder. "Well, for a while there, it seemed there was a chance. There was genuine sentiment in the East for a humane peace policy toward the Indians. But, of course, everything's blown up now. The way Custer slaughtered Cheyennes on the Washita after the Medicine Lodge Treaty, the way the railroads have rammed on through Indian lands in violation of other treaties . . . But I hope you won't give up."

"I won't," Sundance said. "The fate of the Indians won't be decided out here in the West. It'll be decided in Washington, in Congress, in the White House."

"But you can't outbid and outspend railroads and banks—"

"No," Sundance said. "They're throwing millions into trying to get the Government to adopt a policy of extermination. But there are people on the other side. The Quakers, a few other groups—"

"And you," Crook said softly.

"You and my lobbyist are the only two who know where that money comes from," Sundance said. "You'll keep it quiet."

"Of course. I only wish that there were more."

"Well, there isn't. I earn what I can taking on tough jobs, charging all the traffic will bear. I know it's still a drop in the bucket, but I hope—General, I realize now the Indians can't win. Maybe I don't even want them to. But when they lose, I want them to have a square shake. That's why I do it."

"I know," Crook said. He went back to his desk. "That's the reason I sent for you. I see a chance for you to earn maybe twenty thousand dollars; anyhow, a lot of money."

"Twenty thousand?" Sundance's brows went up.

"Not only that," Crook said, "but solve a problem for me. Get me off the hook. It's a matter, Jim, of international importance. But dangerous; dangerous as hell. You interested?"

"For twenty thousand," Sundance said, "you're damned right I'm interested."

Crook smiled faintly. "I thought you would

be." Then he went to the office door, opened it and stuck his head through. "Captain Bourke. Would you be good enough to go upstairs and ask Baron von Markau and the Baroness to join us?"

When he closed the door and turned, Sundance looked at him blankly. "Baron von Markau?"

"Personal emissary from His Excellency, Franz Joseph, Emperor of Austria," Crook said. "I told you it was of international importance."

"But what—?"

Crook held up a hand. "Wait. I'll let them explain it. You'll find the Baron is a most impressive man." A strange expression crossed his face. "His wife is an even more impressive woman. Be careful of her."

"Listen," Sundance said, but before he could go on, somebody knocked at the door. Then Bourke, Crook's young aide, opened it. "General," he said, "the Baron and Baroness von Markau."

As Bourke stood aside, Sundance turned and carefully sized up the man and woman who entered.

Crook made the presentations gracefully. "Your Excellencies, may I present Mr. Jim

51

Sundance? Mr. Sundance, Baron Walther von Markau."

Von Markau was a big man in a dark suit and white shirt. He was as tall as Sundance, wide in the shoulders, thick in the torso, narrow in waist and legs, his beard and temples silver-gray, his face square and rugged. He clicked his heels with a sound like a pistol shot and put out a big hand, shook hands vigorously with Sundance. "Mr. Sundance. A great pleasure. I've heard much about you from the General." His English was good, almost unaccented. "May I present my wife, the Baroness. Herta my dear, Mr. Sundance."

The woman came forward. She had dark hair, enormous dark eyes set in an oval face. Von Markau was perhaps forty-five and she was not more than half his age. She was one of the most beautiful women Sundance had ever seen. Her skin was ivory white, her mouth full and red, her throat a smooth curve. Beneath her tight black dress, her breasts were high and neither large nor small, but separately outlined; her waist was tiny. She put out a small, white hand, lifting it instinctively, but looked surprised when Sundance took it and kissed it quite correctly.

When he raised his head, her eyes met his boldly and quite without reserve. She ran them over him, taking in the blond hair, the coppery hawk's face, the beaded buckskin shirt, the gun and knife and ax, the denim pants and moccasins; something moved in her eyes and her lips parted slightly, and Sundance knew now why Crook had said to be careful of her. He released her hand, took a step backward.

Crook motioned them all to chairs. "Captain Bourke, will you bring us brandy?" He sat down behind his desk. The woman kept flicking her eyes to Sundance and away again. "Now, Baron von Markau. Sundance is the only one I know of who might possibly be able to help you. I warn you, though, he comes dear. But he's worth his hire."

"I'm sure he is," Herta von Markau murmured.

Her husband looked quickly at her, then away, stroked his beard. "Very well," he said, addressing Sundance. "Then suppose I come straight to the point."

He leaned forward slightly. "As the General has told you, I come from the Court of Franz Joseph, Emperor of the Austro-

Hungarian Empire, one of the mightiest of Europe."

Sundance nodded. "Not quite mighty enough," he said, "to set Franz Joseph's brother up as Emperor of Mexico."

"Ah, I see you're well informed. Yes, that was very unfortunate." Von Markau hesitated, looking a little embarrassed. "Still, international politics may sometimes be risky. You know the story of Maximilian."

"I know it. There was Civil War in Mexico, the Constitutionalists led by Juárez won. The big landholders' estates were being broken up. They turned to Napoleon III, Emperor of France, asked him for help, offered him the crown of Emperor of Mexico in return."

He waited as Bourke brought brandy, sipped it and found it excellent. "So Napoleon III sent help, a French army and the Austrian archduke, Ferdinand Maximilian, to be his figurehead emperor, rule Mexico for him. Thought he could get away with taking over Mexico while the American Civil War was on; thought they might even make an alliance with the Confederacy. Of course, Lincoln fought the whole idea, and when the North won, that changed the picture. The

United States put pressure on the French, and Juárez was still fighting and winning against Maximilian, who'd crowned himself Maximilian the First. After the Civil War ended, Washington sent a big army to the Mexican border. There were troubles in Europe, too, and Napoleon and Franz Joseph couldn't help Maximilian any more. The French pulled out, leaving him stranded. Juárez beat what Mexican forces Maximilian had and executed Maximilian by firing squad at Querétaro. Maximilian was brave, what they call in Mexico, *muy hombre*. But it didn't help him after his backers deserted him."

Von Markau was silent for a moment. "A rather brutal summary," he said presently, "but perhaps accurate. Yes, the whole thing was an unfortunate episode. The only bright spot was that Maximilian's wife, Carlotta, managed to escape, returned to Europe before the collapse came. Unfortunately, her mind broke under the strain." He finished his brandy. "Well, be that as it may, Maximilian died three years ago; now Juárez rules Mexico, the episode is ended. Except for one matter, which, Mr. Sundance, brought me to Washington, on orders from the Emperor of

Austria. Washington in turn sent me to General Crook, and the General has brought you to me."

"And this one matter is—?"

Von Markau set down his glass. "A matter of certain royal jewels belonging to the House of Hapsburg, which were in possession of Maximilian when he was besieged in Querétaro by Juárez, and which, after his capture and execution, were never found. Jewels worth a fortune, Mr. Sundance. And I have reason to believe they are hidden in the territory of the Chiricahua Apaches of southern Arizona. If you can help me find them and gain possession of them for their rightful owner, the Emperor of Austria, I am prepared to pay you very well indeed."

For a moment, Crook's office was silent. Then Sundance said, "Go on." He felt a flame of excitement which had nothing to do with the brandy.

"You understand, of course, that the House of Hapsburg has ruled Austria for centuries. In addition, at various times, Hapsburgs have been Kings of Spain, the Netherlands, and—well, gold, silver, precious stones: these are the trappings with which kings and emperors impress their subjects.

The House of Hapsburg has long been rich in them, and as a prince of royal blood, Maximilian inherited his share of these family jewels."

He arose, went to the brandy, poured. "Unless one has seen them, one cannot conceive of their richness and splendor. In terms of American dollars, they are worth hundreds of thousands; perhaps millions. In terms of historical value and traditions, they are worth even more."

He turned to face Sundance. "Maximilian brought these jewels with him to Mexico. In the last days, he was besieged, then executed by Juárez. And those jewels, Mr. Sundance, disappeared. They were not returned to Europe with Maximilian's other possessions, which he dispatched on the last French ship to leave Mexico. Secret agents have convinced us that Juárez and the Mexicans did not get them. They simply vanished, and no one knew their whereabouts—until recently."

He sat down. "Now, the mystery is solved. I have in my possession a map which shows their location. As I said, it's in southern Arizona, in territory dominated by the Apaches. I cannot tell you more, of course, until we reach an agreement that you will help me. What I propose to do is go after them, Mr. Sundance, find their hiding place, and reclaim them for the Emperor of Austria. To do that, I need a man who knows the country and the Apaches, a man who can bargain or fight against the Indians as necessary. One whom I can trust completely. General Crook tells me you are that man. He also tells me that it's certain death to attempt this venture without your help—and, quite possibly, even with it. Still, I have my orders from the Emperor and I obey. Mr. Sundance, if you will assist me, I'll pay you five thousand American dollars in advance. If we retrieve the jewels and return them to the Emperor's Court safely, you'll get another ten thousand. Well, sir, I await your answer with eagerness."

Sundance smiled faintly. Then he said, "My answer, Baron, is no."

Von Markau stared at him, face reddening. "Mr. Sundance, I understood from General Crook—"

"You understood right," Sundance said. "I'm for hire, and I can fight. Southern Arizona: I know it like the back of my hand, and I've lived among the Chiricahuas, speak their language, know their customs. If anybody could get you in there and back out again, I could do it. And as for the risk—well, danger is my business, risk my stock in trade." He got up, went to the brandy himself. "But not at the price you're talking, Baron."

Von Markau made a strangled sound. "Fifteen thousand dollars? A fortune."

"Not to me," Sundance said. "Those jewels are worth millions, you said. Fifteen thousand's a pretty puny sum when you figure that. Not enough, anyhow, to make me want to risk my hair."

He took a sip of brandy, rolled it on his tongue. Crook had mentioned twenty thousand; von Markau was horse-trading. Sundance said, "I want fifteen thousand down, twenty more when the jewels are delivered in Vienna."

Von Markau's jaw dropped. *"Thirty-five thousand dollars?"*

"That's the way I add it up," Sundance said. He shot a sidelong glance at Crook; even the General sat stunned.

Sundance drained the glass, put it down. "Listen," he said. "I don't know where they're hidden. But if they're in Chiricahua territory, there are three ways to get them out. Get General Crook to give you an escort of maybe five hundred men—"

"I have requested of your War Department, and they have refused."

"Hire an army of your own—another five hundred—which would cost you more than the thirty-five thousand I'm asking by half. And if you can find five hundred men in Arizona who'll ride into Apache country with you and not cut your throat for the jewels once you have 'em, good luck. The third way is to hire me and pay me what I ask. If I get killed, you're out fifteen thousand. If I live, you get the jewels and you're out twenty more. It's your decision, Baron."

"I do not have such sums with me."

"You've got the fifteen thousand, I'm pretty sure. As for the rest, the credit of the Emperor of Austria's good with me. After you sign my contract, of course."

Von Markau's jaw dropped further. "Your *contract*?"

"Certainly," Sundance said. "I'm a businessman. I never work without a contract—unless the Indians hire me to do a job. Them, I don't worry about; they keep their word. But white men—well, there's something about this red skin of mine that makes 'em

60

careless. As if a bargain with a halfbreed doesn't count. So I never work for a white man without a paper that'll stand up, iron-clad, in court."

Von Markau stood up suddenly, sputtering. "You dare question my word, the Emperor's word—? You, an ignorant frontiersman?"

Crook cut in. "Careful, von Markau. You're talking to a man who could probably match whatever standing you've got in Austria, if he cared to claim his heritage in England." He stood up. "The price is a matter between the two of you. All I'll say is what I've told you before, Baron. I don't have the soldiers to help you. Sundance is the only man I know of who can. But you're welcome to try to find another." He paused. "I will point out one thing: The Apaches still remember Sundance and respect him; I've learned that much since coming to Arizona. He may be able to find those jewels for you and bring them out without your having to fight at all. Nobody else can do that."

Von Markau stood tensely, looking from Sundance to Crook. Then he sighed. "Very well. It seems there is no alternative. Draw up your contract, Mr. Sundance. After we have signed it, I shall pay you your fifteen thousand and tell you where we have to go and what we must do to find the jewels of Maximilian."

Sundance turned to Crook. "General," he said, "May I borrow paper and a pen?"

4

THE Arizona desert was made for dying. A vast space without water, any water, just dry creek and river beds—dry except for once, twice a year when they turn into conduits carrying roaring, deadly flash floods that vanish as quickly as they come; floods that can drown a man who, seconds before, was dying of thirst.

The terrain itself is almost incapable of supporting life—it is made up of titanic quantities of sand and jagged rock; lava, black, pitted with razor-sharp projections; alkali sprinkled in every crevice. But this land does indeed support life, a grisly life of thorns and spikes—saguaro, prickly pear, pita, ocotillo, yucca; and cholla, from which the thorns seem to leap out at human flesh, in which, once lodged, they leave wounds that fester for days.

If all this does not kill the white man who foolishly ventures into these endless miles of merciless sun, the inhabitants probably will—the rattlesnakes, Gila monsters, scorpions, and the Apache, the only man who can survive in the murderous Dragoon Mountains. And the Apache does not like company.

Four days after the conference in Crook's office, Sundance, like a gigantic lizard, sprawled on a ledge above the mouth of a narrow canyon deep in the Dragoons, watching his backtrail, while, below, Walther von Markau slept.

The Baron, Sundance thought, was either a very ignorant man or a very brave one. Either way, he was not one to waste time. He had put his signature to the contract Sundance had drawn up, after reading it very carefully. Then he had strode out; ten minutes later, he returned bearing two large canvas bags; they chinked as he dropped them on the table. "Fifteen thousand in gold, Mr. Sundance. And so . . . we are bound to each other. My copy of the contract, if you please."

Sundance gave it to him, and the Baron thrust it into his coat. "Now, the remainder of the story. Maximilian knew he was doomed, but the Hapsburgs are brave men, and he made up his mind to go down fighting, as befits a prince. He took his Austrian jewels with him as emblems of his heritage, and they were with him at Querétaro. When he saw the end was near, he determined to get them back to Vienna somehow, rather than let them fall into Juárez's hands. He gave them to a trusted priest, a Mexican, Father Tomás Hernando."

"Go on," Sundance said.

"Father Tomás disguised himself, managed to get through Juárez's lines with the jewels. He feared to go north because of the American Army camped on the Rio Grande. Instead, he turned west to Sonora, where a French and Austrian colony yet remained. But before he reached it, it too came under attack; and he swung north into Arizona, enduring dreadful hardships, traveling across the mountains and the desert on foot."

"With a heavy load," Sundance said.

"On a burro, which he led. He reached Arizona; then, near a stream called San Simon Creek, the Apaches caught him. He managed to elude them long enough to hide the jewels, memorize the necessary landmarks. Then he was taken by Indians, tortured and abused most dreadfully."

"They don't like Mexicans," Sundance

said. "The Mexican government used to pay a bounty for Chiricahua scalps."

"I understand. At any rate, Father Tomás finally managed to escape, at last reached refuge here in Tucson. Unfortunately, his ordeal had erased his memory, affected his mind. He lived in the Mission here, virtually an idiot, until he sickened. Then, somehow, his mind cleared and it all came back. He drew a most detailed map of the jewels' hiding place, sent it with a letter to the Emperor of Austria. His Majesty immediately dispatched me to Tucson to contact Father Tomás. Malaria, on top of the effects of his ordeal, carried the priest off, but not before I had conferred with him, convincing myself of the authenticity of his story and of the map. The jewels are there, Mr. Sundance, well hidden. Now you and I together will go to reclaim them." He took out a wallet, unfolded a sheet of paper it contained. "Here is the map." He spread it out. "San Simon Creek. This huge mountain which I have identified as Chiricahua Peak."

Sundance nodded. "Right smack in the middle of Apache country."

"And here," von Markau said, finger moving along, "is where the jewels are

66

hidden in a crevice in a mountainside. A wall of what, I believe, is here called a canyon. General Crook's experts have been kind enough to identify the canyon for me. It is, I understand, called by the Mexicans *Cañon del Muerto*. Or, in English, Dead Man's Canyon."

"I know it," Sundance said, and he let out a low, whistling breath. "Right in the middle of the Peloncillos, some of the worst country in Arizona and every bit of it swarming with Apaches."

"Precisely." Von Markau laughed bitterly. "I think you shall earn your exorbitant fee before we come out with the jewels."

Sundance raised his head. *"We?* This is a job for me to do alone."

"Nein," von Markau said flatly. "For the two of us. As the Emperor's Representative, I go with you."

"Baron, that's no place for an amateur!" Sundance stood up straight, voice crackling.

Von Markau smiled. "I assure you, I am not an amateur. I am a soldier and a hunter, Mr. Sundance. I have fought in many battles, have stalked chamois in the Alps, brown bear in Bohemia, wild boar in the Vienna Woods. I've traversed the barren Russian steppes and journeyed through bleak Siberia. I do not fear either the landscape or the inhabitants of Arizona."

Sundance looked at him, saw he meant it. "And you want to make sure I don't doublecross you and take off with the jewels."

"I think that is my responsibility."

"All right," Sundance said. "Then you go along. But under my orders all the way."

"Very well," von Markau said. "It is decided. When do we leave?"

"I'll go into Tucson tonight, start to get an outfit together. Maybe tomorrow, maybe the day after. As soon as possible." Sundance was struck by a thought. He looked at the woman. "What about the Baroness?"

"She remains here, under the protection of General Crook."

Herta von Markau stood up, spoke for the first time. "Walther! I want to go along. Please! I can ride and shoot!"

"My dear, you stay here."

She came to Sundance. "Mr. Sundance, please." She stood very close to him, almost close enough for the tips of her breasts to touch him. There was a kind of glow in her eyes as they met his, deep, sultry, persuasive.

"It will be such an adventure, and I love adventure. I beg you—"

"No," Sundance said. "No women. This is no job for women."

Her mouth thinned, now her eyes glittered. "I am not an ordinary woman."

"I don't doubt that," Sundance said. "All the same, you follow your husband's orders. You stay here, where General Crook can see to you."

His voice was flat, unyielding, though he could feel the effect of her closeness. She was, he thought, as dangerous as Crook had implied, young, vital, married to a man twice her age, like a bomb, pent-up power ready to explode. She was the last thing he wanted on such an expedition. He looked back at her coldly; and under his gaze, her eyes lowered; she bit her lip.

"Very well," she murmured. "You men—" Back straight, she turned away.

Von Markau was looking from Sundance to his wife. He let out a long breath. "My wife is young, Mr. Sundance, and easily bored. She does not understand that such an expedition is not an afternoon tea."

"It isn't," Sundance said. "Listen, Baron—besides General Crook, myself, your

69

wife, who else knows why you're here?"

"Absolutely no one." Von Markau frowned. "Do you think I am a fool?"

"No. The point is, I can deal with the Apaches—maybe. But Tucson's full of white men who'd cut your throat for a two-bit piece, much less a fortune in jewels. Hardcases, gunmen, outlaws. Nobody deals with them. Let one whisper of this get out, they'll be swarming into the Dragoons like heelflies after a calf. Apaches or no Apaches. And we'll be lucky to get out with our hides, much less the jewels."

"I can assure you, Mr. Sundance, that no whisper of this *will* get out." He turned to his wife. "Herta, I trust you understand the importance of what Sundance says. Our very lives depend on secrecy."

She took his hand. "Darling, you know—"

"Yes, of course. I only wanted to emphasize. Well, Mr. Sundance, hurry your preparations. I should like to leave as soon as possible."

Sundance had hurried, all right, but not at the cost of thoroughness. He and his friend Don Estevan Ochoa, a leading merchant of Tucson, had spent all night checking and rechecking the list Sundance made up. Then

Estevan had sent the goods to Fort Lowell as if delivering supplies to the post. Crook himself had provided von Markau's horse and the three pack mules. They would, Sundance explained, ride at night and hole up in daytime. They had made their departure from the fort at midnight.

Herta von Markau's lovely face was pale, her eyes enormous as she clung to her husband, who was dressed now in Arizona clothes: slouch hat, leather jacket, woolen pants, high boots, a Smith and Wesson top-break .44 revolver on his hip. Crook and Sundance looked away while the Austrians made their good-byes. "Jim," Crook asked, "what are your plans?"

Sundance shrugged. "It would be ridiculous to try to find that stuff and get it out without getting permission from the Apaches first. When we're in the Dragoons and I'm sure we're not followed, I'll make contact with the Chiricahuas. Maybe I can even get an escort from Cochise. Anyhow, everything depends on the Indians."

Crook's hand was hard as it clamped his. "Well, good luck."

"We'll need it." Sundance had picked up

71

his Winchester. "Baron, if you're ready, we'd better ride."

So far, Sundance thought, the Austrian, allowing for his inexperience in the desert, had been a good traveler. His experience in the Alps made him an excellent mountaineer; and he had courage, plus the knack of observing everything around him. Leave him out here long enough, Sundance thought, and he'd make a damned good scout.

He himself was under no illusions about what they were up against. He knew the Apaches, yes. Once he had been respected and loved by them, but that had been in a different world, when they were the undisputed rulers of Arizona, not yet pushed into a corner by a flood of white men. They might feel differently now. Men like Gannon and Jessup hated him for his red skin, but after what the Chiricahuas had been through, they might hate him with equal fervor for his yellow hair.

It was a strange arrangement, he thought. Crook had filled him in on it. Crook's assignment was to subdue the other Apaches of Arizona. But he had no authority over the Chiricahuas. They were being dickered with by a special emissary from Washington. It

72

was said that he intended to let them have the Dragoons and the Huachucas for their range and guarantee them safety from the Army. The bargain implicit in that was that they could use those mountains for their bases, so long as they confined their raids to Mexico, left Arizona alone. Sundance did not think it would work. Crook could never tame the other bands—the Tontos, Mescaleros, Gilas, Yavapais, White Mountains—so long as the Chiricahuas ran wild and free. It would have been better if they had let Crook deal with Cochise, too: fairly and honestly, as he always dealt with Indians. Then, perhaps, he could bring them all in together.

Well, that was not the problem now. The problem was that this was the undisputed stronghold of the Chiricahua, and if they got in trouble, no help could be expected from the Army. Still, Sundance thought he could bring it off. Cochise had been his father's friend; he could deal with the Apaches—if only nothing happened, if only no other white men came into the Dragoons and mucked everything up.

Before him the Dragoons shimmered in the heat. Nothing moved out there to excite his suspicion; apparently they'd brought it off all right, the backtrail was clear. And now it was time for him to eat and get some sleep, time for von Markau to stand watch.

Sundance wriggled off the ledge, slid soundlessly back down into the canyon. There, where a pathetic seep of water trickled from a rock, the horses were picketed and von Markau sat on his blankets, eating, with a look of distaste on his face, cold biscuits and jerky, washing it down with a sip of water from his canteen, a gulp of cognac from a bottle he'd brought with him.

Sundance looked at the bottle. "Not too much of that," he said harshly. "You've got no idea what this heat will do to you with that in you."

"I miss my coffee," von Markau said. "We Viennese are great coffee drinkers. If we could only build a fire—"

"No fire," Sundance said. "Until this is over, we live off jerky and biscuits and airtights."

"Then I must have my occasional sip of cognac. Is everything quiet above?"

"So far," Sundance said. He ate biscuits, jerky, took a moderate swallow of water from a canteen. "You'd better get on up there, though, and keep your eyes peeled.

Remember, no shots. You see anything, you roll down a rock. And leave that bottle here."

"*Jawohl,*" von Markau said.

"Keep a special watch on our backtrail. The Indians we can't do much about; if they're around, they'll be on us before we see them. But if there are any whites in these mountains, I want to spot 'em first."

Von Markau nodded, then hesitated, a strange expression on his face. "Sundance," he said, "I do not believe you trust my wife."

Sundance looked up at him. "I didn't say that."

"But you imply it. Only the General, whom I know you trust, and Herta could possibly tell our secret. If you do not think the General will, then it must be in your mind that Herta might betray us."

Sundance searched for words that would convey what he thought without enraging von Markau. He could not say, *von Markau, let's face it. You're twice as old as the Baroness and I know a woman with dynamite in her pants when I see her. For all I know, your wife may be sleeping with someone else right now. And women talk to the men they sleep with.*

"Among the Indians," he said, "they say that a woman's mind is a pool of water. And her tongue is the stream that carries it out for everyone to drink of it. All women are alike, von Markau, Austrian, Cheyenne, Apache; they don't keep secrets well."

The Baron's mouth thinned. "I do not think you know my wife well, or you would not say that. I know of no woman I would trust more implicitly. In the three years of our marriage, she has never given me cause to doubt her discretion."

Sundance laid aside the canteen, took cigarette papers from his loincloth, and a tobacco pouch. Carefully, he went about the business of building a cigarette, but it was not tobacco he shook into the paper. Marijuana, a weed he had learned to smoke from the Mexicans; he could not trust himself with whiskey or the Baron's cognac, but one cigarette of this would ease him, make him sleep, and still not interfere with his reflexes if he had to wake in a hurry. He said, "Three years? That's how long you've been married?"

"*Ja*. For a long time, I resisted marriage. Then I met her. Her family was very high-born, but far from wealthy. I settled their debts, and she has been very grateful to me for that; with all she owes me, I know she would not betray me. Besides, she loves me."

"Sure she does," Sundance said, and snapped a match on his thumbnail, lit the cigarette. "I didn't mean to imply she didn't. Only, in a business like this, you take no chances. That's why you'd better get up on guard right now."

"I will do that," von Markau said. He turned.

"The bottle," Sundance said. "Leave it behind."

"Oh, yes, I forgot." Von Markau put down the bottle; then, rifle in hand, he climbed up the rubble-strewn, cactus-clad canyon wall.

Sundance drew the marijuana smoke deeply into his lungs, and he thought of Two Roads Woman, Barbara Colfax. She had been captured by the Cheyennes on the Santa Fe Trail a few years before; he had brought her back to her wealthy father. But, like his own sire, she had fallen in love with the Indian way of life, and one night he had taken her back to the camp of the Southern Cheyenne band that had adopted her. She was still there, unmarried, yet living happily as part of a society in which she was valued, useful, instead of the sterile cocoon of ease and riches and boredom in which, in New York, she had been wrapped and stifled. He had seen her on his trip south from Laramie, and even now he could almost feel the eager mouth on his, the body moving beneath him, as they had made love in the willows along the Republican River. *Oh, Jim, if you would only come back to these people, where you belong, where we both belong—*

And he said aloud what he had said to her then: "I can't, yet. Too much to do." She had understood, but that had not eased the pain of separation. The marijuana helped a little.

While he smoked it, Sundance drew the buffalo-hide panniers that he had unslung from Eagle to him, opened them. He fished in the first one, cylindrical, about four feet long, and brought out a bow. Made of juniper, wrapped with bison sinew and tipped with horn, it was a weapon he had learned to use in childhood, was still master of. With it, he could send an arrow four hundred yards, drive one through a full-grown buffalo—or a man. He had done that, too, more than once, especially as a Dog Soldier of the Cheyennes in battle against the Crows and Blackfeet.

He ran his hands over the bowstave, checking for any possible split, checked the dangling string, too, for defects, found none. He laid the bow aside, took out an arrow

78

quiver made of panther skin, the tail still attached. It held more than thirty arrows, each a yard long, feathered with vulture quills, tipped with flint points worked to razor sharpness. The making of flint arrowheads was almost a lost art; those Indians not armed with rifles used arrowheads of steel. But a flint point inflicted a more grievous, deadly wound, had greater stopping power; and he had his reasons for clinging to the old style arrowheads, even though they were hard to get and cost him a premium.

He laid those aside with the bow. There were other things in the pannier, but he did not take them out. Instead, he pulled up the other bag, which was round. Opening it, he withdrew the shield.

To a Cheyenne, a shield is sacred. This one, painted with a Thunderbird, had required much ritual and sacrifice to complete and make holy. Thick hide of a buffalo bull's neck drawn over a wooden hoop, a pad of grass added and antelope skin sewn over that, it was round, with a loop that would slide up his left arm. It would stop a musket ball or an arrow, but was useless against a bullet from a modern rifle. That did not matter; he believed in it, as he believed in the medicine in the otter-skin pouch on a thong around his neck, just as some men believed in saints' medals and crucifixes worn the same way. He looked up at the sun. All medicine came from the same source; it did not matter what a man believed, so long as he believed in something.

He dug deeper in the sack, took out other gear. Then he put his sombrero aside, peeled off the buckskin shirt and pants and moccasins. A few minutes later, he was dressed in a loose-fitting spotted calico shirt, a loin cloth, and high Apache leggings that reached nearly to his groin. His yellow hair was bound with a red band. From now on, Apaches might come at any moment. When they did, maybe he would be recognized from a distance if he dressed this way. If he were not recognized from far off, he might be shot from far off. Maybe he would be, anyhow; maybe nobody remembered Jim Sundance among the Chiricahuas anymore, or if they did, maybe his yellow hair made him their enemy now.

He put back the shield, stored the bow and arrows. His cigarette almost finished, he looked at von Markau on the ledge above. He

80

had to trust the man; but there was no chance in hell of von Markau seeing Apaches before they were ready to let themselves be seen; if any alarm were given, it would have to come from Eagle.

Sundance draped his pistol belt around the horn of the saddle he'd use for a pillow. He put the rifle in his crooked arm, pulled up a blanket to shield him from the brutal sun, dust, and gnats. Then he slept.

Like an animal, he came awake, knowing at once by the sun that three hours had passed, that something was wrong. The moment he opened his eyes, he was totally alert, but he did not spring from his blanket with his rifle, only sat up slowly. Von Markau was still on guard up on the ledge. Sundance looked at Eagle.

Then he understood what had brought him out of sleep. Eagle sidled restlessly, raising his head, testing the air. His ears pointed straight up.

Sundance laid aside the rifle. "Von Markau," he called softly.

The Baron stirred, turned. "*Ja*, Sundance?"

"Lay your gun aside. Slowly, carefully. Put

81

your pistol with it. Then come down here."

Von Markau's face was a white, amazed blot in the sunlight. "What? Are you quite—"

Sundance's voice was low and even, yet hard as iron. "Do what I say. Now. This minute. Don't ask questions. Just lay your guns aside and come down here with your hands up." He himself got slowly to his feet, moved away from the saddle and all his weapons. Stood there with hands slightly raised, open palms outward.

Rock clattered and dust roiled as von Markau came down the slope. Sundance let out a breath of relief as he saw that the Baron had obeyed, was unarmed. Then von Markau came up to him, face pale. "What—?"

"Stand still," Sundance said. "Very still. They're here."

"They?"

"The Chiricahuas," Sundance said.

Von Markau blurted something. "I don't see—"

"They're here." He raised his eyes to the razor-backed canyon walls above them, their flanks scabbed with boulders and slides of rock, overgrown with every sort of thorny plant, plus a few junipers stunted for lack of water. The sun was high, cruel; the wind through the canyon's mouth was like the blast from a furnace. Eagle moved restlessly, and now the mules had raised their heads as well. The ears of the animals pricked forward as they swung around at the ends of their picket ropes. "They're all around us."

Von Markau sucked in a breath. "And we just stand here, wait for them to murder us?"

"That's it," Sundance said. "It's what the Emperor of Austria has asked of you." He broke off. "I heard one."

"I heard nothing."

"You weren't listening. Cartridge clicking in a bandolier, behind us, to the left, up high. Don't move. Let them look us over. They'll look us over for a long time. Then I'll talk to them."

He himself had not looked up, had made no attempt to find them in the cover on the hillsides, the canyon walls. He knew it was useless anyway. They would not let him see them unless they chose to.

The silence stretched on, charged and deadly, for five more minutes. Sundance felt a prickling in the short hair on his neck, a twitching along the spine. Well, he thought, now or never. He cleared his throat, and then, in Chiricahua dialect, he called out: "My brothers, it is I, Sundance, the Cheyenne, the yellow-headed Indian. It is I, Sundance, who comes among you again. It is I, Sundance, who comes in peace and who brings presents. I wish now to talk with you. I have brought a friend, a white-eye friend. He wishes to talk with you, too. Will you come down and smoke and talk? I have tobacco, plenty of tobacco. My brothers, the Chiricahuas, I come in peace. I seek Cochise."

There was silence. The furnace wind rustled the stalks of ocotillo. Now, Sundance thought. Now they will either talk or shoot. Every muscle in his body was tense, strung tight.

Then, in Chiricahua, a voice called down. "Sundance. It is I, Uklenni."

"Uklenni." Sundance drew in a long breath. "My brother Uklenni. Fifteen years ago, in the Sierra Madre, when we were young. We killed a bear together. A great grizzly. We divided the claws and teeth between us."

"I still wear the claws and teeth," the voice said. "It was the only grizzly I have ever killed. But I have killed some white-eyes since." The voice hardened. "You are my

84

brother. But the white-eye with you is not my brother; he is my enemy."

"No. He is my friend and would be yours. He comes in peace from a far place. He has brought presents for the Chiricahuas—blankets, knives, axes, tobacco, cloth and conchas for your women. My heart is good for the Apaches and so is his."

"Maybe. Maybe not. We can kill him and take the presents anyhow. And the horses and the guns."

"Then you would have to kill me, too, because I would fight you then. Why should Sundance and Uklenni fight? Look, we have laid aside our guns. We seek friendship with the Chiricahuas, and their help, not war."

There was silence. Sundance looked at von Markau. The big man stood rigid, sweat pouring down his face. But he cast a glance at Sundance's guns, over by the saddle. He trembled slightly.

Sundance whispered: "Don't break. You break, you're dead." And he called out, "Come down, Uklenni. I have been lonesome for you. I would see you again."

The silence held a moment more. Then Uklenni said, "I come. But the others remain up here. You are covered, Sundance."

"I know," Sundance said.

There was no sound, not a whisper of it, but now Eagle snorted. Sundance growled an order at the warhorse, as it laid back its ears, bared its teeth; and, obediently, it eased. Then, silently as a puff of smoke, Uklenni was there.

5

THE Apache was in his thirties, Sundance's age. He was shorter than the halfbreed by six or seven inches, but enormously broad across the shoulders, his chest a massive barrel. His coppery thighs bulged with muscle above his leggings. His face was square, his nose flat, his skin the color of chocolate. He wore a shapeless deerskin hat in which a few turkey feathers had been fixed. He carried an old Spencer carbine. As he moved around the two men, coming up from behind, stepping in front of them, he held it pointed at Sundance's belly.

He and Sundance stared at one another.

Sundance smiled faintly. "It's good to see my brother again," he said.

Uklenni's face did not change; his eyes, black, hard, intelligent, probed Sundance, then shifted to von Markau, seemed to cut through him with their intensity. Von Markau met them, held them bravely, and even managed a ghost of a smile, a nod.

Uklenni looked back at Sundance. He drew

in a breath, huge chest heaving. Then, suddenly, he laid down the gun, leaped forward, and embraced Jim Sundance.

Sundance laughed and caught him up in the same manner. The Apache was hard as rock, smelled of sand and sweat and grease and smoke. Sundance thought of the cornered bear, of Uklenni and himself moving in on opposite sides, each challenging the grizzly, diverting him, so the other could sink in an arrow. It had been a great deed for two boys to kill such an animal. The camp had resounded with jubilation in their honor all night long. Nicholas Sundance had been very proud of his son, and so had Uklenni's father.

Then Uklenni broke away, stepped back, and now he was grinning, eyes shining. "Ah, Sundance, by the Mountain Gods, it's really you! But you've grown up."

"You too." Sundance laughed, clapped him on the shoulder. "How many women have you now?"

"Two! And you?"

"None, yet." Then Sundance sobered. "Uklenni, you speak the Mexican language."

"*Si.*"

"My white brother also speaks Spanish." Changing to that language, he went on:

"Uklenni, this is my white brother Walther. If you love me, you will love him, too. He is not an American white-eye nor a Spanish one, but from a different place across the water. His people have never made war against Apaches. My brother Walther, my brother Uklenni of the Chiricahuas."

The Indian turned to von Markau, saying in border Spanish, "Sundance's brother is mine, if his heart is good."

Von Markau caught on quickly. "My heart is good," he replied slowly, carefully, in Castilian. "I have many presents for the Apaches."

"We are not Apaches. We are *Tenneh*—The People."

"I am glad to be among the Tenneh."

Uklenni stared at him a moment longer. Then he smiled. "*Bueno*. Welcome to the country of the Chiricahua." And he put out his hand.

Sundance sighed with relief as the Austrian and the Apache vigorously sealed their friendship.

Then Uklenni turned away. "It is good," he called softly. "Come down, all. Except One-ear and Dreams-too-Much. The two of you keep watch at the canyon mouth."

And then the Apaches materialized. From behind rocks and clumps of brush that seemed too small to hide a rabbit, much less a human being, they arose. Von Markau gasped as one stood up not ten feet from where he had lain on watch. Then, they leaped nimbly down the hillsides, five, ten, fifteen of them, dislodging hardly a pebble in their progress to the canyon floor.

For some time after that, there was confusion as Uklenni explained to those who had never heard of Sundance about the Indian with the yellow hair, proclaimed him his brother, and the white man from a strange country his brother also. One Indian climbed to the ledge, brought down von Markau's weapons.

"There are presents," Sundance told the Apaches. He and von Markau went to the packs, returned with a knife, ax and pouch of tobacco for each brave. Then, after they had thanked him ceremoniously, as delighted as children with the Bowies and hatchets, Sundance said, "Uklenni. We must talk."

"I think the same. Will you eat with us?"

"Yes," Sundance said. "Have you seen any other white men in the Dragoons?"

"No," Uklenni said. "You are the first white-eyes we have seen in weeks."

"Then it should be all right to build a fire." Sundance gestured. "If you would like a mule . . ."

Uklenni's eyes brightened. "Excellent!" He snapped an order. The men looked pleased. They examined the mules, chose the smallest and least prepossessing. Then von Markau let out a strangled sound as one leaped on the animal's back and cut its throat. It fell, kicking, and the others swarmed over it like ants. It was dead at once. With magical speed, they butchered it and began to roast its flesh over fires of brush so dry it made hardly any smoke. Von Markau swallowed hard. "Roast *mule*?"

"Eat it," Sundance said. "The custom of the country—and one of the Apache's favorite foods." He grinned. "Don't look so green. They feel the same way about fish and pork that you do about mule. The very thought of eating bacon would turn their stomachs inside out."

Von Markau nodded. "When in Rome, then . . ." And he bravely ate his share. Then he turned, reached for his saddle bag. Sundance caught the gesture just in time.

"Baron!" he snapped. "Don't bring that bottle out where they can see it!" He spoke in English, softly, furiously.

Von Markau blinked, then understood. "Yes, of course. I see the risk." He masked the gesture by finding a scarf, wiping his mouth. Uklenni, stomach bulging, face smeared with grease, looked curiously from one to the other. "I think it is better if the two of you talk Mexican," he said.

Sundance nodded.

Uklenni went on. "You are lucky I was with this band. It might have been different if no one had been here who knew you. I recognized you at once, but"—his face sobered—"one never knows nowadays who is his friend and who his enemy." He fingered the bear-claw necklace around his throat. "You took a long risk. Even in Apache clothes, that yellow hair might have cost your life." Now he was very serious. "Sundance, what brings you here?"

"Big Medicine," Sundance said. "I must see Cochise. Is he nearby?"

"No," said Uklenni. "He is far away."

"Bad luck. A matter of much importance. How far away?"

"North, to the edge of Mescalero country.

Food is scarce in the Dragoons. We band with the Mescaleros in cooking mescal, growing corn. After that, the sacred festivals."

Sundance considered. That would be two days' good ride, maybe more and the same back, plus talking time. Five days lost, anyhow. And with people like Red Gannon in Tucson and rumors floating around an army post, five days was a lot of time.

Before he could continue, Uklenni went on. "But while Cochise is away, I speak for him here. My men and I scout the country and wait for raiding parties who are off in Mexico. Otherwise, the Dragoons are for the moment empty of Chiricahua. That is why you were not found sooner yourself."

Sundance nodded. These were Cochise's rear guard, to give alarm if soldiers or vigilantes entered his territory. Even though he talked peace with representatives from Washington, Cochise did not trust the Army or any other white men; and Sundance did not blame him. But maybe this was a break; Uklenni might be easier to deal with. "Then," he said simply, "I will tell you what business I had with Cochise. After which, you will decide whether we must see him before we go on—or turn back."

93

"I listen," Uklenni said, slicing off another chunk of mule with his knife.

Slowly, carefully, Sundance explained about the jewels of Maximilian. From time to time, Uklenni asked questions; Sundance answered each painstakingly and with utter honesty; lying to Apaches was a dangerous business, for they seemed to have a sixth sense that told them when someone was trying to bamboozle them.

When he was finished, Uklenni sat for several minutes without speaking. "I think," he said at last, "that such things would be worth very much in trade to white men, or the Mexicans. I have seen such things in their churches and sometimes on their women. For the like, they would trade many cattle, lots of food, guns, knives, cloth"—his eyes glittered—"and whiskey."

"That is true," Sundance said.

"And these precious things you seek are in Apache country. Thus they belong to the Apaches. Why should you be free to take them out when we can trade them to the Americans ourselves?"

"What you say is true and wise," Sundance said. They spoke in Spanish and von Markau

94

sat straight up, shot a startled look at him. "Except for this. The Americans would not deal with the Apaches for things of such value. They would not recognize your right to them. They would say, 'Why should an Indian have such things?' And they would take them from you."

Uklenni laughed defiantly. "Hah! Take them from the Chiricahua?"

Sundance nodded. "If you went to a fort with them, the soldiers would take them from you with their guns; if you asked white men in here to trade, they would bring an army to steal them from you, a big army, and you would have to fight and many of your tribe would die. I tell you, Uklenni, these are big medicine things, they would bring every fighting man in Arizona into the Dragoons if it were known that they were here. Just as gold has brought men into the territory of the Sioux so that they must fight a war."

"Hah! And we are not Sioux!" Then Uklenni sobered. "But I see what you mean. These are white men's medicine and bad luck for Indians. If they were cows or horses . . . Yes, I see. They are like the kind of rock on the desert that draws down the lightning when the storms come. You are right, Sundance. This is a matter for Cochise to decide."

"Then," Sundance said, "let's do this. You and your men go with us to the place where the jewels are. When we find them, we will all go to Cochise together. Show them to him and he can decide. If he will let me take them out, I will pay the Chiricahua much white man's money. The money they can safely trade, a little at a time. I will pay the Chiricahua enough to buy a cow for everyone in the tribe."

Uklenni's eyes glittered. He picked his teeth with the point of his knife. Von Markau looked as if he would protest, then held his peace at Sundance's gesture.

Then the Apache nodded decisively. "It is good," he said. "We will go with you, find this sacred treasure, and take it to Cochise for his decision. But San Simon Creek is a long way." He jumped to his feet. "We should start at once."

"Fine!" Sundance arose. "Do you ride or run?"

"We run. Food is too scarce to ride; we eat what horses we can get."

"Then I will run with you. But the white man must ride. And he must lead my stallion.

That is my warhorse, and he is not to be eaten."

"Be it so," Uklenni said. He squinted at the sun. "Then pack your things and let us go. We can make many miles by nightfall."

Sundance had almost forgotten what it was like to run with Apaches. They were not horsemen in the sense the Cheyennes were, although they could ride anything with hair on it. For them, horses were not property to be cherished, but food to fill their bellies. When they laid their hands on stolen mounts, they would ride them to death, then eat them. Otherwise, they traveled on foot, through country in which a horse was often a liability. Generations of such a life had produced a race with immensely powerful legs and lungs half again the size of those of ordinary men. Like wolves, they could lope for hours, uphill or down, without tiring.

Sundance, on the other hand, had grown up, lived, on horseback. Yet, in his time, he had run with the Chiricahuas. He still remembered—indeed, would never forget—passing one of the strictest tests of Apache boyhood: filling his mouth with water, running five miles across the desert, and

97

returning to the starting point to spit it out and prove he had not swallowed it.

But that had been long ago, and loping eastward beside Uklenni through sun-blasted valleys, up gravelly hillsides, over lava flats and across ridges, legs accustomed to the saddle knotted, lungs unused to such demands ached. But he was careful to betray no sign of distress. For what lay ahead, he must have the complete respect of the Chiricahuas. And it was worth the temporary discomfort to be assured of their protection and good will.

It was no wonder, he thought, that American cavalry with all its gear and trappings had so little luck in running down Apaches. The Indians carried almost nothing except their weapons. A bit of dried meat, some *piñole* made from ground corn, perhaps water flasks made from reeds and sealed with piñon pitch, the little buckskin bag of *Hoddentin*, the sacred pollen for use in prayers at night and morning, and their various sacred amulets or medicine bags. With no more burden than that, they traveled at the speed of a trotting horse across brutal country.

They made fifteen miles that afternoon; by then, Sundance, who kept himself always in superb shape, had got a second wind and was almost enjoying the run. Von Markau, however, trying to keep up on horseback, was nearly exhausted; more than once, Sundance saw him eyeing the saddlebag that held the cognac and warned him away from it with a glance.

They camped that night in a cleft of rocks in which they and the animals were invisible to any creature without wings, dined off the remainder of the mule meat, which had been packed along. Afterward, while the other Indians laughed over a game of *monté* played with horsehide cards, Sundance and Uklenni talked, with von Markau listening drowsily. Once he put in, a little testily, in English: "Sundance, I can't get all these Indians straight. Chiricahua, Tontos, Mescaleros, Yavapais, Gilas, what's the difference?"

"Don't worry about it," Sundance told him, speaking Spanish as Uklenni wanted him to. "It depends on the range they live on at any time, who their chief is. Sometimes they mix together, sometimes split off, but they're all the Apache nation, and they work together."

"Yes," Uklenni said, firelight glittering on his dark face. "We are all one people. And we

99

will all fight the white-eyes together if they crowd us any more. They will find that out." Then, without a blanket, he lay down in the lee of a rock, promptly went to sleep.

Sundance spread his own blankets, and von Markau made his bed close by, as if for safety. Sundance was soon asleep; he awakened once, roused by von Markau stirring; except for the guards on the rim above, the rest of the Apaches also slept. Sundance heard the gurgling of liquid, von Markau swallow, sigh.

He rolled over, put his mouth close to the Baron's ear. "Listen," he rasped. "Put that damned stuff up and keep it up or I'll pour it out. You let the Chiricahuas see it, they'll take it away from you and drink it, and then all bets are off. If I have to kill one to save your hair—Damn it, you don't know what a drunken Indian's like!"

"I am sorry," von Markau whispered. "But I was so exhausted."

"You're going to be a hell of a lot tireder before this is over. Now keep that out of sight."

He rolled back in his blankets, wondering if it wouldn't be smarter to steal the stuff from von Markau's saddlebags, pour it out. But there was no opportunity to do that now; not without attracting the Chiricahuas' attention. Von Markau didn't have much, only a couple of bottles. But it didn't take much for Indians, himself included. Two, three drinks around and there could be bad trouble. Well, he would keep an eye on those saddlebags.

Anyhow, he thought, cramping his rifle closer to him beneath the blankets, so far all had gone better than he dared to hope. Maybe, if his luck held, they could get the jewels and get out of the Dragoons without having to fight at all. Two more days would see them at Dead Man's Canyon, and another three afterward would bring them to Cochise, and with an escort from the great chief, their safety would be assured.

The highest peaks of the Dragoons clawed up to nearly ten thousand feet. In the center of the range was the stronghold of the Chiricahuas, an impregnable fortress of broken country, deserted, now, Sundance knew from Uklenni, while the Indians sought food elsewhere. The journey through the mountains with the tireless Apaches was a nightmare, even for the whipcord-tough Sundance. They knew all the gaps and passes, but even these were rugged; moreover, they did not always use them. They never let down their guard, preferring sometimes to take the longer, harder way around rather than risk a passage where ambush was possible, even though there were supposed to be no white men in their range. Sometimes they split up, part of the band traveling by one route, part by another, meeting again at a prearranged point, to confuse anyone who might strike their trail.

Tough as it was, Sundance ran on with them. When they paused to hunt, the mule meat gone, he joined them. There was food enough on the remaining pack mules for himself and von Markau, but not for all the Indians; besides, he preferred to share their hunting and their rations to maintain his acceptance by them.

He brought down quail and jackrabbits with arrows or helped the Apaches run them down on foot. But he could not match their fleetness. Trained from boyhood in running, they were all incredibly swift, could overtake a fleeing hare and kill it with a stick.

They ate rats, too, flushing them out of burrows by closing the escape exits, breaking the rat's neck with a deft movement of a curved stick when it popped out of the main hole. Gutted, roasted, the little animals were devoured eagerly. Von Markau tried not to watch, refused to sample them, though Sundance pointed out that they fed only on seeds and fruits, were cleaner than any pig or chicken.

Indeed, everything was grist for the Apaches' mill. Hardly a plant grew or living creature moved that they had not learned to eat. And when nothing was at hand, they fasted and ignored their hunger.

Now they traveled down the eastern slopes of the Dragoons to the valley of San Simon Creek. Ahead loomed the rugged outline of the Peloncillos—and somewhere in there was Dead Man's Canyon; and somewhere in Dead Man's Canyon were the jewels of Maximilian.

They crossed a furnace plain on which dust devils swirled and capered. Once a minor sandstorm halted them; they hunkered behind rocks until its gritty cloud had passed. They reached the creek; it was dry, but they dug deep enough in the sand to find water for themselves and animals. And they scouted, looking for the signs of passage of any strangers, found none.

"I think we're going to bring it off," Sundance said. "That is, if Cochise will let us take them out of his country. And I believe he will. He's smart enough to know that if word gets around that there's a treasure like that in here, he'll be overrun."

"I hope so," von Markau said fervently. He was a vastly different man from the one who, less than a week before, had ridden out of Tucson. He had lost weight, his body seemed shrunken on its frame, all surplus water and extra fat boiled out of it. His face was sun-blistered, his lips cracked and swollen. Still, he was tough, did not complain, even though Sundance knew that saddle galls were festering on his thighs; and although he must have longed for a drink, he had not touched the bottles in his saddlebags.

They moved on, into the rough country of the Peloncillos. Uklenni and Sundance conferred, turned south through a devil's broth of broken rock and cactus and stunted juniper. They wound through a narrow defile so rugged that von Markau had to dismount, the horses and mules had to be led.

"Gott in Himmel!" von Markau panted. "How much farther?" He squinted at the brazen sky, in which the sun seemed pinned

like a fiery medallion. It was just past noon, the hottest time of day. "Can't we rest awhile?"

Sundance grinned, white teeth flashing in a face burned by the desert to a deeper bronze. "If we keep on, by nightfall we ought to have the jewels. Time enough to rest then."

The Baron pulled at his horse's reins. "In that case," he said determinedly, "let's go."

The gorge narrowed, became even rougher. The Apaches scouted ahead, soundlessly, tirelessly, like wraiths. Sundance led Eagle over piles and barriers of boulders, through thickets of every sort of spiny growth. Von Markau stumbled along behind, and more Indians brought up the rear.

That nightmare journey lasted for two hours more. Then, suddenly, the gorge turned, widened. In its east wall, a great split appeared, a gap, the mouth of a lateral canyon. Above towered rugged, saw-toothed peaks and ridges.

Uklenni halted atop a rock, a figure seemingly carved from mahogany. He waited until Sundance and the Baron came up. Then he pointed. "There," he said. "I think that is the place you seek. Once the Apaches, the old men say, killed very many men there, strange

105

men with iron shells upon their bodies. Since then, it has had its name. That is the mouth of Dead Man's Canyon."

Von Markau leaned against the rock, panting, gasping, sweat running down his face in rivulets. "At last," he whispered. He jerked his horse's reins, staggered forward, moving ahead of all the rest toward the dark, forbidding place to which his Emperor had ordered him. But Sundance stopped him. "No," he said. "Wait. Let me and the Apaches scout the place first. We've come too far to take any chances now."

Sundance rode cautiously, rifle at the ready, while the Chiricahuas loped ahead. A quarter of a mile beyond the entrance, Dead Man's Canyon fanned out to a width of a half mile; it stretched on, as Sundance remembered, for five or six times that in length, boxed at the other end. The walls above it were steep, jagged piles of rock, although its floor was comparatively level and sandy.

He kept his eyes on the right wall. Somewhere up there, about halfway down the canyon, was a boulder bigger than a house, shaped like a cone. Above it a hundred yards, there should be a ledge. And twenty paces east along that ledge, there was a crack too narrow to be called a cave. In that, concealed by a small landslide of stones and gravel, Father Tomás had supposedly hidden the jewels of Maximilian.

But the jewels could rest for now. Indians fanned out on either wall, disappeared into the rocks. Sundance watched the skyline, saw nothing suspicious on it. But an army could hide up on that broken rim. He crisscrossed the canyon floor, seeking sign of passage by any white man, found none. Then, from far away, there was the sound of a hunting hawk. Thin, mewing, it quavered once, twice, thrice in the silence.

Sundance wheeled Eagle, galloped back along the canyon. Then he signaled with his rifle to von Markau, waiting with a few Indians at the mouth. The coast was clear, and as von Markau read that message, he spurred his horse, put it into a dead run. The map was in his hand when he pulled up beside the halfbreed.

"Have you seen it yet? The rock? The landmark?"

Sundance pointed with the rifle barrel. Just before he had turned around, he had caught sight of it, high on the canyon wall. "Down there," he said; touched Eagle with his heels;

and rode. Von Markau galloped beside him. When they were at midpoint in the canyon's length, he reined in. "That's it!" he cried. He stood in his stirrups, pointed. "That's it!"

"Yes," Sundance said. "Let's go up."

The sun was like a torch as, on foot, they scrambled up the nearly vertical slope, Apaches climbing with them. Above, the great boulder pointed toward the sky like the crown of an enormous hat. They reached its base, stopped for breath; even Uklenni was winded, chest heaving as they paused in its shade. He grinned at Sundance, pointed. "Look," he said. "One of the old iron shells."

Sundance followed his gesture. There, lodged in rocks on the canyon wall, the cuirass of a suit of Spanish armor, now hardly more than an arch of red rust, lay among the cactus. A few white bones, protruding from the sand around it, were stark.

Impatiently, the Baron scrabbled on up the wall, sending down a fall of talus. "Dammit," Sundance snapped, "you want to start a rock-slide?" But he and Uklenni hurried after. He was feeling an excitement that matched the Baron's own, a strange, greedy eagerness.

"Here's the ledge!" von Markau crowed. He

stood erect on a shelf about four feet wide, lined himself with the center of the boulder, faced east and, as Sundance and Uklenni came behind, began to pace. "One, two, three . . ." His voice was tense as he stalked carefully along. Sundance at his heels. "Seventeen, eighteen, nineteen . . . twenty!" He halted, whirled and faced the cliff. There, a pile of rubble, no different from a thousand others like it along the canyon walls, had fallen down, lodged on the shelf. Von Markau made a sound in his throat, fell to his knees, began to dig with his bare hands, throwing rock aside. Sundance and Uklenni joined him. Rock crashed and rebounded off the shelf as they made their excavation. Then von Markau crowed again. His hand disappeared through the rocks, he leaned forward, his arm vanished to the shoulder. "We're through!" Hastily, they rammed the remaining stones aside, to reveal a cleft perhaps a yard long, half that high.

"Wait!" Sundance snapped. "We've got to probe that for snakes!"

But he was too late. Sweating, von Markau was already reaching in with both hands. The Austrian grunted, tugged. Sundance and the Apache scrambled back, gave him room. Von

Markau tugged harder. Then it came: a great leather bag, an *aparejo* of the kind used by Spanish packers. It seemed to be very heavy, and it was cracked and split with dryness. Through one of the splits, Sundance caught a dull, golden gleam.

Then it was free, coming so swiftly that von Markau nearly went back off the ledge. He jumped to his feet, picked it up, showing the strain of its weight as he did so: at least a hundred pounds and likely more. His face was wreathed in smiles, glowed. He gave a triumphant laugh. "Sundance! Look! We've got it!" He bent to unfasten its lashings.

"Wait," Sundance said. "Let's get it down the slope. Lay it out on the level." Despite himself, his own hands trembled as he helped von Markau pick it up. What he held was truly a king's ransom. Together, Uklenni following, they lugged the rotting bag down the canyon wall, slipping and sliding. As they reached the level, where their horses were tied, the other Apaches came running, as excited as themselves. They clustered around, chatting excitedly, as Sundance and von Markau gently laid the *aparejo* down. Then they stood back as, with trembling fingers, von Markau unfastened the straps. He seized the bag and lifted, and it came tumbling out into the sand: the treasure of the House of Hapsburg.

Sundance stared, awed, as diamonds, opals, rubies winked in the desert sunlight, as beautifully wrought gold and finely crafted silver fell into the dust. A crown, a chaplet, a brooch, a crucifix, a sceptre, medallions: all rich metal, magnificent jewels. And more, it tumbled out seemingly without end, until the space all around von Markau's booted feet shone with its glory. The Apaches, gasped, put their hands over their mouths. Sundance licked his lips involuntarily.

Von Markau backed away, stood there a moment, staring down at that vast treasure in a kind of awestruck reverence. Slowly, he crossed himself. He seemed in a kind of daze. Then he turned away, went to his own saddlebags. Sundance hardly noticed, kneeling to touch a great, cold-glittering diamond set in a cross of gold and ivory.

Then von Markau's voice rang out in the silence. "Gentlemen!" he cried exuberantly, "I give you the Archduke Ferdinand Maximilian, crown prince of Austria, Emperor of Mexico, God rest his soul!"

Sundance looked up, too late, and froze, as he saw von Markau pull the cork from the cognac bottle, put it to his mouth and drink.

6

SO far there had been no killings.

A big fire burned in the center of the canyon like a beacon. One Indian sat pounding on a saddle bag as if it were a drum; another rhythmically hit an empty cognac bottle with a knife blade. Five more danced unsteadily around the fire; two lay sound asleep, and one of those was Uklenni. The rest of the Apaches giggled and quarreled over a *monté* game like kindergarten children, their weapons laid aside. Sundance stared in fury at von Markau. "You see?" he rasped in English. "Now do you see what I meant?"

The Baron stared at the spectacle of fifteen Indians roaring drunk on four bottles of cognac. "Sundance, I am sorry, I did not realize—"

"Realize! I—" He stopped. "Well, the damage is done."

Von Markau's hands caressed the huge bag between his feet. "Perhaps not so much. The cognac's all gone. One night's carouse. Is that so harmful?"

"You'd better hope it isn't." Sundance cast an eye at the shadowed rimrock all around them. "You'd better damned well hope there's nobody else on the track of this treasure or even in these mountains. Because that fire and all this racket will bring 'em like buzzards to a carcass." He spat disgustedly. "And I can't even leave you to scout. If I did, I'd probably come back and find your throat cut."

Von Markau touched his pistol. "I can take care of myself."

"Oh, sure. You saw how they went for that booze." The minute the Apaches had seen the bottle in von Markau's hand, they had been like wolves on the hot scent of game. And Uklenni had been the first and worst of all. Even as the Baron had lowered the quart of cognac, still nearly full, the Apache leader had, quite without ceremony, snatched it from his hand. "Thank you, brother," he grunted in his own dialect, rammed the bottle in his mouth, drank long and deeply. And in that instant, the others had already swarmed about von Markau's horse, rummaging in his saddle bags.

He had brought four bottles, and they found them all. And there has been nothing

114

Sundance could do. Once someone was his friend, an Apache would die before stealing from him. But whiskey was different. That was a rare treat, to be seized and shared, and they swarmed all over the four quarts, arguing, laughing, drinking greedily, everything else forgotten. The cognac was high proof, the sun strong, their bodies dehydrated and their systems unused to alcohol; the effect was instantaneous. Fifteen white men sharing four bottles might have become a little tipsy; the Apaches were quickly dead drunk.

"Yeah," Sundance grated, "you can take care of yourself, all right. Listen, they're mean, now, not responsible for their actions. One comes at you, you'd have to put a bullet in him to stop him. Then the rest would be all over you and—" He made a chopping gesture. "You'd better just hope they don't decide they want to divvy up all that pretty stuff in the bag. They're liable to kill both of us if they do—and then be sorry in the morning when it's too late."

He sat down beside von Markau. "Well, I'll side you." His rifle was cradled across his knees, and Eagle, the warhorse, guarded his rear. "Let's hope they just stay good-humored. And tomorrow morning, they're gonna feel like hell and—" He stiffened. One of the Apaches, a brave named Bû, the Owl, had left the card game, was lurching across the firelight toward them. His voice was thick, his eyes glittering, as he mumbled in Chiricahua dialect: "*Tiswin*. More *tiswin*."

"There is no more *tiswin*."

Bû knew a little English. "Goddammit," he growled, "you give me one time *tiswin*. You got more. Pletty damn much more . . ."

"I said there is no more!" Sundance snapped.

Bû swayed, mouth a slit in a mask of a face. "Lie," he grunted, in Apache language once again. "Yellow-headed Apache is no Apache, only white-eye liar. And wants *tiswin* for himself." His hand dropped to a sheathed knife. Sundance swung the rifle muzzle around, centered it on his chest.

The gunshot was thunderous in the confines of the canyon.

Bû stood on tiptoes, eyes wide, clutched his back. He opened his mouth and blood poured from it. Then he fell sideways, dead before he hit the ground.

"Sundance!" von Markau cried in horror.

Sundance stood frozen for a split second, the unfired rifle still in his hand. Then he roared: "Out of the light!" He fell backwards, too, hit von Markau, seized the man's shirt, dragged him over. They rolled out of the circle of yellow fire gleam just as the canyon wall to the right came alive with spitting orange gunflashes, and the sound of rifles crashed from rock to rock like thunder.

Sundance rolled again, landed on his belly, tilted up the Winchester, worked the lever. Around the fire, the dancing Apaches halted dazedly. Then every one of them went down beneath a withering sleet of lead. The man who beat the saddlebags screamed, fell backward. The cognac bottle in the hand of the other dissolved in shards as a bullet struck it. Then the next blew off the top of his head.

Sundance saw that much as he returned the fire from the slope above, pumping round after round from the Winchester at those orange flashes. He heard a man cry out up there, a thin, reedy sound, but the shooting went on. The card players had scrambled to their feet, leaped for their weapons. None made it; he saw them whirl, crumple, fall. It was as if a mighty hand had slapped them all. Then Uklenni and the other sleeping Indian were on their feet. Uklenni, dazed, took one step forward. A rifle bullet caught him in the mouth. He was jerked backwards into darkness beyond the firelight. The last Apache fell across his feet, three bullets in his chest; and now Sundance's gun was empty. He rolled over, scrabbling desperately for cartridges from his belt, shoving them through the loading port. But while he did that, the canyon fell silent, save for the frightened snorting of the animals.

Sundance rammed in the last cartridge the gun would hold, rolled back into firing position. "Von Markau," he began, "swing around outside the firelight. See if you can get Uklenni's rifle. Don't try for your own, it's where they can see you. There's ten, maybe fifteen men up there and—"

A voice sliced through his words. "Sundance," it roared from up above, and in the chill night, the echoes bounced it back and forth from cliff to cliff. *"Sundance, Sundance . . ."*

Sundance froze. "They know your name," von Markau whispered.

The voice came again. "Sundance! Von Markau! This is Gannon!"

"And yours," Sundance rasped.

"Gannon? Who—?"

"The one man I was afraid of. In Tucson

118

with a bunch of hardcases when we left. Somehow he got wind—"

"*Sundance!* We know you're down there, you and the Dutchy! We know you got the treasure, too! You might as well give up! All your Injun friends are dead, and we got the canyon mouth blocked. Neither one of you has got a prayer! We can come and take you any time we want to."

Sundance clenched his teeth. Wild fury flamed in him. "Then come ahead!" he roared back defiantly. "Maybe you'll get us, but we'll get some of you!"

"Shore!" Gannon yelled back from the slope above. "But there's a joker in the deck. A damn purty one! Her name's Miz von Markau, and if you and that Dutchman don't give up, we're gonna cut her throat! You see, we got her with us up here, and either you throw down your guns, or you and her husband can listen to her scream awhile before we finish her!"

Beside Sundance, von Markau made a strangled sound. "Herta? How—? *Mein Gott—*"

"You don't believe us?" Gannon bellowed. "Listen!"

There was a second's silence before the

night was shattered by a woman's scream. *"Walther!"* she wailed. "Walther, in the name of heaven—"

"It *is* she!" von Markau rasped. "How did they get her?" Then he got to his knees. "Herta!" he cried. "Herta, are you there?"

His answer was another scream. "Walther, please—"

"Get down," Sundance rasped. "You can't help her now."

"Yes. Yes, I can." Suddenly Sundance felt a hard pressure in his ribs. He recognized it at once, the muzzle of a pistol.

Von Markau's voice was hard, cold. "Those fiends up there have my wife. I don't know how they got her, but I'll not have her tortured. Drop your gun, Sundance. We give up."

"Von Markau, don't be a fool. We can get out of here in the dark, then have a chance—"

"And Herta may be dead." The Baron's voice rose, quavered, and the pistol barrel burrowed harder into Sundance's ribs. "No . . ." Von Markau's voice broke. "I have ruined it, ruined everything, and for that I am very sorry. But now I must think of my wife. On your feet, Jim, without your gun."

There was nothing to do but obey.

Sundance let go the rifle. As he got up, he felt von Markau pull revolver, knife and ax from his belt, throw them out into the firelight. Then von Markau rammed the pistol in his back. The Austrian's voice was full of grief. "Out where they can see us, Jim."

"All right," Sundance said thinly. He raised his hands and, prodded by von Markau, walked slowly into the firelight, bracing himself for the bullet that he was sure would come. To his astonishment, it did not.

"You're a smart man, Dutchy!" Gannon yelled. Then Sundance heard him say, "All right, boys, let's go down."

Ten minutes, fifteen, passed. Sundance stood there beside the fire, von Markau's pistol in his back. Once the Baron said, in a trembling voice, "Jim, you must understand—"

Sundance did not answer. There was nothing to say. It was bitched, all bitched, and fifteen good men were dead, thanks to von Markau's patriotic fervor and stupidity. If the Apaches had been sober, no one would have got within rifle shot of them without the alarm being given. He only stood there, stoically, as the outer darkness came alive with the sound of many men approaching.

121

Gannon's gang came into the firelight. The red-bearded man himself was first to appear, a rifle leveled. His handsome face had wholly recovered from the effects of Sundance's beating. His teeth gleamed white in his ginger beard as he trained the gun on Sundance. "All right, Dutchy. We take over now. You can throw that pistol away."

Von Markau made a sobbing sound. Then he threw the Smith and Wesson into the darkness. At that instant, the rest of them were there with drawn guns, surrounding them. Sundance saw the man called Jessup, Gannon's black-mustached major-domo. At first he thought Jessup wrestled ahead of him a Mexican boy, arm held in a hammerlock. Then he tensed. That was no boy: it was Herta von Markau, eyes wide, face pale, hair falling from beneath her sombrero, breasts heaving under her tight shirt.

When he saw her, the Baron gave a wordless cry, took a step forward. Gannon swung the gun. "Stand hitched, Dutchy."

Under the threat, von Markau froze. He and the woman looked at one another. "Herta," he whispered, "how—"

She turned her face away.

Gannon moved forward, still grinning.

122

"That's a right hot little piece you got there, Dutchy!" He jerked up the gun as the Baron rocked forward. "She didn't hang around the fort long after you and Sundance took off. No, sir, she went into Tucson, where the action is."

"Herta," von Markau groaned, voice despairing. "You—"

She shook her head, staring at the ground. "Walther, I am sorry. I did not mean—"

"You betrayed me," he whispered.

Gannon laughed again. "You're damned well right she did. Come into town a-prowling. I spotted her right off. I mean, I can recognize a slut like her from a mile away, and I moved in. I'm a good sweet-talker, von Markau, and she was kind of all stirred up by what she called a 'real frontiersman'. On top of which, I'm ten years younger than you. You're a little long in the tooth for a kid like this, ain't been keepin' her happy, seems like—"

"He lies," Herta von Markau whimpered. "It was only . . . I was lonely."

"Lonely," the Baron said, and the contempt in the single word was like a blow.

"Oh, she was lonesome all right. Lonesome enough to bed down and git drunk with me.

She don't hold her likker well, Dutchy. She talks a lot. Told me about a treasure, even had a map—"

"I gave her a duplicate," von Markau said dully, "in case something happened to me—"

"Shore. When I got my hands on it, me and my boys took off right away, brought her with us. Figured she might come in handy for bargainin' in case things got tight. Besides, she keeps the blankets warm at night." Gannon chuckled. "We trailed pretty far behind, but we made it up fast. Saw a damn fire, heard all sorts of drummin' and singin', knew it must be you and Sundance and them Apaches we cut sign of. But we shore never expected to find 'em all sittin' ducks for us. When we finally come up, we saw 'em finishin' off the bottles. Figured it would be dead easy, and it was."

His mocking grin vanished. "Tie 'em up!" he snapped. "Hands behind their backs. And some of you check them Injuns. Put a bullet through every head, whether they look dead or not; we'll take no chances." And he swung his gun toward von Markau once again. "Where's the jools?"

As men moved behind Sundance, jerked his hands back, wrapped thongs around them, the Baron's glance went to the leather bag. "Ahhh," Red Gannon said, lust thick in his voice. He knelt beside it, gun still on the Austrian, opened the straps. Then he stood up, seized the bag, shook out its contents. A moan went up from the gunmen around the fire. Gannon crowed: "I told you boys, you stick with me, you'd strike it rich! Feast your eyes on that, but keep your damn hands off it. Nobody touches it until we fence it to a guy I know in Frisco!"

Sundance was tightly bound. Men whipped thongs around von Markau's wrists. The Baron looked at his wife, and his voice trembled. "Herta, how could you do this to me?"

She only stared down at her boot toes, unable to meet his gaze. "All I can say," she breathed, "is forgive me. If you can, forgive me. I can never forgive myself." She shuddered. "I thought . . . It was so lonely at the fort. An innocent affair. Like in Vienna."

"Tucson is not Vienna," von Markau said.

Gannon giggled. "Shore as hell ain't."

The Baron turned on him. Suddenly the Austrian's face was scarlet. "And you, you swine!" He flung himself, bound, at Gannon. Gannon's rifle barrel came up, as the red-

125

bearded man nimbly stepped aside. It made a sodden sound on von Markau's skull. The Austrian pitched forward, lay unconscious beside the fire. Gannon looked down at him. "Well, ain't he rambunctious? I got plans for Sundance, but on second thought, I don't see no reason to bother with a Goddamn Dutchman. Hell, might as well cut his throat right now." And he drew his Bowie from his boot.

Sundance lurched forward. "Gannon!"

Gannon hit him between the eyes. Sundance, stunned, fell backward. "Shut up," Gannon rasped, "or you git the same medicine." Then he rolled von Markau over, knelt beside him. The knife blade flashed in firelight.

Herta screamed, over and over, until Jessup hit her and knocked her out.

7

THE buzzards were black dots in the sky's stainless blue. Sundance saw them circling high above the canyon. His head felt as if it were splitting. That had been a bad move, a foolish one, he thought, but the act had been instinctive. As Gannon had cut von Markau's throat, he had thrown himself at the man. And Jessup had slammed him with a rifle butt, and the world had vanished in a burst of light.

He tried to move. Could not. Slowly, painfully, lifted his head. Then saw that he was spread-eagled, wrists lashed to pegs driven deep in the canyon floor, ankles tied in the same way. And he was naked, stripped of every garment.

He closed his eyes, let the pain subside, opened them again. Then he was looking into the grinning face of Gannon. The man crouched above him, von Markau's Smith and Wesson in his hand.

"Well, good mornin', Sundance," he said. "Don't you look purty all laid out like that?"

His sardonic grin vanished. "You think I forgot that beatin' you handed me at Duppa's? Gannon forgets nothin'. I coulda cut your throat last night, too, but that woulda been so easy. And easy ain't the way I want you to die."

He stood erect. "So I got you fixed good, now. Lots of bodies around to draw the vultures. You and her, Sundance. Because I'm through with her now, too, and so are all the boys. She might as well go the way you do, after what she called me last night. See?" He gestured. Sundance rolled his head.

Like himself, the woman was spread-eagled naked on the canyon floor, not five feet away. She lay with her head turned, eyes closed, and she was crying silently.

"Slow," Gannon said. "That's the word, Sundance. Slow. And hard, goddam hard." He jerked a thumb upward. "The *zopilotes*, the buzzards. There are sixteen bodies here, Sundance, good buzzard bait. Bring every vulture in the territory. It won't take long for them to eat the bones clean. You understand? First, the dead men. Then you and her."

He grinned down at Sundance. "You ever seen buzzards pick a carcass? They come

128

down in flocks, rip, tear at it, fight each other over it. The coyotes come in, too, and fight with 'em. It don't take long to pick a body clean. And the thing about it is, halfbreed, the body don't even have to be dead. Jest so long as it don't move, that's all."

He spun the cylinder of the Smith and Wesson. "A damned good gun." Then he holstered it. "A fortune in jools, a fine pistol; a profitable trip. Not to mention the fun I had with *her*." Then he said, "They go for the soft parts first, Sundance. Your eyes, your lips, down there . . . rip them out with their beaks. It will take you a long time to die. Both of you. But, what the hell. I've seen Apaches stake out white men like that. And you ain't even white."

He waited for Sundance to say something. When there was no answer, he went on. "Well, I'll drink to your bones in San Francisco with the money from the jools. We ride out of here the way we came in. Fast and hard, and God help anybody that tries to stop us. Incidentally, that appaloosie stallion of yours . . . the sonofabitch charged me last night; I shot him. Mean bastard. I didn't kill him, but I'm purty shore I broke his leg. He'll die slow out here, same as you . . ." He turned away. "Jessup!" he yelled. "Everything ready to move out?"

"All ready, boss."

"Then mount up." Gannon stood spraddle-legged over Herta von Markau. "Hey, Dutch woman."

She did not answer, but Sundance could hear the rasp of her breathing.

"All right," Gannon said. "Good-bye, then." And he kicked her, hard. She made a muffled sound, still did not speak.

Sundance rolled his head, saw Gannon and his men mount up. He saw the leather bag tied behind Gannon's saddle. Gannon reined his horse around, tipped his hat sardonically. *"Hasta la vista,"* he said. Then, with big Chihuahua rowels, he spurred the animal so hard it reared. At the head of his band, he galloped out of Dead Man's Canyon.

Sundance lay there, listening to the sound of hoofbeats fading. When they had died, he raised his head, straining his arms against the ropes that bound his wrists.

From where Gannon had staked him out, he could see the bodies scattered everywhere, already turning from red to black in the ferocious heat. He dropped back, looked straight up. The black dots were larger now,

130

like bits of charred paper, swooping and soaring in the hot air that arose from the canyon. Ten, fifteen, more than twenty of them . . . And more appearing over the rim. A feast, he thought, a feast for vultures.

He strained against the ropes that bound his wrists, his feet. Nothing gave; Gannon's men were experts; the stakes were driven deep, the thongs lashed and double-lashed. He wrestled, tugged, until he was exhausted. Then he gave up, sank back. Now he could see the outlines of the wings of the lower tier of birds.

"Herta," he said.

She only groaned.

"Damn it, Herta, come alive."

Her voice was dull. "I do not want to live. I do not deserve to live."

"You don't want to die, either. Not this way. Those buzzards are getting lower. Do you want them to rip out your eyes? Try your ropes. Maybe they didn't tie you as hard?"

He could watch her from the corners of his eyes, see her naked body, already reddening from the brutal sun, writhe and curl. Then she sank back. "I cannot free myself."

Sundance lay with eyes closed. Well, he thought, it was a bad way to die. He opened his eyes again, and the vultures were nearer now.

With a kind of fascination, he watched the birds circle and swoop down. Now that there was no sign of life below, they descended swiftly. He licked his lips, mouth dry, afflicted with a terrible thirst. He sucked in his belly, had a ferocious desire to cross his legs, protect himself. But, of course, he could not move.

"Herta, are you *sure* . . ." He himself wrenched against the bonds again.

He heard her struggling. "I'm sure," she panted, moments later.

Sundance said, "All right. I guess this is it."

She was silent for a moment. Then she said, "Sundance. I do not care what happens to me. Whatever happens, I have earned. But for Walther, I grieve. And for you. It was so different . . . In Vienna, one flirts, it means nothing. I . . . was bored, went into Tucson. Yes. Yes, he was very strong and very . . . different. He . . . aroused me. I am sorry."

Sundance said nothing. Two vultures passed over his line of sight, low enough for him to see every detail of their wing feathers, the sun glinting off of raw, red heads. Then

132

he heard the flutter of their pinions as they landed, each on a corpse outside his range of vision. He heard other sounds, too, closed his mind to them.

There was a chance, he thought, if they were lucky, that they themselves would be dead before the vultures got to them. He knew too well how quickly the sun could kill a man motionless in its full light, with no water to replace the moisture it squeezed out of him. He said, "Herta. Stay awake. Try to stay awake. If a bird lands on you, tries to land, raise up your head and scream. Scream as loud as you can."

"Yes," she answered dully. "All right."

They lay motionless for a while. More vultures flapped down. One tried to land on Sundance. He saw the outstretched talons, the ugly beak, made for ripping, the obscene head. Just as it descended, he jerked his own head up, howled with all his might. Startled, the bird slid sideways, landed, ran over to the dead men.

The scene was repeated. More vultures swirled down. Twisting his head, he saw one about to settle on Herta von Markau. He bellowed; she came out of a daze just in time. Before the talons touched her belly, she jerked up her head, screamed shrilly. The ghastly bird veered off.

But now the sky was full of them above the canyon; this was a feast the carrion-eaters rarely found. It seemed that every vulture in this part of Arizona had caught the smell of death. Instinctively, most of them made for the bloating corpses. But some went for Sundance and for Herta. The two living victims yelled until their throats were hoarse, their voices only croaks. And as the sound they made diminished, and as the corpses around them were occupied by other birds, fighting, croaking horribly over their carrion harvest, the vultures came straight for them. Sundance, in a heatstruck daze, felt a wing brush his face, opened his eyes to stare into the eyes of a vulture, beak outstretched. He croaked, turned his head, and the bird hopped aside. But it came back, circling him slowly. And another lit beside it, and another.

And now, he knew, it was almost over. He jerked his head around, saw Herta von Markau ringed with hunched forms in black. She moaned listlessly, just enough to keep them at bay.

Sundance made one last frantic effort, straining at the ropes and stakes. Earth and sky alike were furnaces, mingling in brazen flames in his vision. He knew he could not last many minutes longer. His dark bronze body writhed, twisted, in one last desperate effort, as a huge black bird, talons outspread, blotted out the sun, about to settle on his head. He yelled at it, but the yell was only a whisper. He felt the cold touch of its claws on his face, the gouge of the horny nails protruding from each one. Then the buzzard had settled on his head. Its body stank terrifically. He rolled his head, but it held on; all he could see was blackness.

Sundance summoned every last ounce of strength, jerked up his head once more, convulsed his body, screamed. The vulture hopped back, and now it was standing on his stomach; he could see it in every obscene detail. His wrists moved in their bonds; then he stiffened. Something had cut his skin.

Not a rope. Something hard, metallic.

He turned his right wrist again. Yes, there, on the back of his hand. When he revolved the wrist, it scraped across the ropes, scraped his hand.

The vulture put its beak down on his belly. Sundance arched his body. "Herta!" he cried. "Keep them off! Keep them off as long as you can! Herta, wake up!"

He rolled his head, saw, through a shimmering haze, the girl rise and twist as another vulture tried to land on her. It dodged, settled beside her, began to walk awkwardly around her. "I've found something," Sundance gasped. He revolved his wrist again. The thing slid back and forth across his bonds; rather, his ropes slid back and forth across it. It had to have a cutting edge, because it slashed the skin.

Now he moved his wrist faster. He felt metal gouge into the back of it, slide across his hand, tearing at the buckskin thongs simultaneously. A buzzard lowered its beak toward his eyes; he bucked his head up and it drew back. But it squatted there, watching him. The one on his stomach challenged it, ran forward, flapping its wings. The two birds fought, all over and around Sundance's face. Their talons gouged his cheeks, barely missed his eyes.

But something was happening now. The sharp object that gashed his arm and hand was chewing into rawhide. Suddenly he felt a thong go. He jerked, the other thongs slid. He pulled harder, folding his hand into a cone. The bonds loosened; his right hand came free. Sundance whooped a hoarse Cheyenne warcry, lashed out with the hand. It struck the vultures. Surprised at the assault, both staggered back, flapped their wings, ran away. Sundance raised his hand high, waved it. "Herta!" he cried. "Herta, I'm loose."

The motion of his waving arm frightened the birds around the girl. One ran, another took slow, flapping, noisy flight. Herta von Markau turned her head, looked dully at Sundance. She was past comprehending.

Blood ran down Sundance's gashed wrist. He did not care. He fumbled awkwardly at the thongs that bound his other hand. It took some time to get them free. But he could use his mouth, his sharp teeth, now that he could raise his right shoulder. The rawhide parted; then, dizzy, he sat up.

All the buzzards took flight then, flapped high, then dropped down on the corpses.

Sundance fumbled with the ropes on his ankles. He got them loose after an eternity; his hands were numb and awkward. Then he scrabbled to his feet, swaying with fatigue.

He stood there a moment, waiting for strength to come back. Then he dropped beside the naked girl, attacked the binding that held her. When her arms were free, he saw life come back into dull eyes. Slowly, she sat up, rubbing her wrists. "What—?" she murmured groggily. Her flowing hair was full of sand.

"We're loose," Sundance whispered. "Wait . . ." He whirled, scratched in the sand for the object that had cut the thongs on his right wrist. He found it, brought it out. It was an enormous spur, with a rowel bigger than the palm of his hand, each point filed by a hand long since dust to saber sharpness. What rusting had taken place in this dry canyon over centuries had not completely dulled the brutal cutting edge. Sundance thought of the cuirass, the piece of armor, on the slope. Once this spur had belonged to a *conquistador*, a Spanish invader of the Apache empire.

Very many men, Sundance thought. Uklenni had said that the Apaches had killed a lot of Spaniards here. Their bones and armor would be scattered up and down the canyon. This spur, long since covered by sand, had been hidden for centuries until the convulsive twisting of his wrist had worked loose the dirt that shielded it. Dead Man's

Canyon, he thought; and a man dead for two centuries or more had saved his life.

The rawhide that bound Herta von Markau's ankles parted easily under the rusty but razor-sharp points of the ancient spur. But she, still dazed, did not move. She had fainted.

Sundance got unsteadily to his feet, blood dripping from his right wrist and the talon-scratches on body and face. All around the ashes of the dead campfire, feeding vultures made a blackness. They squabbled, fought, beaks dripping remnants of their gory meal. Sundance, a little crazy, ran at them, shouting, waving arms, windmilling. The buzzards took fright, lifted off, flapping heavy wings with a sound like water pouring over a fall. He saw them rise, confused, circle, climb higher.

He tried not to look at what they had left. Right now, what he needed was water. There was none in Dead Man's Canyon, and Gannon had taken every bit of his own gear, including the full goatskin on one of the mules. But then he found what he sought: an Apache wicker water bottle. He picked it up, shook it, heard a faint slosh within. He opened it, took enough from it to moisten his lips and mouth. Then he went back to where Herta lay unconscious. He trickled a little over her lips, then ran some down her mouth. There was hardly more than two swallows in the bottle anyhow—a day's ration for an Apache.

The long lashes of her eyelids fluttered as the liquid seeped down her throat. Then she opened her mouth to scream as memory returned.

"Hush," Sundance said. "It's all right. We're not buzzard bait yet." He stood there, naked, bleeding, sun-blistered, looking toward the west. "We'll get out of here somehow. And then I'll find Gannon."

The floor of the canyon around the dead ashes of the fire was a shambles. Sundance searched it carefully for anything of use, especially for weapons. But in this country, rifles, pistols, knives and axes were too precious to be left behind, even by men who possessed a treasure. Not a scrap of armament was left.

But he found clothes. The *vaquero* outfit in which Herta had been disguised so she could be smuggled past Army patrols had been thrown aside. She got into it, as Sundance

140

wrapped his loins in the cloth Gannon had stripped from them, pulled on his Apache moccasins which Gannon had left behind. Nagged by a feeling that there should be something else, he trotted on a wider circuit of the area. Then he saw them: the bullhide panniers he usually carried behind his saddle.

They had been slit open. His shield had been thrown into some nearby rocks. He ran to it, picked it up; this was good luck, part of his medicine. From it dangled six scalps, three black as crows' wings, one brown, one red, one yellow as his own. The last scalps he had ever taken. Those of the six who had murdered his parents north of Bent's Fort.

The other pannier, which had held his bow, arrows, his pipe and a few other items important to him, lay ripped and empty nearby. Sundance climbed up on a rock, looked around carefully. Then a flash of color caught his eye, fifteen yards away, in the rubble. He scrambled over to it, grinned wolfishly as he picked up a Cheyenne arrow, brilliantly painted to make it easy to find in just such circumstances. He continued his search, found a dozen more like it. All pointed in the same direction, though they were widely scattered. Apparently, Gannon's

141

men had amused themselves by shooting his bow.

He backtracked in the direction from which the arrows had come. Thirty yards away, behind another rock, he found the bow, strung, and the quiver, holding the rest of the shafts. Sundance laughed soundlessly, and his face was not a pleasant thing to look upon. The time might come when Gannon would be very sorry indeed that he had not broken these arrows.

He felt better, infused with new strength. He strode back to where Herta sat, hands covering her face. "They left us something, anyhow. Now, we've got to start, walk out of here."

"But, Walther . . ." Her shoulders shook. "He must be . . . buried."

"No," Sundance said harshly. "We don't have water enough to waste our strength on anything like that." His voice gentled. "I'm sorry. I would like to bury Uklenni, too." He pulled her to her feet, held her up, and wordlessly she leaned against him as they began to walk.

Gannon's sign was plain, leading out of the canyon, he and his men traveling fast. They would not, Sundance thought, head back to Tucson nor near any other Army post. Crook would be frantic now, wondering what had happened to the woman he had been supposed to guard, and he would have every soldier under his command seeking trace of her, stopping every traveler. No, if Gannon were smart—and he was—he would head north, then swing west, keeping to the broken country of the Mogollons, taking his chances with Apaches. It was risky, but the risk was worth it for a treasure like the jewels of Maximilian. Anyhow, he would be making all the time he could; no need to worry about an ambush on his backtrail for a while.

They reached the canyon mouth, and then, for a nightmare hour, Sundance pulled and dragged the fainting Herta von Markau, who was still in shock, over rocks and through brush along the gorge. Presently he was exhausted, sank gasping by a boulder, staring down the defile with its barricades of stone and cactus thickets dazedly. His heart sank; he could make it, but the woman—? He had no illusions about what lay ahead. He knew where he was going, and alone, even on foot, he could get there, somehow. But could he get there with her?

Still, he had to try. They started out again, and this time she was more help, but still not enough. After two more miles, Sundance was again exhausted; and it was plain now that she would never make it. Well, this was no place to spend the night, this far from water, but she must rest.

Then he tensed, and with a swift motion drew an arrow from the panther-skin quiver, nocked it to the bow. "Get down," he hissed, and shoved Herta behind a rock, disappeared behind another, seeming to melt into the terrain. From down the gorge, the sound came again, faint, yet unmistakable: the click of shod hoof on rock. Sundance held his breath, waited.

Then he caught a glimpse of color in that wild jumble of rock and scrub. Suddenly he relaxed, then jumped to his feet. He gave a low whistle, like that of a prairie lark.

From behind a pile of boulders, something like a trumpet answered him, and a surge of joy went through Sundance, followed by apprehension. Herta forgotten for the moment, he leaped over the rock, plunged down the gorge, stumbling, his flesh ripped by thorns. At the same time, hoofs scrabbled on stone; then Eagle appeared, stripped of bridle and saddle, broken picket rope trailing.

And yet, as he approached the horse, a kind of coldness filled Sundance. *I'm pretty sure I broke his leg.* If that were true, he would have to use an arrow on the stallion—

He halted, watched the horse's movement as it plunged toward him. Yes, he thought bitterly, its off hind leg was crippled. Then he ran again, and he and the horse came together. Eagle thrust his head against Sundance, bowing crested neck, nickered softly. Sundance rubbed his forelock, then, with a heart that seemed to stop beating, went to Eagle's rump.

Then something unknotted within him. A bullet had gouged a huge chunk of flesh from the hind-quarter; and flies and gnats already swarmed around the ghastly wound. But it had broken no bone, cut no important tendon. If the wound did not fester, Eagle would recover, though he would have trouble traveling for a while.

"Wait," he told the stallion. It nickered as he went back to where Herta slumped behind a rock, scrambled after him. He picked up the girl, slapped her awake out of her exhaustion, dragged her down the gorge. Somehow he got her on the horse's back.

It was going to be hard on Eagle, but he knew the animal's endurance. He rubbed the velvet muzzle, scratched the topknot. Then he started down the gorge again, and Eagle limped behind, the girl slumped across his neck, clinging to his mane.

They finally reached the gorge's end. Now they were in comparatively open country. Sundance scouted; there was no sign of Gannon. He began to lope, like an Apache. Eagle hobbled along behind.

Sundance turned not west, toward Tucson, but north. He thought of Uklenni, von Markau, and of the vulture standing on his face; and the hatred within him was a flame. Everything else could wait; but he was not letting Gannon get away.

He could not fight fifteen men alone, unarmed, so he had to go north, find Cochise, up in the Mogollons with the Mescaleros, and seek his help.

8

TORMENTED by flies around the healing bullet wound, despite the juniper pitch with which Sundance had smeared it, Eagle hobbled as he ascended the steep slope of the Mogollon rim. But it was cooler here; at this altitude, the trees were bigger, juniper giving way occasionally to pine; the harsh sacaton yielded to nutritious grama, on which Eagle gorged himself; sometimes there was running water, bubbling springs or flowing streams. In these, Sundance and Herta von Markau drank their fill and, naked, let the current wash and cool their scraped, dusty, exhausted bodies.

Three days it had taken them to gain the Mogollons; and slowly the girl was coming out of shock. But, Sundance thought, maybe it would have been better if she hadn't. She had recovered physically, but tortured by regret, she was in mental agony. As she lay resting on a rock, after a swim in a stream, while Sundance broiled a wild turkey he had

147

brought down with an arrow, she drew the jacket of the *vaquero* outfit around her, shivered, and covered her face with her hands. "Sundance." Her voice was muffled.

"Yes." He fed the fire.

"How can I ever forgive myself?"

He was silent for a moment. Then he said, "You didn't know. You couldn't know about what kind of country this is, you'd never met a man like Gannon. You made a mistake, but von Markau made some, too. The first was buying you like a piece of property—he told me about that, how he paid your family's debts—and expecting your love and loyalty for that. The second was bringing you to Arizona with him. The third was disobeying me, breaking out that cognac; if he hadn't, Gannon would never have caught us off guard. What neither one of you knew is that this is a country that doesn't allow you even one mistake."

"Still, I did betray him. And now he is dead. A lot of men are."

"People die all the time in Arizona; death is a part of this country, like the mountains, the deserts. The Apaches mourn their dead and never speak their names again, and sometimes even burn their villages. After death,

148

they wipe out everything, make a fresh start. Out here, it's the only way to survive. Regret won't bring von Markau back; but the lesson you've learned may save somebody else someday. Come and eat; we've got a long way to travel before the sun goes down."

She looked at him strangely as she sat down across the fire from him. "I have never met a man like you, either," she said. "Thank you for your kindness. Kindness is not something I have come to expect from men. All my life, I have only been something men wanted, felt they had to have, not someone to whom they should be kind. Perhaps that made me bitter, perhaps I wanted to get revenge on them . . ." She touched her hair. "I feel better, now."

And after that, she began to come to life again. They rode on that afternoon, camped that night. The next day, they found Cochise.

Or rather, his scouts, as Sundance had expected, found them. When Sundance awakened at daybreak, shivering from the cold, he sat up to look straight into the eyes of an Apache hunkered over him, rifle pointed at him. Three more squatted in a circle all around them.

"So you are awake," the Apache said. "An

149

Indian with yellow hair. And a white-eye woman. What is this?"

He betrayed no surprise when Sundance answered in fluent Chiricahua. "My name is Sundance, of the Cheyennes; but I am also an adopted Chiricahua. Cochise is my godfather, and I have news for him, bad news, of Uklenni and Uklenni's people, and I would ask you to take me to him."

"Sundance." The Apache considered. "I think I have heard of you. *Inju.* Good. On your feet. We'll take you to Cochise. But be very careful, do not make one wrong move."

They crested a ridge, pine-clad and grassy, rode down a long, broken slope into a deep basin. There smokes, a dozen of them, curled skyward in thin, steady columns. In a fold by a creek on the basin floor, they found the *ranchería*, the Apache village.

As they rounded a ridge and it came in sight, Sundance drew in a long breath. It was almost like coming home.

The camp was a big one, the Chiricahuas and the Tontos and Mescaleros having come together. Sundance recognized the brush shelters of the first two bands, rude domes of limbs and foliage over which cloth and deerhides had been thrown to help cut the

150

wind, spread out along the stream. Farther away were the teepees of the Mescaleros, who, ranging out onto the plains, had adopted that sort of shelter from the buffalo tribes. Three hundred people, maybe more, Sundance judged, as Choddi—Antelope—the chief of the patrol, led them into the village.

Not many men were present; they hunted or scouted or, perhaps, even raided somewhere far enough not to draw down revenge upon the *ranchería*. Women were everywhere, working hard, dressed in deerskins or in cloth bought in trade, their garments voluminous, modest. The smokes came from great pits in which mescal cooked; it was the staple food of the tribe. Leaves, stalks, and the central bulb, like a huge onion, were all baked together in the pits for three days, producing a sweet gluey mixture which the Apaches loved, and which they dried in sheets. Other women tended small cornfields, and still others, Sundance knew, would be on the mountainsides, digging wild potatoes and gathering piñon nuts, acorns, black walnuts, grass seeds, *nopal* fruit, and sunflower seeds which they would combine with mesquite beans to make a rich bread. Weavers were at work, too, making the tightly woven, superb

Apache basketry. A few men were busy sewing buckskin; that was a peculiarity of the tribe; the men were all expert tailors, sewed beautifully. Some others gambled, tossing painted sticks in the game of *Tze-chis*; and children, mostly naked, were everywhere, the boys practicing throwing lances, the girls playing with dolls or helping their mothers gather firewood.

Choddi called out as they entered the village. Everyone looked up, all activity ceased. The people crowded forward, staring curiously at the strange spectacle: an Apache with yellow hair and a beautiful white woman in Mexican clothes mounted on an appaloosa stallion. They chattered in wonder, and the children stood open-mouthed. Sundance searched for familiar faces in the crowd, saw none.

Choddi gestured to him to stop the stallion. Sundance, walking beside Eagle, halted him with a touch. Now the crowd moved in closer, and one woman with a strange deformity reached out, touched Herta von Markau's boot.

Herta shrank back. "Sundance," she whispered, "what happened to her?"

Sundance looked at the woman. "She was

caught in adultery," he said flatly. "Her husband cut off the end of her nose."

"Oh," Herta said faintly and, shuddering, put one hand over her face.

Then a hush fell over the crowd. It parted, and Sundance looked around. People made way for a tall, wide-shouldered man with iron-gray hair. He wore a buckskin shirt, loin cloth, leggings, some hawk's plumage in the band bound around his head. A Colt revolver was strapped around his waist. He came forward, square-faced, massive, halted before Sundance, legs spraddled. Black eyes probed Sundance's face, ranged over the scarred, coppery body.

They stood like that for a long moment, looking at one another.

"My father," Sundance said softly.

The hard face broke; thin lips smiled. Suddenly the eyes gleamed with pleasure. "My son. It is good to see you." Then Cochise, chief of the Chiricahuas, stepped forward and embraced Jim Sundance.

Cochise had two wives. They led Herta von Markau off to another house, after spreading food before Cochise and Sundance in the chief's dwelling. The dome-shaped place

153

smelled of smoke and grease and drying mesquite and juniper. The two men sat cross-legged opposite each other, and Cochise listened without speaking while Sundance talked. With each minute that passed, the Apache's face grew more stern and dour.

Then Sundance had finished. Cochise tamped a pipe, lit it. "It was bad for you and Uklenni to go after the treasure without first coming to me. But, no matter; what is done is done. Uklenni should not have drunk the *tiswin*, either."

He paused. "For the treasure, I care nothing. I well know the value of a white man's dollar; I have done business with them, cutting wood for the fort at Bowie and being paid for it. But I know much else about the white man, too. If, as you say, this is worth more dollars than we can imagine, it is bad, bad medicine. If we had it, we could not sell it. They would say, *you Goddam dirty Injun sonofabitch*," and here he lapsed into English, mockingly, "*this belongs to us. You stole it, we'll put you in jail and hang you.* The more valuable it is, the more ways they would find to kill Indians for it. I say the treasure is well out of our country; I do not want it."

Sundance nodded.

154

"Of course," Cochise said, "you are half white. If we took it, maybe you could sell it for us."

Sundance laughed bitterly. "Father, I am half Indian, too. They would say, *you Goddam dirty halfbreed sonofabitch*, and then it would be the same thing." He sobered. "But if I can take the treasure, I will get money which I will pay to the people in the council of the Grandfather in Washington. Money that will make the Grandfather's heart good toward the *Tenneh*."

Cochise spat into the fire. "Nothing makes the Grandfather's heart good but money, does it? What kind of man is he, what sort of heart does he have?" Then he said harshly. "I would not pay the Grandfather anything. He has sent his man Colyer to me, we bargain. But if I must pay to bargain with the Grandfather—"

"You do not understand," Sundance said.

"And you don't, either. You do not understand what it is to be a chief, hold so much responsibility in your hand. Colyer comes to me, he says: 'Cochise, we will give you the Dragoons and Huachucas for your own land. But you must not raid the Americans. We do not care how much you raid the Mexicans if

155

you leave the Americans alone.' And now, if I kill fifteen Americans—"

"Who killed fifteen Chiricahuas," Sundance said harshly.

"Who should not have gone with you before talking to me. Who should not have drunk the *tiswin*. Who are dead and cannot be brought back." Cochise gestured. "Look," he said. "We camp with the Tontos and the Mescaleros. They are never safe from the Army, they live in fear. We Chiricahuas are stronger, fiercer, than they, and so the white-eyes bargain with us. The Tontos and the Mescaleros have nothing; we have the Dragoons and Huachucas, anyhow . . ."

"What you're saying," Sundance rasped, "is that you don't want to give me any men."

"I'm saying," Cochise told him, "that we have a chance to hold our land. Everything in me cries out for vengeance for Uklenni and the others. But I am a chief, and that is not an easy thing to be. I must balance one thing against another. This is something the Chiricahuas must stay out of."

Sundance, understanding, but astounded by Cochise's self-control, sat up straight. "All right," he said. "This is the country of the Tontos, anyhow. I will go to them."

"It'll do you no good. They listen to me. I am trying to make peace for them also, save some land for them. I will tell them not to go with you. And the Mescaleros, too. Not now. Not right at this moment. It would turn over all our bargaining with the man Colyer from the Grandfather. It is not our medicine; it is white man's medicine." He laid down his pipe, looked at Sundance, grinned. "You see," he said, "there is nothing I can do. Our people talk too much, drink too much, brag too much, and if we killed fifteen white men everyone would know it. But I do not drink or talk or brag too much, and neither do you. Suppose we two, only we, went on a hunt. And came back from it and said nothing."

Sundance stared at him. "Father," he whispered, "do you mean—?"

Cochise's grin broadened. "Your father was my brother. Always you have been my son, and my heart is good for you." He stood up. "Besides, being a chief and talking much is hard on the nerves. Sometimes a man needs excitement. And I did not get to be chief of the Chiricahuas because I am so gentle and such an old woman. Do you understand? Sundance, it has been long since we hunted together. I think we should hunt again."

Sundance looked at him in admiration. "The two of us? Against fifteen?"

Cochise grinned. "Without help, you'd have gone alone, wouldn't you?"

"Yes," Sundance said.

"Then we've cut the odds by half." Cochise laughed. "Now go rest. I've had a lodge prepared for you and your woman. Meanwhile, I'll send out scouts to cut their trail. When I have news, I'll let you know, and you and I will hunt together once again. And what game we kill, no one shall know but us."

It does not take long to make an Apache brush house; this one was brand new, spread with robes and bedding, food provided; venison, mescal, mesquite bread. When Sundance entered it, she was waiting, sitting cross-legged on a deerskin, her face grave. "They say that I am your woman."

"No," Sundance said. "I already have a woman, with the Cheyennes."

Herta von Markau took off the sombrero, laid it aside, began to smooth her hair with a brush made from sacaton stems. It glistened as she worked the kinks from its dark lushness. "Of course," she said. "And you would not want to touch me anyhow, not after what I did."

Sundance looked at her. "I told you. It was everyone's mistake."

"If I were an Apache, I would have my nose cut off." She laid the brush aside. "And would deserve it. *Christus* knows, I would. And yet . . . suppose . . . suppose I had met you before I met Walther. Suppose I had met the one kind man I have ever known. I can't get that out of my mind. If I had ever met a man really kind to me, in time—" Her voice harshened. "Sundance, you're lucky you're not a beautiful woman. Your life is simple."

Sundance sat down opposite her. He said: "You're mixed up already. I don't want to mix you up worse."

Herta looked down at the hide on which she sat. "Maybe it wouldn't mix me up. Maybe it would straighten me out. I know it's shameless, with Walther dead, and it my fault, but . . ." Her voice broke. "I don't seem to be able to grieve for him anymore. He bought me like a cow at market, commanded me to love him, and I tried and . . . couldn't. And now . . ." She raised her head, eyes shining. "I would like to do one thing in my life," she whispered, "that was right, and right because I knew it was. I would like to carry one memory out of here with me to offset all the rest."

And then she came to him. "Jim," she said. "Jim, please."

Sundance looked into eyes that begged him. But that was not the point. The point was that he wanted her. At least for now. Maybe it would be bad for her or both of them, maybe good; he did not know. But for right now, this moment . . .

He pushed her away, turned, pulled down the deerhide flap that closed the door. Then he turned again. Her face shone in the dimness. She lay back on the deerskin, and her hands went to the buttons of the shirt . . .

Later, he knew that it had been good for her, purged her of something, maybe tension. She clung to him as they both dressed. Then he said, "Let's walk around. I'll be riding tomorrow, maybe. Cochise and I are going hunting."

"Hunting?" Her voice echoed disbelief.

"Hunting," Sundance said. "You'll be here while I'm gone, so you'd better learn what's expected of you. Come on."

Dressed again, but this time with Herta in a

simple buckskin skirt that Cochise's wives had given her instead of the *vaquero* outfit, they strolled around the camp.

"The first thing to learn about Apaches," Sundance said, "is that they never lie to one another and never steal from one another. They always keep their word and expect other people to do so, too. That's why they've had trouble ever since the Spaniards came."

Cooking fires curled up from before the wikiups and the teepees. Children ran and laughed; from inside one lodge came the sound of chanting. "Medicine man," said Sundance. "Somebody's sick in there. He'll use all the herbs and roots he knows of, and all the chants and prayers. And if they die, still, he'll accuse some poor old woman of witchcraft, and if he can make it stick, they might burn her or stone her to death."

"Ghastly," Herta whispered.

Sundance's mouth twisted. "Yeah. Did you ever hear of a girl called Joan of Arc?"

"I have heard so many horrible things about Apaches . . ."

"All true," said Sundance.

"Killing babies . . ."

"Yes. Kill all children too small to travel, when they take captives. Those big enough to

161

keep up, they spare, adopt into the tribe. Same thing with women. They learned their lesson well, learned it from the Spaniards and the Mexicans—and the Americans. You know about the scalp bounties?"

"No."

"Thirty years ago, Mexico put a bounty on Apache scalps. Men, women, children, it made no difference. Hunters went out after 'em. As a matter of fact, a lot of Mexicans died. You can't tell one black scalp from another. But the Apaches learned from that. And the *piñole* feasts."

"The what?"

"*Piñole* feasts. *Piñole* is a mush made from ground corn. The Apaches love it. The Mexicans, and the Americans, too, used to invite them to love feasts, served all the *piñole* they could eat. One little trick: the hosts put strychnine in the *piñole*. Poisoned dozens, hundreds, of Apaches at a time, before the Indians caught on."

"How ghastly," Herta breathed.

"Well, it taught the Apaches another lesson." Sundance paused, looked around the village. "They're no better, no worse, than other people. They do unto others as others would do unto them. They value their women, chastity is important to them. You won't find Apache whores hanging around trading posts. But, yes. They're tough and mean. This is a tough land, a mean one; you know that by now."

They walked up a hillside; there, in the fading light, women still attacked the mescal plants. They stripped away the thorn-hooked, fleshy leaves, chopped off the stalks. Then they severed the body of the plant from its roots with pointed sticks, which they drove in with hatchets. The bulb, halfway between a cabbage and an onion, that was left, they carried down the hill. "Everyone works in an Apache camp," Sundance said. "The men hunt, raid, make war. The women gather food. In this society, it takes a lot of work to stay alive. Nobody lives off of anyone else, unless he's old or sick or crippled. And they worship all the Gods. If they kill a Christian, they'll take his crucifix and wear it. No point in angering anybody. But the Mountain Gods, the *Kan*—they're very powerful. You ought to see the ceremony. A great dance, goes on for days. The masks they wear are fantastic. The Apaches are a very religious, superstitious people. When Uklenni and I hunted the bear, we always had to be careful to call him Old Man Bear. A term of respect If you're not respectful, you lose your luck."

They swung back through the camp, paused to watch a Mescalero woman adjust the smokeflaps of her teepee. "Anyhow," Sundance said, "one thing about being an Indian. You're never alone and helpless."

"The whole tribe, it's one big family?"

"Yes," said Sundance.

"Nobody ever tries to get rich off of anybody else?"

"They don't even understand the idea," Sundance said. "How can you cheat your brother?" He grinned. "Still, it gets tricky sometimes. An Apache husband must never meet his mother-in-law face to face. A mean mother-in-law can drive a man out of his mind, chase him all over the country, to keep from breaking that rule. But they say that if you never have to talk to your mother-in-law or even look at her, your marriage is happier."

Herta laughed bitterly. "As a woman once married, that I can understand."

Then they were back in the brush shelter built for them. Outside, it was nearly dark.

"Jim," said Herta. Her eyes were enormous, shining in the murky light.

164

Sundance looked at her. "Yes."

She pulled the deerskin dress over her head. Her body gleamed in the dusk. "I am still your woman," she whispered. "For a little while, anyhow."

9

COCHISE reined in his horse. "There," he said. "You see?"

Sundance saw, but no one not Indian-bred would have noticed the half dozen blades of grass turned the wrong way, dew glistening on their bottoms, not on their tops. "The ground is hard," Cochise went on, "but our game went this way, I think."

"I think so, too." They were in the high country of the Mogollon plateau, he and Cochise. The Chiricahua chief, mounted on a stolen Arabian, carried a Winchester across his saddle; his torso was swathed with a bandolier of cartridges, and the Colt was slung low on his hip.

Sundance rode Eagle. Despite the great, scabbed wound on his hip, the stallion was still more horse than any other in the Apache remuda. He could depend on Eagle; besides, the exercise was good for the wounded animal, kept him from getting stiff. Sundance was still dressed Apache style, having added

166

only a buckskin shirt to the rest of his gear. Cochise had given him a Winchester and a Colt and a knife made from an old brittle piece of steel, but he still wore the quiver of Cheyenne arrows on his back and the powerful juniper-wood bow slung across his shoulder.

"Not far, either," Cochise said. "They passed this way just before daylight this morning."

Sundance turned Eagle, looked at the high broken country of the Mogollons that lay before them. "Let's move, Father," he said. "Let's keep on." Eagerness fluttered within him. In a few more hours, they could overtake Gannon and his men.

It had not taken long for the Chiricahua scouts to cut their trail. Fifteen men left a lot of sign behind, especially white men. Fifteen horses gave off a lot of droppings and urine puddles; and there were the stubs of ground-out cigarettes thrown aside. You could almost smell it, Sundance thought: the trail white men made going through a wilderness.

Not that, by their lights, Gannon's men were careless. They worked hard to disguise their passage, sent out flankers, scouts, rear guards. They were determined to ward against surprise; obviously, Gannon had traveled through Apache country before. He was good, but he was no Apache.

And so, no matter how hard Gannon tried, Sundance and Cochise could follow him. When he struck a stream, led his band down its bed, the two of them split up, always found, sooner or later, where Gannon's crew had emerged. When he took advantage of a lava flow or rock flat, shod hooves still left scars, turned over pebbles.

And so there was no way he could escape. Like a pair of implacable hounds, Sundance and Cochise stuck to his trail.

And gained. Gannon was not sure of his country. Sundance knew it fairly well; Cochise knew it as he knew his wives' bodies, every fold, hollow, byway.

They struck another stream—cold, shallow, swift-running—and the trail disappeared. Again, they split up. Sundance had not traveled fifty feet before he saw the blades of grass on the bank, ends cropped short by a horse's teeth. Gannon, he thought, if you knew your business, you'd tell your men to keep the heads of their mounts up. Then he cawed like a jay to summon Cochise.

The Apache chief splashed across the

creek, rode up its far bank. Presently he reined in, grunted. Sundance crossed, saw the trail leading out. Water still gleamed in the hoofprints, though the wind blew dry and strong.

"Not far now," Cochise said. He laughed softly. "Sundance, I love to hunt. And this is the best hunting of all."

"Father," Sundance said, "don't get over-confident. These men are clever, dangerous." He held Eagle in check, squinted at the jagged, piney ridges ahead. "Where are they bound now. Down into Deer Canyon?"

"I think so." Cochise wagged his iron-gray head.

"As I remember," Sundance said, "there are two rock towers where the trail leads down. A good place to set a rear guard, watch the backtrail."

Again Cochise nodded. "Yes. I had thought of that."

"One pile of rock to the right, one on the left," Sundance said. "I should think at least one man on each. The trail goes between, leads down. Do you want the right or the left?"

"It makes no difference," Cochise said.

"Only this," Sundance answered. "We

must make no noise. Nothing to alarm the rest."

The Apache chuckled. He drew a long knife from a sheath on his hip.

Sundance touched his own. "Then let's leave the horses here and go on foot."

They swung down, tied the mounts. Not to large trees, but to small ones. If something happened, if they did not come back, the horses could uproot those and go home. It was a little thing, but the kind of thing an Apache thought of. Then they fanned out, moving through the pines.

Sundance's moccasined feet made no sound on the carpet of needles. He went from trunk to trunk, pausing behind each to survey the land ahead. Overhead, wind soughed in the branches, sadly, cleanly, steadily. There was always a chance, of course, that Gannon might leave a guard where one was not expected.

Sundance could no longer see Cochise, knew the Apache could not see him. Both of them traveled through the pine forests like wisps of drifting fog, just that quietly and insubstantially. Sundance crouched low behind the bole of a great tree, hundreds of feet high, centuries old. Ahead, the forest thinned, vanished suddenly. Clouds drifted level with the rim of Deer Canyon. And rearing high at the only passage over the cliff, was a vast pile of rock, a great, tortured jumble of it, like the watchtower of a castle he had seen in a picture in one of his father's books.

If Gannon were smart, there would be a man posted there.

Sundance grinned unpleasantly. His thumb ran along the blade, sharply honed, of the crude knife Cochise had given him. Then he veered off far to the right, dodging sound-lessly through the dim forest. He ran a hundred yards, two hundred, and came to the canyon rim, where he threw himself flat behind a clump of brush.

Below him, Deer Canyon spilled away in awesome immensity, a hole that some Eastern states could have been slipped into entirely. Its slopes and floors were thickly timbered. The outlet at its far end was a notch between high peaks. Sundance looked down on circling hawks and eagles, hunting the canyon floor.

Then he slid over the rim.

His soft-shod feet gripped an outcropping. The canyon's wall was a steep cliff, save for the slope down which the trail that passed between the two towers led. From where he hunkered against the rock, Sundance could see that trail, caught just a flicker of motion as, at its end, men rode into the timber.

Gannon. Well, his guards had to be put out of action before they could fire a rifle shot. You could hear a gunshot for miles in this echo-sounding-board.

Sundance's feet grasped the outcrop, moved along. He struck a ledge not more than a foot wide. Like a cat, he traversed it, laden as he was with guns, his shield, his bow, his quiver. He did not walk, he ran, sure-footed and fearless when it came to heights. One misstep would have plunged him down into that great timbered, cloud-smoky hole. He did not even think about that as he worked along the cliff.

Then, a few feet away, he saw the tower rearing high on the rimrock. And he saw, too, the man who lay behind the rubble, watching the backtrail. Saw him turn his head, rub his jaw restlessly, recognized the dark, black-mustached face of Jessup, Gannon's second-in-command.

Sundance had reached for the bow, but now he took his hand away. With the knife poised, he crept along just below the edge of the rimrock. Now he was under the rock tower. He looked up. Intent on the backtrail, Jessup dragged on a Mexican cigarette, pulled the butt from his mouth, tossed it out in space. Showering sparks, it sailed over Sundance's shoulder. Sundance, knife tightly gripped, began to climb.

It was a slow business. He must be careful not to dislodge a single pebble and send it rattling down. At any moment, Jessup might turn, see him, fire a shot and blast him off the canyon wall.

Sundance played it tight, examining every foot- and hand-hold before he moved. Jessup, Winchester ready, lay motionless, watching the woods.

Then, from very far away, came a cry, cut off short, so low and short it might almost have been a marmot's squeak. Sundance's lips peeled back from his teeth. Cochise might be older, but he was faster.

Jessup shifted uneasily, looked toward the other tower. "Gray?" he called softly. "Hey, Gray—"

There was no answer. Jessup shifted restlessly. "Hey, Gray—"

Sundance came up over the rim fast and

hard, and without making a sound until a single pebble rolled and clicked. By that time, he was almost on Jessup. But the man whirled, threw up his gun, saw Sundance, recognized him. He opened his mouth to scream. Sundance rammed his left hand between the jaws and took the bite and shoved forward with his right and felt the knife slash deep in Jessup's throat.

He left it there, jerked his hand away, seized Jessup's gun just before the man—convulsively—could fire, ripped it from nerveless hands, threw it aside, then gripped the knife again. But it was already over. Gagging, Jessup slid down the pile of rock.

Sundance pulled free the blade, thrust it home again, this time through Jessup's heart.

That ended it. Jessup kicked, sent a few rocks clattering, was dead.

Sundance looked at the body, recognized the belt Jessup wore: his gun, his knife, his ax. He seized the buckle, unlatched it. Lashed it on his own waist, strapping the cartridge belt above it. He left the poor Chiricahua knife in Jessup's body, took out his own fourteen-inch-Bowie, hefted it, restored it to its sheath. Feeling stronger, better, he climbed the rimrock, made contact with Cochise.

"It was so easy," Cochise said. "Mine had already gone to sleep. He never even twitched."

"Mine was wide awake," Sundance said. "It took a little longer."

They rode down the trail into the canyon. Cochise said, "My son, the hunting has been good so far. I think, come dusk, it will be even better."

"Where will they camp?"

Cochise, leaning back in his antelope-hide saddle, gestured, as the Arabian slid down the canyon wall on its haunches.

"Below there's an opening in the forest, a clearing. Considering the time, the little light left, they'll camp there. We always do when we come into Deer Canyon."

"Then they won't," Sundance said.

Cochise jerked his head around. "Why not?"

"It would be full of Apache sign. White-eyes would never camp in a place like that. Afraid the Indians might come back. They'll go on, be in the woods below."

"Maybe," Cochise said, not convinced. "We'll see."

It seemed to take forever for their horses to reach the bottom of the canyon. On its floor, they had to halt, let them blow. Dusk swirled in the great canyon, an hour sooner than on the rim above, when they rode on.

In the dim light, Cochise and Sundance looked at one another and grinned. Both were full now of the hunting spirit. Then Sundance reined in. "If they don't camp in the clearing, where should we look for them?"

"A creek runs through here. Further up it, there are great slabs of rock on either side, level and big enough for all of them to sleep on. My guess would be there."

Sundance swung down off Eagle. "Then let us wait."

Cochise stared at him, then also dismounted. "Yes. After all, there are thirteen of them and only two of us. Probably it would be better if we waited."

They ate jerky, piñole, a little mesquite-bean bread, in the shadow of the pines. Even in the canyon, they were at an altitude of nearly eight thousand feet. The wind was cold. Thinking of what lay ahead, neither felt it.

Sundance leaned back against a pine bole, watched a sickle moon climb over the rimrock. Midnight, he guessed, then one o'clock. Cochise, older, a little fatigued by the day, dozed in a blanket.

Sundance stood up, shook Cochise's shoulder. "My father. It is time."

Cochise awakened. He rose, looked at the moon. "Yes," he said, "well past midnight."

"An hour," Sundance said.

"Everyone is low, then," said Cochise. "No man is at his best at that time. It is the time to strike, when the guards are tired."

"Yes," Sundance said. He touched Cochise's thick wrist. "Father."

"My son?"

"Gannon, the leader, has a red beard. This I want from you: However it falls out, you are not to kill him, unless I am already dead. He is mine."

"You hate him so much?"

"It is a thing between us," Sundance said.

"Then he's yours. Let's go."

They ran through the pines, rifles up. Presently, they reached the big clearing. Except for the tumble-down remnants of the old Apache wikiups, it was empty. They skirted it, went on, following the bank of the stream that brawled and tumbled coldly through the canyon.

A hiss from Cochise stopped Sundance. He edged over to the Chiricahua.

"Listen," Cochise whispered. "We are near the other camping place. They will have guards out."

"I will deal with them," Sundance said. He unslung the bow.

Cochise grinned. "I was once pretty good with that myself. But I have used guns so long . . ." He touched Sundance on the shoulder. "Be careful. When you are ready, give the cry of the white owl."

"Yes," Sundance said, and with an arrow nocked, he ran forward through the trees, keeping always to cover, a darker shadow among the shadows in the forest.

Circling, he soon found the place: the creek roared down, foaming, between two giant slabs of rock on either bank, and he saw the dull glow of the dying embers of a campfire on the slab on his side. In the murk, that was all he could see. He faded back, searched for the guards.

As he had expected, one squatted on the

very edge of the slab, a gun across his knees. His head drooped low; he was half asleep.

Sundance coursed through the trees, found the other. He was beyond the camp, upstream, sitting with his back against a pine. He was supposed to be watching the upstream side, but he had gone to sleep.

Sundance's lips peeled back in a feral grin. He moved soundlessly on moccasined feet across the pine straw. He pulled the Bowie knife and, when he was in position, dropped to his knees. His left hand clamped across a startled mouth; his right raised the knife and drove it home.

He stood up, drifted back down the creek. The guard at the end of the rock slab still dozed. Sundance unslung the bow, slipped a buzzard-quill feathered arrow on the string, drew back until his thumb touched his cheek-bone, aiming carefully in the tricky moon-silvered, pine-shadowed light. Then he loosed the shaft.

The guard lurched sideways, without a sound, as the flint point drove through his skull. Sprawled grotesquely, he didn't even kick.

Sundance ran back through the forest.

Cochise was a moving shadow in deeper blackness. "Now?" he whispered.

"Now," Sundance said.

The old chief turned. Rifle high, bandolier full, he splashed out into the roaring stream. The icy water swirled around his knees; Sundance watched Cochise lest he be swept off his feet. But he never faltered, his moccasins gripping the slippery stones with certainty. Then he emerged on the far bank and, like a ghost, vanished into the pines.

Silently, Sundance ran up the near bank, threw himself down where he could overlook the slab of rock stretching into the stream. Blanketed men were huddled blobs; across the creek, picketed horses, catching his scent, snorted. No one stirred. Sundance waited, rifle ready.

Then he heard it; the sound of pounding hooves. Cochise had cut the picket rope, stampeded the mounts of Gannon's men. Sundance laid aside his rifle, whipped an arrow from its quiver, notched it to his bow. The frightened horses whinnied, and men came boiling up out of their blankets.

Sundance unloosed the arrow; before it was on its way, he had another on the bowstring. A man scrambling to his knees cried out, fell

180

back, as the first shaft went home. A second rolled in agony, an arrow through his belly up to the feathers. Then they were all on their feet, bringing up the guns never far from their sides. Sundance let go another arrow and another. One missed, the second slashed through the gun arm of a tall figure raising its rifle.

Sundance smiled coldly as he put another arrow to the bow. Out there on the rock, the men were running aimlessly, like ants in a kicked-over hill. That was the beauty of the bow: no muzzle-flame, no sound. There was nothing they could shoot back at. Panic-stricken, they dived for cover, and a voice Sundance recognized yelled: "Injuns! Head fer th' woods!"

At that instant, Cochise opened up with his rifle from the far bank. As men scrambled for the wooded slope above, they toppled, fell. Others, seeing a target at last, turned, fired as they climbed the bank, shooting at Cochise's muzzle flame. Their own gun flashes gave Sundance targets; his hand moved rhyth-mically, whipping arrows from the quiver. It was nothing for an experienced bowman to have three or four in the air simultaneously;

he could aim and shoot them as fast as most men could fire a repeating rifle.

But some went wild. The light was tricky and all his targets were in frantic motion, and now the quiver was getting lighter, almost empty. He slipped the bow on his shoulder, picked up the rifle. At that instant, he saw a lean figure leg across the rocks, vanish among the trees. He recognized it, and then he forgot the others, ran into darkness, chasing Gannon.

No moonlight could penetrate the thickly interlocked heads of the great pines; in here, blackness was total. Sundance dodged between the tree trunks, headed toward the spot where Gannon had disappeared. Away from the creek, the ground sloped sharply upward; his legs labored as he climbed. After a few yards he halted, held his breath, cocked his head. He heard nothing except the steady, pumping drumroll of fire from Cochise's weapon, and the sporadic uncertain return of it from what men were left down there.

Sundance ran on, angling up the hill. He held his rifle ready, halted. There was no trace of Gannon.

Sundance roared his name. "Gannon!" His voice rang through the woods, echoed from the cliffs dying, fading: *"Gannon ... Gannon ... Gannnnoonnn ..."*

No sound, no answer. "Gannon!" he bellowed once more. "This is Sundance! You hear? Jim Sundance! Gannon, come out and fight!"

He turned around, eyes searching the stygian woods. "What's the matter, Gannon? You afraid of a halfbreed? You and me, we're on the same side of the creek. And I'm alone over here. You won't come out and fight, white man? Here I am. Here's your target! All you got to do is shoot!" And he fired a shot straight up, his muzzle-flame a signal, and then he stepped wide aside; and in that instant the answering shot came, from up the hill, followed by two more. Sundance saw the orange tongues of gunflame, heard the whine of slugs.

He grinned savagely, took cover behind a tree, and emptied his rifle at the place, a hundred yards up the hill, from which Gannon's shots had come. He sprayed lead in a wide pattern, knowing Gannon would have rolled after firing.

Nothing happened; from above there was no sound, no movement, no answering shot. Sundance shoved more rounds into his gun and slowly, carefully, began to climb the hill, sheltering behind the thick boles of pines as he went.

He waited a moment behind one immense tree, then ran swiftly, soundlessly forward toward another. As he crossed the open space between, suddenly, from his right, a gun flamed, and lead ripped all around him as Gannon fired and fired and fired again, and Sundance pitched forward, hugging the pine needles. Then, as quickly as it had come, the fire pinched off; the woods were still again.

Sundance drew in a deep breath, smiled tightly. Gannon was smart and Gannon was no coward. While Sundance had stalked him, he had stalked Sundance. And now he was over there to the right, not even certain, probably, whether he had fired at a man or a shadow. He would be crouched there, waiting, listening, maybe praying—if such men prayed—that Sundance would return his fire, give him a gunflash for target.

Instead, Sundance laid the rifle aside. For what he intended to do now, it would only hamper him. He pulled the sixgun from its holster, laid it with the rifle. That was no bravado; he wanted nothing that would drag or catch when he began to crawl. He took the arrows from his quiver, clenched them in his hand so they would not click together, discarded the quiver. He cradled the bow in his arm. Then he snaked forward on his belly toward the source of Gannon's shots.

He made ten yards, waited, holding his breath, listening. Wind mourned in the pines overhead, but he paid no attention to it. Two minutes passed, three. Then he heard it, from not more than fifty feet ahead and to his left: a faint, metallic tick of sound. He knew what it was: a cartridge being rammed into the loading port of a Winchester.

Sundance crawled on, teeth bared in a kind of snarl. The darkness was still absolute; down at the creek, all firing had ceased. But he had Gannon pin-pointed; now all he had to do was break Gannon's nerve. He nocked an arrow, drew the bow, and loosed the shaft.

Its point chunked loudly into a tree trunk somewhere near where Gannon should be hidden. When it hit, Sundance heard a gasp. He already had another arrow on the string; he let it go in the direction of the sound. He fired the third just after it, and notched the fourth and last, and held it, and then it happened. Gannon leaped to his feet, and now Sundance could see him as movement in the darkness, and suddenly, frantically, Gannon began to shoot. He whirled, with no idea from whence the arrows were coming, and he pumped the lever of his Winchester and sprayed bullets in a circle, and Sundance could hear him cursing. "Goddamn you, Sundance," Gannon yelled, "come out and fight!" And Sundance lay flat until he heard the rifle snick on empty. And now he could see Gannon and sprang to his feet and pulled back the bowstring. "Gannon," he said. "Over here. This is where it's coming from." Gannon whirled and reached for his Colt as Sundance loosed the arrow.

It caught Gannon in the chest, sank to its feathers. The red-bearded man gave a strange, muffled cry, fell to his knees, tugging at the shaft, then rolled over on his side. Sundance drew the hatchet, ran to him with the weapon ready.

But there was no need for it. He bent over Gannon, staring into a contorted face, able to discern pain-filled eyes. Gannon's lips moved. "I thought the buzzards—"

"No," Sundance whispered, no mercy for Gannon in him. "It's you they'll eat, not me."

"You damned halfbreed," Gannon said

faintly, in a voice full of hate. With that curse on his lips, he died.

Sundance stood up, breathing hard, knees suddenly weak. Then he tensed, sensing rather than hearing someone coming up the hill behind him. Suddenly he bent, seized Gannon's Colt, brought it up. Then he lowered it as he heard the soft mournful hoot of an owl.

He answered it, and Cochise was there, panting from the climb. "My son, you're all right?" He looked down at Gannon.

"I am all right. He almost got me one time, but I got around him."

Cochise nodded, looking at the shaft protruding from Gannon's chest. "For hunting men in darkness, the bow is always best." He paused, looked down the hill. "The others—most of them are dead. A few escaped into the timber. On foot, they count for nothing. We must be watchful of them, but . . . I can send men after them later. They will be here. And what you sought—It is down there, in its bag. I cached it beneath some rocks before I came up here."

"Then I think it's time to go," said Sundance.

"I think so, too." He hesitated. "The hunting has been good tonight, and yet my heart is heavy. I am an old man now, and maybe when one is old, one has had enough of war. I no longer enjoy it as I did when I was young. Let us go and get your treasure and ride out of here and leave this place before daylight and the vultures come."

"Yes," Sundance said. He worked back through the woods until he found his rifle and sixgun, Cochise bringing Gannon's weapons. Then he and the Apache went down the hill together in darkness, both alert, to get the treasure from its hiding place.

10

THE dancing and feasting had been going on for four days around the arbor made of scrub-oak and the sacred house built on a framework of mescal stalks. The coming-of-age ceremony of the young Apache women was one of the greatest festivals of the tribe, as big a thing, and as serious, as the Sun Dance and Medicine Lodge ceremony of the Plains Indians.

Together, Sundance and Herta von Markau had watched it all: the blessing of the girls with sacred pollen by the medicine men and the godmothers of the maidens, the blessing of the tribe, in turn, by the girls, the dancing of the maidens, the ritual of the Medicine Basket. The basin in the mountains resounded day and night with drums and chanting and the click of deer-hoof rattles.

The Austrian woman was impressed. "I think that it is a great thing to be an Apache girl."

"Women are powerful in the tribe, and honored," Sundance told her. He had already explained the demands made on the girls of twelve, thirteen, fourteen, how they must drink only through reeds during the ceremony, must avoid water on their bodies, must not look at the sky or lose their tempers or laugh excessively, and how they must dance and dance to the point of exhaustion. "When a girl has been through all this, she knows she has earned her womanhood."

Now, though, it was late, and time for the dance of the Mountain Gods. This was the high point of the ceremony. A huge fire blazed in the center of the camp, before the sacred dwelling. Then a group of singers began an age-old chant:

Big Blue Mountain Spirit
The home made of blue clouds,
The cross made of the blue mirage,
There you have begun to live,
There is the life of goodness,
I thank you for all made of goodness
* there . . .*

Then the dancers costumed as Gods, the *"gahe-nde,"* came stamping out, heads concealed by weird black wooden masks, save for one masked in white. Dressed in buckskin, each brandished a wooden sword and danced around the fire. Five of them:

They cast fantastic shadows as they charged back and forth, toward the flames, at each other, and at the crowd, with their swords. Soon they were joined by five more, and another five after that, and the drums throbbed and reed whistles blew and rattles clattered dryly as the fantastic figures continued the wild dance of the mountain ghosts.

Leaning against Sundance, Herta watched raptly. Sundance had already told her the legend of the two young men, one blind, one crippled, abandoned in a mountain cave by their tribe; how they were saved by the four black Gods, the one white one, the blind man's sight restored, the cripple's lameness cured; and how ever since, the Apaches had danced this dance in honor of those mountain spirits, to insure health and good fortune in the coming year.

Later, the ceremonial dancing was over, and the whole tribe gathered around the fire to dance, forming a circle, men and women holding hands. Sundance and Herta joined them, sidestepping to the beat of drums. They did the back and forth dance, long ranks of people swaying forward and back, in the firelight, to the drumming.

191

He looked at her. In the ten days they had spent here, she had recovered from her ordeal; her blistered face had healed, the bruises left her body. Now, in sheer exuberance, she laughed, great eyes shining, white teeth gleaming. Her hand squeezed his as they swayed back and forth, and her hip, clad in an Apache buckskin dress, brushed against him.

Then it was over. Tired yet exhilarated, they returned at dawn to their own house. Herta threw herself down on the buckskin matting of it, laughed, then looked up at Sundance above her. She sat up suddenly, pulled off the skirt. "Jim . . ." she whispered.

Later, she lay in Sundance's arms. "Must we leave tomorrow?" she whispered.

"Yes," Sundance said.

"But I do not want to go, to return to the Emperor's court. Here I feel so alive, so real. Sundance, could I stay here? Be an Apache woman? And you . . ."

"No," he said. "I have work to do. And you, Herta. It's fun for you now. But later, it'll be different." He paused, and his face hardened. "Later, they'll all be hunted. Men, women, children. I know Crook. His job is to fight them and beat them and bring them in. And he will do it. All I hope is that they'll also let him settle them and civilize them. He's a good man; he knows what they need and want and how to get it for them. But if he's going to do that, it's going to take pressure in Washington, and that's my job, to provide the money for that." He raised himself on one elbow, looked out the door; the drumming and chanting still went on. "They don't know what's ahead of them, what they're going to have to cope with." His voice was sad. "I do."

She clung to him, then sank back. "Yes, I suppose you're right. I belong back in Vienna. This much I can do for Walther, save his honor by seeing that the jewels get back where they belong, and that the emperor pays your money promptly. Still . . . I will always remember this as my time of greatest grief and greatest happiness."

Her nails dug into his flesh. "Jim. Jim, please come with me."

"No," he said. "I can't."

She was silent; then she sighed. "Of course not. Then all we can do is take what time we have left." She pulled him to her again.

And now it was done; the feasting was over and the mescal cooked and dried and stored, and the tribes split up, the Tontos to go back to their basin, the Mescaleros to return to the White Mountain and the Davis Mountains further east, the Chiricahuas to head for the Dragoons and Peloncillos and Huachucas.

Except for ten. Led by Choddi, the ten warriors sat horses in the center of the village—which was rapidly being dismantled—an escort for Sundance and Herta von Markau back to Fort Lowell. Sundance adjusted the lashings of the leather bag on the back of the pack animal, its weight of gold and silver and jewelry, a mule sufficient for the load. Then he checked the fastenings of the panniers that held his bows, arrows, and shield, behind Eagle's saddle.

He also checked the rifle in his saddle scabbard, the sixgun at his waist, the knife and hatchet on his belt. Everything was in order. The sun gleamed on his coppery body, his golden hair, as he helped Herta into the saddle of a fine gelding, son of Cochise's Arabian, then swung up on Eagle.

He looked around, holding the appaloosa's reins tightly gathered. Then he saw the man for whom his eyes had searched. Cochise

194

strode toward him, tall, graceful, thick-chested, hair frosted with gray. He came up by Eagle, raised one hand.

"My son," he said, "I do not know when we will see one another again. Perhaps never. Perhaps in the Shadow Land. But whatever you can do for us with the white-eyes, we will be thankful for. And if the white-eyes become too much for you and you have a stomach full—then your home is always here, with the Chiricahua, in the Mogollons, the Dragoons, or the Sierra Madre. We will be free for many years yet, that I promise you."

"I hope so, Father," Sundance said; and they shook hands.

"Now," said Cochise, "a safe journey and good hunting." He swung up on his Arabian. "I will ride a distance with you." At the head of the column, he gave a signal, and all moved out.

They filed down through a sloping canyon, which brought them off the Mogollon rim and back to the desert again. There Cochise reined in.

"I leave you now," he said. Only that, no more.

Then he wheeled his horse and galloped off alone.

They rode on. Sundance turned in the saddle, looked back. The Mogollon rim was a high, jagged, tree-clad escarpment, its top dominated by a great butte. As he watched, a lone horseman climbed that, gained the crest, turned his white mount around, sat, rifle cradled across his arm, watching the cavalcade file down the slope and turn west toward Tucson.

Sundance stood in Eagle's stirrups, raised his arm.

The silhouetted figure on the rim saw the gesture, raised high one hand in reply. Then it wheeled and rode away, vanished amidst boulders.

On the third day, they were in the desert. Sundance, at the column's head, reined in.

Ahead, a dust cloud roiled. It was moving toward them.

Sundance turned to Choddi. "*Sikisn,* brother. Someone comes."

"Yes," Choddi said.

Then they heard the sound of bugles.

"It's the Army," Sundance said. "Time for you to leave us."

"I will do that," Choddi said. He put out his hand, clasped Sundance's. Then he

196

snapped orders to his band; they wheeled and galloped off.

Herta von Maukau looked at Sundance sadly as the bugle sounded again, closer. "It really is over," she said.

"Yes," Sundance said. "But remember. I depend on you to get me justice from the Emperor. My money. The Indians' money."

"I will do it. I can do that much, anyhow."

"Then let's go," said Sundance, and he touched Eagle with his heels. The packhorse, laden with the treasure of Maximilian, trotted behind as they rode to meet the column with General Crook at its head.

BRING ME
HIS SCALP

1

HE'D never counted on dying in bed. Sliding more rounds into the .44 Winchester, Sundance squinted through the heat glare. Down the slope, the six men had taken good cover behind the boulders, some as big as houses, littering the hill's flank. Occasionally they loosed a round at him just to make him keep his head down. They were in no hurry. They had him penned up here like a calf in a barnyard; there was no escape, and they knew it. He knew it, too.

What he did not know was who they were or why they wanted to kill him. For the moment, that made no difference. Their intentions were clear, attested to by the bullet slash across his shoulder, the hunk of meat another slug had taken from the hind quarter of the big Appaloosa stallion which, nickering softly with excitement and thirst, was just behind him in the shallow cave. Whoever they were and for whatever reason, they wanted Jim Sundance dead.

Well, Sundance thought, sliding down behind the rocks that shielded the cave's mouth, he was not dead yet. Maybe by nightfall or come tomorrow morning, he would be. But, he vowed grimly, in that case he would not be the only one.

With the rifle ready, himself lying in the prone position, he watched the slope. He was a big man, his sprawled body inches more than six feet in length, shoulders bulking wide beneath a buckskin shirt fringed and beaded in the Cheyenne way. Beneath his old Stetson, his face was that of an Indian warrior, high of cheekbone, big of nose, wide of mouth, strong of chin, and his skin the color of weathered copper. Startlingly, his eyes were blue, the hair that fell to the collar of the shirt blond, almost the color of gold. The hair and eyes were his legacy of his English father, the skin and features from his Cheyenne mother.

There were other weapons beside him on the ground behind the rocks. He had laid them out to be ready for whatever came: a short, recurved bow of juniper, powerful enough to drive an arrow clean through a bull buffalo—or a man—and a quiver full of shafts for it, their heads of barbed flint or obsidian, ugly and razor sharp. Then there was the Colt in the gunbelt, which he had taken off but left close at hand, and the Bowie in its beaded sheath. There was, too, a steel-bladed hatchet with a straight handle, perfectly balanced for throwing. A canteen lay nearby, too, but it was useless, punctured by a bullet, its contents long since drained away.

He had been here on this slope in the Godforsaken wasteland of the deep Big Bend country of Texas for four hours, now, ever since the wound in the Appaloosa's leg had forced him to go to ground after a long chase. The sun, as always down here at any season, was as brutal as a sledgehammer, the temperature better than a hundred even in the mouth of the shallow cave, maybe twenty degrees hotter outside. But they—the six attackers down the slope—could stand the heat indefinitely, for they had plenty of water left. He had none, and he could feel the moisture baking out of his body with every minute that passed. It had been six hours since his last drink. The sun would not go down for at least another six. There would still be life in him by then, but not the kind of fighting energy he would need. He had been trained by Apaches in desert warfare and

203

could go a full day without water, but he knew what twelve hours in the sun without a drink would do to his vision and coordination. By then he would lose his alertness, see movement where none existed, and his hands would no longer be rocksteady. And, of course, if they could hold him here for another twelve hours beyond that, through the night, come morning he would be all theirs.

The cave was a dead end, not more than a big hole fifteen or twenty feet deep in sunbaked rock. It held a few old bones and flints, relics of Indians who had camped there, but there was no water.

Picking up a small pebble, Jim Sundance slid it beneath his tongue to generate saliva, waited, and tried to make sense out of what had happened. At first he'd thought they were simply robbers, highwaymen ready to ambush any random traveler for horse, gun, and whatever money might be on his person. Now he knew better. They were going to too much trouble for that. They had another reason for wanting him.

Whatever it was, they had been waiting for him on the north side of the Boquillas crossing of the Rio Grande.

He'd had business down in Mexico. He had business wherever there were Indians, and this had involved the Yaquis, who were still treated as hostiles by the Mexican government. It had been the matter of a negotiation of a new treaty with the government, and the Yaquis had wanted Jim Sundance on their side. He had done the best he could for them, although he knew all about treaties by now. Governments made them with Indians only to be broken, and in that, Mexico was no different from the United States. Still, he had got the terms he asked for, after a lot of hard bargaining and the meeting had ended with apparent good will on both sides. Maybe, for a little while anyway, this one would hold.

After that, he had ridden north. He knew people in Mexico, a lot of them, ranging from Yaqui and Tarahumara villagers to rich *haciendados*. Most of them were glad to see Jim Sundance, whose business was doing what he could to solve the problems and iron out the conflicts between Indians and whites, a man noted for his honesty, his fairness, and his services to both sides. Feared, perhaps, too, for he was, after all, not only an expert gunman, but a Cheyenne Dog Soldier in good standing, as much professional fighting man as peacemaker. But then, sometimes, it took a lot of fighting before you could make peace . . .

Anyhow, the ride north had been uneventful, even pleasant. He had stopped in the sleepy little village of Boquillas, in the shadow of the great, colorful escarpment of the Del Carmens, for the night, and early in the morning, he had put Eagle, his big Appaloosa stallion across the shallow ford.

As always, no matter how apparently peaceful the surroundings, he rode alertly, with his rifle across his saddle. He had not lived until his middle thirties by being careless or taking anything for granted. In this case, as it had more than once, that habitual caution saved his bacon.

The north bank of the Rio here was edged with reeds, and there were some woods along the stream. The eight *Americanos*, Texans all, had been in ambush there. They must have taken station in the night, or the Mexicans would have known about them. The wind was in their favor, or the stallion would have scented them and given the alarm. As it was, they still did not quite catch Sundance cold.

As the big stallion headed for a well-defined trail leading up the north bank through reeds and brush, a mockingbird flew across the river, and, a flash of gray and white, spread its wings and tail to land. Then it gave a mewing cry, veered away. Even as the stallion reached the bank, Sundance knew that something was in that thicket. He reacted instinctively; he jerked the horse around with its hindlegs still in water, and he lined the gun.

That action saved his life. In that instant, the whole bank of the Rio Grande seemed to explode in gunfire.

Lead whipped through the air where Sundance's head and body had just been. He turned in the saddle, working the Winchester's lever, returning fire. The stallion plunged upstream through the shallows, close by the bank—no chance of crossing back to Mexico, Sundance knew. They'd burn him down in midstream.

And now they themselves poured down the bank and out into the river, eight of them, all well-mounted, and the first to hit the water caught a slug from Sundance's rifle and lurched sideways from his saddle, arms flung wide, gun dropping. That slowed the others, and Sundance grunted something to the stallion and touched the reins, and the big horse made a fantastic leap.

The bank was high, sheer, here, but its forefeet caught, and like a cat it, brought its hindlegs up. Sundance leaned low, the others were out in the middle of the river now, and a sleetstorm of lead whipped around him, chopping reeds and bushes along the bank. Then the stallion gave one more great shove and it was up and out and plunging into the cover of the undergrowth, and as the brush closed behind Sundance, the ambushers turned their horses and raced back for the trail at the ford to cut him off.

The Appaloosa went through the brush like a wild hog, smashing what it could not slide past, at a dead run. Then it broke out into the open, less than a hundred yards from the ford. At the same time, only slightly behind, the seven riders now boiled out of cover, still firing. Sundance turned the stallion, bent low in the saddle, sent the spotted stud racing across the bottomland, sand dunes and thin grass, heading for the cover of another line of trees. Behind him, the riders came just as hard, the three in the lead still firing. Sundance knew there was no time to shoot back; he had to gain distance.

The stallion, eight years old and in its prime, gained it for him. Long legs stretched, mane and tail flying, it devoured ground at a dead run, making nothing of the drag of deep sand beneath its hooves. The band of trees neared, where a small stream ran down to join the Rio. The stallion had gained two hundred yards when they broke into it.

Sundance did not halt. The big horse leaped the narrow wash, landed at full speed, raced on without faltering or slacking. Sundance reined him north, away from the river.

In that direction, heatwaves shimmered like a veil before one of the most brutal wastelands in the West. Miles away, the great blue hump of the Chisos Mountains reared, like a giant island in a sea of sand and rock and gravel. Other mountains, raw and naked, reared to the east, rockstrewn flats, arroyos, canyons, baking in the sun, clad only with cactus, a few sparse junipers, occasional thin grass. A vast land and an empty one, until recently domain only of Apaches, men on the dodge from the States, and the Comanches whose war trail to Mexico led straight through the Boquillas Ford and which Sundance had intended to follow north.

But they had him blocked from that and they were coming hard, and he put the stallion toward the Chisos. He knew those mountains well; if he could make that sanctuary, there were a dozen places where he could lose them or, if necessary, stand them off.

But they stuck to him, even though the Appaloosa widened the lead, taking him well beyond a stray pistol shot, making it unlikely that anyone could drop him with a rifle. Now, for the first time, he had leeway to turn in the saddle, look back, trying to make sense of it all.

He had the vision of a hawk, and even through the heat and boiling dust, he did not think he had seen any of them before. They were strung out in a long line, and the man in front wore a checkered shirt, blue and white, a good target, Sundance thought, when and if he had time to snap off a shot. For now, though, more leeway, the sanctuary of the Chisos, room to fight in.

He was full into the desert now, and they were still behind him. But as the lead widened, the checker-shirted man yelled something that came to Sundance as a tatter of sound. He saw checker-shirt pull his horse aside, while the other six came on inexorably. Checker-shirt dragged his rifle from its scabbard, dismounted, knelt, took a rest, tracking Sundance. Then he fired.

Sundance felt the impact of the bullet striking home. The horse grunted, missed a stride, ran on. Something warm and wet ran over Sundance's leg. He looked down, saw water pouring from the canteen that had taken the bullet. He had a lead now of about four hundred yards. Checker-shirt was steadying himself for another shot.

Sundance whirled the stallion. He snapped an order; the big horse stood fast. Checker-shirt's second bullet missed. Sundance raised his own rifle, as Checker-shirt levered in another round, got off a snapshot. With marksman's instinct, he knew even before the gun recoiled that his aim was good. Checker-shirt sat down hard, then fell over on his back. But the remaining six didn't even slow.

Sundance had no time for another shot. He pulled the stud around, sent it into a run again.

Good as the stallion was, not he, nor any horse, could keep up such a pace for long in this heat. Already his body was white with lather, Sundance's denim pants were soaked with it. Five more minutes, he thought, knowing the horse's capacities as well as he knew his own. That much time and then he'd have to slow. But, surely, by then their mounts would be exhausted, too.

In five minutes, the stallion had bought him another hundred yards. A glance back showed that the pursuers were slowing down. Beneath Sundance's thighs, the great Appaloosa's huge barrel pumped and Sundance could feel the beating of its heart. It would run until that heart broke if he asked it to, but that would do him no good.

The main thing was simply to keep ahead of them until he made decent cover. Gain a few yards here, a few there, and when he had room to turn and fight—

He slowed the stallion to a hand gallop and then to a trot. Behind him, the pursuers eased off, too. They had missed their quick chance, the mockingbird had cost them that, and now they were settling down for a long run. Sundance watched as three of them matched their pace to his and the other three dropped behind, reining in to let their horses blow.

His mouth tightened. They were professionals. They would follow him in relays, three at a time, the way coyotes followed a swifter antelope. With half their horses always rested, soon they would run the big stallion into the ground.

It was an eerie sort of race now. Sundance looked back, pacing the stallion's gait to that of his pursuers. They came on at a determined trot, and he held the stallion in, saving it. Three or four miles of that, and then the others made their play. With a man in a red shirt in the lead, they came up from behind and as the first three dropped back, reining in blown horses, they lashed their mounts into a gallop.

Sundance asked the stallion to give some more. It did, rested by the slower pace, stretching itself, drawing away easily. The men behind made no real effort to overtake; they knew the accuracy of that rifle. All they wanted to do was keep on pushing him.

They did, and when their own horses were done in, the first trio came up again in relay and demanded that the stallion run again. Amazingly, it responded vigorously, but Sundance knew that this could not go on. He looked toward the blue hulk of the Chisos, closer now, but still too far away. But he knew a place in the foothills where a spring came out of living rock and he could command the low ground with a fine field of fire, and if he could make that . . . The thing to do was to make the try right now, asked the stallion for all it had.

He did, and the horse seemed to find another notch to let itself out. With seeming effortlessness, it drew away from its pursuers, although they began to lash their mounts. Confidence rose in Jim Sundance. It would work, he would make it work, Eagle would carry him to safety—

And then they began, in rage and frustration, to shoot again. It was not their marksmanship, only luck: but as Eagle raced across a flat, he suddenly grunted, faltered. He tried to regain step, go on, but now there was a bad limp in his off hind leg, and Sundance, twisting in the saddle, cursed.

The slug had torn a huge chunk of meat from the horse's ham, chopping the great muscle there. It was not a permanently crippling wound, if given time to heal, but right now it could mean the death of Jim Sundance. No horse could run with a wound like that. The race was over, and the Chisos were far away.

So now he had to go to ground wherever he could. He reined in the bleeding stallion, ignoring the riders coming hard behind, rose in the stirrups, surveyed the land. A map of this desolate back corner of hell seemed to unreel behind his eyes. Then he remembered the butte and the cave.

A mile away, the butte thrust up out of the level desert floor, its lower slopes like a vast gravel heap strewn with enormous boulders. Thrusting out of the gravel was a tower of solid rock, soaring straight up for another forty feet. And there was, Sundance recollected from days spent down here with the Apaches, a hole in that rock big enough to shelter man and horse. But there was no water there, and once in, no way out if they chose to guard the slope.

But at least he would have the high ground, a field of fire that would make it costly for them to come after him.

He whacked off a couple of shots at them to slow them, missed, and then he patted the stallion's neck. Then he touched it with the heels of his moccasins and it broke into a gallant, shambling awkward run.

Sundance heard, behind him, a yell of triumph. They saw now that the horse was wounded. He cursed them, and as Eagle made the best progress he could, turned in his saddle and began to lay down fire to slow them.

That tactic worked. Realizing they had no further need to take chances, they dropped back. With what seemed to Sundance dreadful slowness and heart-breaking effort, Eagle made it across the flat. The graveled, boulder-studded slope loomed up just ahead, its only living growth a few prickly pear, some cholla and some wands of ocotillo. Where the rock tower emerged from the gravel, Sundance saw a thin dark line that, he knew, was the cave beneath a beetling overhang.

Not knowing that the cave was there, to the pursuers it must have seemed like a mountain lion going up a tree in desperation. He could not possibly climb that rock tower. All they had to do was be very careful and not get themselves shot and presently they would have him. Already, they were fanning out to encircle the butte.

At the base of the gravel hill, Sundance swung down. "Eagle," he whispered, "just one more good climb." Bent low, leading the horse, he scrambled up the slope. The stallion came behind, grunting with pain. Below, the men closed in; a few fired their rifles, and bullets whanged off rock, but the range was great for saddle guns.

And then Sundance reached the cave. Panting, he saw opening up the big hole beneath the shelf, huge enough for a horse to stand upright in. He led the stallion inside, knowing the danger from ricochets, but with no help for that. Eagle, in the shade and comparative cool of the shelter, dropped his head, and his breathing was like the pumping of a mighty bellows. Sundance uncinched two bullhide panniers from behind the saddle cantle, threw them down behind some rocks which made a natural barricade at the cave's mouth. From the long *parfleche*, he withdrew the bow and quiver, hooked taut the string of twisted buffalo sinew, laid the arrows beside him. Removing his gunbelt for greater comfort lying on the rocks, he put it beside him, too, with the hatchet and his spare ammunition. Then, careful to keep sand out of the rifle, he burrowed down behind the rocks, prepared to sell his life. He did not know why those six *pistoleros* wanted it, but he knew this: before they had it, it was going to cost them.

Again he noted their professionalism, as they

settled down for a siege. One man took their horses out of range and picketed them. Two others kept up a steady covering fire while three more moved up the slope, into position behind the boulders. The beetle of rock above the cave's mouth saved the horse and the barricade protected Sundance, but he could not raise his head, had no chance for a fair shot. When the first three were in place half-way up the slope, sheltered behind rocks big enough to hide them entirely, even standing, they laid down a barrage of their own with rifles, and the remaining trio came up and scattered out. Now all six were in place down there, in front and on the flanks, and their horses out of reach of either Sundance's bullets or of himself if he tried to run for it. They had seen him roll into the cave; they knew it did not come out anywhere else on the butte; they guessed it was only a hole. They had him and they knew it.

The day wore on, the heat ever more brutal, Sundance's mouth as dry as if stuffed full of cotton. He improved his barricade, keeping low and working carefully to give himself the necessary field of fire. Down there on the slope, the six men waited with the patience of wolves. They occasionally pumped lead around their shelters to remind Sundance they were there. He fired only an occasional round in return, saving his ammunition. They made no demand on him to surrender, gave him no indication of why they had to have him dead. Nor did he yell down to ask them.

If he'd been an outlaw with a price on his head, he could have understood it. But, although he had made a fair share of powerful enemies in his time, he was clean with the law; there was no bounty outstanding on him. No legal one, that is. But, with time to think, he began to understand. There *was* a bounty. Someone wanted him dead, and whoever it was had laid out enough money to pay eight men to come deep into the Texas desert and risk their lives to kill him.

That would not be peanuts. That would be a lot of money. Men like these did not come cheap.

Sundance tried to think of who might have posted such a reward. There were lots of possibilities. He had stepped on many powerful and sensitive toes in his career. The nature of his work made that inevitable.

This was, after all, a time when possession of the West still hung in the balance. Now, in

1874, from the Canadian border to the Rio Grande, the Indians, the high plains tribes and the desert bands, still clung to their most valuable hunting grounds.

The Sioux still claimed most of Dakota Territory as their reserve, including the fabulous Black Hills. The Cheyennes, Northern and Southern, allied with them, continued to rule parts of Montana, Wyoming, and hunted south as they pleased to the Canadian and Red Rivers. The Comanches held the Llano Estacado, the vast Staked Plains. West Texas, New Mexico, and Arizona still feared the Apaches, who had made only a tentative and uneasy peace. Smaller, less powerful tribes held reserves of their own and defended them with arms: the Blackfeet, the Nez Perce, the Paiutes, and others. Meanwhile, land-hungry white men eyed their magnificent hunting grounds with greed. True, there were treaties, sacred promises of their governments. But treaties could always be rewritten or, for that matter, completely disregarded. The irresistible force of Westward expansion had run slam into the immovable object of Indian love of their traditional lands. And Jim Sundance, half white, half Cheyenne, was caught square in the middle.

In the beginning, it had seemed to him that there was plenty of room in this vast country for red and white to live together. He knew that each had culture and knowledge, as well as goods and products, that the other needed. In the beginning, he had dreamed of a peaceable intermingling of the races, founded on mutual respect and honesty, and he had worked hard to bridge the gap between them, to help each side as seemed necessary. When he had thought it furthered that dream, he had scouted for the Army. Just as readily, when they needed his help, he had ridden with the Indians. It was, to him, a matter of justice, of fairness to both sides. Because he understood both races, it had seemed to him he had a mission to bring them together in peace.

Now, lying behind the rocks in the desert sun, his mouth curled in a savage grin not unlike a wolf's. The dream was dead. He knew now that there would be no peace. What the white man wanted was everything the Indians had. And Jim Sundance was determined to do his best, use his brains and guns both, to keep them from getting it. He had not always been successful, but he'd had his victories, some in combat and some in the

221

politics that went on behind the scenes, and those victories had cost a lot of powerful white men a great deal of potential profit.

So it made sense that they were tired of him. They wanted him out of the way, once and for all. And that was why those men were down there, waiting, well hidden behind those huge rocks. He could think of no other explanation.

He looked at the sky. The sun seemed pasted there, immovable. Maybe when darkness came, he would have a whore's chance; maybe on foot he could slip down the slope and past them. But that would mean leaving the stallion behind, which would be like abandoning his brother. He would also have to leave his gear, and there were things in those *parfleches* that he valued almost as much as his life; indeed, they were part of it. The warbonnet with the eagle feathers he had earned in his youth for counting *coups*, the medicine bag, the sacred shield of buffalo skin; he could not take all of them along. And, likely, he could not make it anyhow. They knew their business, would be alert all night long for any such move. He might get past or kill two or three, but the others were bound to take him.

No, Sundance thought, looking at the sun, there was only one way to save himself, and that was to kill them all.

2

WITH that decision made, the next step was to figure out how to do it. For the moment, it seemed impossible, but so was escape, and he thus had no choice except to die himself.

He had been in a lot of battles, in many different kinds of combat. His father, an English remittance man, had been a soldier once himself before becoming a trader among the Indians and taking the name Sundance. He had taught the son all he knew about the white man's weapons and ways of fighting. Service as a Cheyenne Dog Soldier had taught Sundance everything about the Indian way. Then, there had been the Civil War: he had fought as a guerilla on the Kansas Missouri border, and that had made a polished gunslinger out of him. In the years that followed, he had been in more pitched battles than he liked to remember on one side or the other between Indians and soldiers. Now, he ran through his mind every way of fighting he had ever known, every tactic he had

224

ever seen used, every weapon he had ever encountered. He searched all his combat lore for any idea, any inspiration, that might yield him chance. But he found none. The way those men were forted up behind the rocks, there was no way of getting at them short of using a cannon, and a howitzer at that, one of those stubby guns that could throw a shell almost straight up and drop it behind a strong position on a hidden enemy.

And, of course, he had no howitzer, so—

Sundance's prone body stiffened. Suddenly that wolf's grin jerked at his lips again. All at once he forgot the thirst, the stiffness and fatigue, the ache of the bullet slash a ricochet had given him.

Now he had a chance. Maybe a slim one, but—

He eased his rifle forward, through the loophole he had made in the barricade. Suddenly he sprayed the slope with bullets. The thunder of the gun echoed and re-echoed in a drumming roar, lead screamed as it bounced off rock.

Immediately the fire was returned. Sundance, cramming fresh cartridges into the gun, watched carefully. He had been pretty sure of each man's position; now powdersmoke verified them for him. One there behind the enormous boulder, another in that great rockburst, another behind that upjutting finger of thick sandstone, the other three in like cover, widely spaced around the gravel slope.

All right, the man behind the big boulder first.

When the gun was fully loaded, Sundance braced it in the loophole. He reached for the bow, laid out three arrows of the two dozen or more the quiver contained. Lying on his back, he nocked an arrow to his bow, drew the string, let the arrow fly. The long quilled shaft went up in a shallow, almost lazy arc. Before it had reached the top, Sundance had sent two more after it, distance nicely calculated, spread exact. He could place an arrow as easily and accurately as a rifle shot. Before the three shafts were coming down, he was at the loophole again with the rifle lined.

He saw the arrows coming down, watched them disappear swiftly behind the huge rock, one after the other, two feet apart. He heard a man's surprised yell, and then he had a target. As the arrows dropped in on the gunman hidden there, the man had to dodge. There was an instant when he exposed his shoulder, red shirt flashing into view behind the granite. Sundance fired.

The bullet caught the shoulder joint: the gunman howled, spun into view, whirled by the impact. An arrow bristled from his other arm. Sundance fired again, and this time the slug caught the gunman in the chest. Its impact jerked him back and down; he landed on the gravel, kicked twice, rolled six feet and he was dead.

"Curt!" somebody yelled. "What the hell?"

But Sundance was already reaching for more arrows. He had the three arcing in a spread again toward the rockburst, the clump of shattered boulders, almost before the first victim's body had quit twitching.

"Curt!" the man in there shouted, and then his shout died in a strange choking sound. He jumped to his feet, reaching behind his head to tug at the arrow embedded in the back of his neck. Sundance shot him between the eyes. He fell forward across a boulder.

Down there the slope exploded in gunfire. The four remaining killers grasped what was happening now. Lead screamed and whined off the brow of the cave and Sundance's barricade. "That sonofabitch!" somebody hollered. "He's droppin' those Goddamn Injun arrers in on us!" But Sundance had three more in the air by then.

As they soared up, the gunfire tapered off. Every man down there was watching those shafts rise and fall. A spread of three whistled down toward the tall finger of sandstone. The man behind it yelled something inarticulate and broke from cover before they landed. Zig-zagging like a startled jackrabbit, he made for another rock. Sundance took a lead on him and fired. The bullet smashed the right leg of the running man and he fell, face plowing into gravel. He tried to rise and Sundance killed him. Then he grasped another arrow.

Suddenly the slope was very quiet. Then a voice rang out. "Hey, Bascomb, you see that? Dead, three of 'em, Curt, Sandy, Jed! I'm gittin' the hell outa range right now!"

"No, you ain't!" Bascomb screamed back from behind a boulder no smaller than a log cabin. "Dig in, damn it, dig in and—" But gravel already rattled. Sundance had an arrow on the string. Then he caught a flash of color. In panic, terrified of those silent killers descending from the sky, one gunman ran, keeping cover between himself and Sundance's gun. But he had one short open space

228

to cross, and— There was no time to reach for the rifle. Sundance brought the bow down, drew the string, aimed, let the arrow go.

As the man dived between two rocks, it caught him, and with it buried in his flank, the head caught low in his entrails, he fell onto the gravel in the open, screaming horribly, clawing at the shaft, twisting and doubling like a worm on a hot stove. And now it was only two against one, and those odds were short enough for Sundance and he was tired of waiting. He threw back his head, and a sound even more awful rose above the screaming of the wounded—a Cheyenne warwhoop. Then, knowing this was the time, while they were demoralized, he grabbed the sixgun, swarmed over the rock barricade, and charged, shrieking that demonic cry.

Zigzagging, he ran and slid at full speeed down the gravel slope. He made a fine target, a beautiful one, Bascomb could not resist it. Clad in flannel shirt and chaps, Bascomb stepped from behind his rock, bearded face twisted in a snarl, rifle at his shoulder. Sundance did not even pause, and the Colt bucked in his hand as he ran on. The bullet zinged off the rock beside Bascomb's head and Bascomb flinched and missed and Sundance fired again, and Bascomb's face disappeared in a wash of scarlet, and now there was only one more, and he was not shooting at all. He was running as hard down the slope as his legs would carry him, tall, thin, tripping over his own spurs. Once he halted, looked back, face white with terror, started to raise his Winchester.

It was a long shot for a Colt. Sundance took careful aim, arm straight out and locked. The kick of the Colt was solid against his palm, its roar like a blast of thunder. Powdersmoke whirled and drifted: when it cleared, a long, thin body lay face down on the gravel. And, except for the diminishing howl of the man with the arrow in his gut, everything was terribly, dreadfully still.

The reaction hit Sundance then. He had raced and fought for his life and had killed eight men since breakfast, eight strangers he had never seen before. All at once, his knees went weak beneath him, he felt hot bile rise stingingly in his throat. He sat down heavily, chest heaving as he swallowed hard and sucked in great lungfuls of the hot dry desert air.

But he allowed himself only a moment to recover. The man with the arrow through him was still crying out. Shakily, Sundance arose, loped across the slope.

The man lay where he had fallen between two rocks, and he was short and stocky and balding and pushing middle age, with the marks of a hard, violent career engraved on his contorted face. Blood ran from the corner of his mouth and through his nostrils, and he still clawed weakly at the arrow and drew his legs up in agony. When Sundance towered over him, he looked up dully at the halfbreed.

"Jesus, Injun—" he managed in a thick, gurgling voice.

Sundance lined the Colt at his head. "I want to know," he said. "Why? Who sent you?"

"Who—?" Another spasm twisted the short man's face.

"Who sent you to kill me?" Sundance roared.

"I—"

"You'll be a long time dying unless you tell me!"

"I—" The man relaxed, gathered every tatter of his faculties. "Dunno. Bascomb. Made the deal."

"Where?"

"Del Rio . . . east of here."

"You don't know who?"

"I said *no*. Injun, in the name of God . . . have mercy."

"Yeah," Sundance said bitterly. "You boys were full of it. All right." He lined the Colt and pulled the trigger. There was no other mercy at his command.

Finding a canteen behind the rock the man had fled, he took a long drink and, with moisture in his mouth again, rolled a cigarette. He sat down with his back against the rock, looking out at the limitless desert, still alert and not neglecting to reload the Colt with spare shells from his pocket. When the cigarette was gone and he was steady, he stood up. Already, black flecks, like tiny bits of soot, circled overhead in the scalding blue.

Sundance went from body to body, checking pockets, searching Bascomb especially thoroughly. Each man had a lot of money on him, either in pockets, belt or poke. The average amount was five hundred dollars a man: Bascomb had a thousand, mostly in greenbacks. Eight men, Sundance thought, counting the two he'd dropped elsewhere. That came to nearly five thousand dollars. Likely the first installment of the bounty. And with probably as much or more payable when proof of his death was delivered; such deals usually worked that way. He frowned. That meant a minimum of ten thousand dollars as the price on Jim Sundance's head. Somebody wanted him dead very badly and had the cash to pay the freight. But . . . Del Rio? Who in that little nothing of a cowtown, which he had only visited once or twice?

Sundance had no qualms about keeping the money, the price for his own head; and he had a good use to which he could put it. He roamed the slope, retrieved all the arrows he could find. They were precious; most Indians nowadays used steel arrowheads. He preferred the ones made of flint or obsidian, for they packed more shocking power, dealt an uglier wound, but they were hard to come by and took a long time to make. When he had them, he went back up the slope, with a load of canteens. At the cave, he let Eagle, unscratched further by all the shooting, drink sparingly. Carefully he packed and loaded all his gear and led the horse back down the hill of gravel. Those black birds dropping lower, plus the coyotes, desert wolves, and kit foxes would take care of the bodies.

Eagle scented the hidden horses of the killers and led him to where they had been picketed. He unsaddled all but the best one and turned them free. The remaining one, a big sorrel with a cream mane and white right forefoot, he mounted. When he turned it east, headed toward Del Rio, Eagle followed without a lead rope.

He could have made the town in three days' hard riding, but he took it slowly and rested often to give Eagle's haunch a chance to heal. It was nearly well by the time he had crossed the Pecos canyon, and a week had passed. During that interval, Jim Sundance had traveled like a hunted animal, which, he knew now, he was. He stayed off the skyline, camped at night in the most remote spots he could find, and, slept with his weapons, as always, within easy reach, depending on the spotted stallion to serve as watchdog and, with its keener senses, warn him of any danger.

He saw no one, save for two wandering cowhands at a long distance, a couple of Mexican shepherds, and a single Caddo, a remnant of a nearly destroyed tribe, who had come into the desert to pray. During his journey, he had plenty of time to think. He had intended to travel north, join the

Cheyennes for their fall hunt, and see his woman again, but the matter of this price on his head took precedence.

Meanwhile, he could come up with no particular name. The Indians had blocked railroad building in Dakota Territory and Montana, as well as elsewhere. They blocked, too, the expansion of the cattle business up through Wyoming and Montana, as well as in West Texas and on the Staked Plains. They blocked vast fortunes to be made in land speculation, and for that matter, in mining. And, since he had helped the Indians and balked in some way or another people involved in all those ventures, it could have been anyone, railroad men or cowmen, miners or land boomers, who had posted the bounty to have him killed. Whoever it was, Sundance intended to deal with them. No matter how long it took, he would run down the source of that reward money. And Del Rio was where he had to start.

A day before reaching it, he turned loose the strange horse and mounted Eagle once more. When he rode in, he wanted nothing that could possibly link him with the killers.

On the evening of the eighth day, he topped a sandy rise and saw the town laid out below him in a bend of the Rio, with its sister hamlet, Villa Acuña, on the other bank. Over there in Mexico, a church bell tolled the hour, and the twilight wind from the river was cool and fresh. Sundance checked his weapons, found them in order, and rode in.

The town had grown since he'd last seen it a few years before. There were more false-fronted buildings of sawed lumber along the wide main street, more saloons and bars, more horses and rigs at the racks. Although this was the middle of the week, there was plenty of action, and the men on the sidewalks or the porches of the saloons were mostly in the range clothes of cattlemen: big hats, neckerchiefs, flannel shirts, chaps, high-heeled boots, spurs, and, of course, the ever-present holstered Colt. But, Sundance thought, putting Eagle warily down the street, not too many of them looked like ordinary cowhands. An expert on such matters, he recognized the stamp of hardcase, of gunman, on too many of them. He could tell by the cool, careful way they followed him with their eyes, and by the way they wore their sideguns; there were plenty of them who carried a pair, lowslung and tied down. They were, he thought, cut from the same cloth as

236

Bascomb and his killers, and his wariness increased. Whoever had made the deal with Bascomb and his men would have no trouble finding eight more just like them—or a dozen—if he were still here.

Well, if they wanted him, let them make another try at him. God knows, they could not help recognizing him, with his Indian features, blond hair, blue eyes and mounted on the Nez Perce stallion. Let them try, and this time he would get more information before they died. Meanwhile, he would not slink in or hide like a hunted wolf. He had been on the trail through the desert too long, he had too many hungers. He wanted a couple of drinks, a meal not cooked over a campfire, a bed with a mattress. There was another hunger, too, long unsatisfied and stronger than all the rest. He would go about his business and see what he could stir up. Here was the game walking squarely into the jaws of their trap. That ought to provoke some action. And this time he would not be taken by surprise; this time, he was ready.

Deliberately, he picked out the biggest saloon, put Eagle to the hitchrack, swung down and tied him. He loosened the Colt in its holster, stepped up on the porch. Three or four toughlooking characters there eyed him with keen appraisal, but none moved or spoke as he passed through them and went in. As soon as he was through the door, he shifted so that a wall shielded his back and went, on a careful route that enabled him to watch the entrance, to the bar.

More of the tough ones were there and others scattered around the room at tables along with a sprinkling of genuine cowpunchers and saddle tramps.

There was room at the counter, but he preferred a table himself where he could sit with his back to the wall. He decided on a beer to cut the dust and after that two shots of whiskey, his limit. Something in him, a heritage from his Indian mother, he supposed, made him susceptible to alcohol; he could not hold his booze. Three drinks of hard stuff and he turned mean and surly, four and he might go crazy, wanting only to fight, destroy, tear things apart. So he held himself to no more than two shots at a time, and he would not drink again until those wore off.

He got the beer, carried it to the table, hitched his chair up hard against the wall, swung his holster around to lie on top of his right thigh in easy reach, and sipped the beer.

238

It was cold and good, and he felt it spread a loosening of the nerves through him, and it sharpened, also, that hunger that had nothing to do with his belly, but that would have to wait.

Meanwhile, he watched the ebb and flow of customers. The place was filling up. Then a kind of murmur went through the crowd. Heads turned, and Sundance's with them.

There was a stairway at the rear, and the woman coming down it took his breath.

She was tall and the red hair, almost the color of flame, piled on her head made her look taller as it glinted in the lantern light. Her eyes were green, her skin pale ivory, the satin dress she wore was green, hugging large breasts, a cinched-in waist, spreading hips, showing the lines of her good, long legs beneath the clinging fabric of the long skirt, which she held up practicedly, like a lady, so it would not drag in the spit and refuse of the sawdust-covered floor. She came down the stairs with grace, like a queen, and the hunger of the men in the otherwise womanless room could almost be felt like a humid, muggy fog suddenly filling the place. Then she was off the stairs and walking toward the bar, and all at once Sundance realized that he knew her.

At almost the same minute, she saw him and halted. A big man in a flannel shirt and California pants, with two guns swung low on his waist, shoved back his chair, came toward her, reached for her arm. "Kate—"

Without looking at him, she pushed his pawing hand away. "Not now, Calder."

"Damn it, Kate—" Calder rumbled. He was in his late twenties, handsome, with a blond mustache, and obviously hard as nails. He wore his blond hair long and slicked back against his head with grease.

"I said, not now. Excuse me." Her voice was sharp. Ignoring Calder, she came toward Sundance, and a smile, faint, enigmatic, began to curve red lips. Calder stood there blinking, staring at her, and then his eyes shifted to Jim Sundance, who was rising from his chair. Calder chewed one end of his mustache. But for the moment, he did not move, only watched.

"Hello, Kate Barclay," Sundance said.

"So you remember me. Only, out here it's Kate Danton." She put out her hand. "Jim, Jim, it's good to see you again."

"You, too," Sundance said, holding back a dozen questions. "Sit down."

"Yes. Shall we have a drink together?"

Sundance grinned, started to raise his hand in a gesture. But she added, "It's on the house. Hey, Grover!"

The bartender turned with alacrity. "Yes, Miss Danton."

"The good bourbon and two glasses."

"Yes, ma'am." He hurried over, set them down, as Kate Danton seated herself. Sundance dropped back into his chair, while the bartender poured, and looked at her, and this time the questions were in his eyes.

She waited until the barkeep had gone, and her smile turned a little wry. "That's right. I own the place."

Sundance's brows went up.

"Shocked? Yeah," she continued. "I suppose so. It's a long way from the Palmer House in Chicago, isn't it?"

"You don't have to tell me anything you don't want to."

"There's no need of hiding it." She picked up her glass, tossed off her drink at a swallow and gestured, and he poured another for her. "I'll never forget," she said, with a touch of bitterness, "the day you walked in there with General Sheridan and the others. Even in a dress suit and pumps, you walked like an Indian, and you made the others look so little and awkward . . . That red skin and blond hair and . . ." Her mouth twisted and she drank half the glass. Sundance shifted his gaze to Calder, who had gone back to his table, poured a drink, and was watching them narrowly. Then he brought his attention back to Kate, but he kept part of his mind on Calder.

"You," she went on, "were there to advise the Army on Indian affairs. That was when you were still in their good graces. And I . . . was with George Phillips, and he had just given me an engagement ring. And I thought I loved him, but the minute I saw you . . . he just shrank to nothing."

"I didn't know you were engaged," Sundance said.

"There were a lot of things I didn't want to tell you about myself. I didn't want to scare you off. I didn't tell you how much money my father had or . . . Well, never mind." She finished the glass of whiskey, gestured once more, and he poured another. "Anyhow, it was a good month while it lasted, wasn't it? Maybe it was even worth it, I don't know."

Sundance was frowning now. "I'm not sure I understand."

"It's simple. Society girl gets big yearning

for magnificent, halfbreed Indian. Society frowns on that sort of thing. Girl plays all sorts of tricks, convinces Indian she's footloose and fancy free, only in it for the fun, all the time she hopes that when the time comes for him to leave he won't go . . . Meanwhile, she deceives her future husband and her parents and nearly everybody. Or thinks she does. Then—" She spread her hands. "Halfbreed goes back West. And she understands that, alongside his work, whatever it is, she never really counted."

Sundance drew in a long breath. "What I had to do out there was important." He hesitated. "I came back as soon as I could. But I couldn't find any trace of you. It was as if you'd just disappeared."

She smiled without humor. "I had. What I didn't know was that George was suspicious and had put a private detective on my trail. He learned the truth and contronted me with it and my parents as well and—everything blew sky high."

"That doesn't explain why you're in Del Rio."

"I think it does. George, of course, threw me over, with every right to. My parents tried to send me to Europe, to hush the scandal. I refused to go. I came West, instead, looking for . . . for somebody."

"Me," Sundance said.

"That's right. I ran away. And—" Again that shrug. "I never went back. Never wrote, never heard from them. Never quite caught up with Jim Sundance, either. But . . . I stayed alive. I made my way."

Sundance asked, "How?" before he thought.

Kate Danton's mouth twisted. "Guess," she said coldly.

3

FOR a moment, silence hung between them. Then Sundance said, quietly, "I'm sorry."

"No need for you to be." She laughed, a little huskily. "It wasn't your fault, you didn't know how serious it was with me. All you knew was that here was a wild girl ready for an affair on any terms, no questions asked, and you had a month in Chicago with lots of spare time. You never really knew the truth about me, my family or . . . a lot of things. No, Jim, I don't hold you to blame."

Sundance didn't answer. "Anyhow," Kate went on in a lighter tone, "it sure as hell hasn't been dull. I've hit all the towns, Jim, from Omaha to Bismarck to San Francisco to Abilene. They ran me out of Abilene last year. Well, I was ready to go. I'd made some money by then, a lot of it. I figured it was time to put it to work, so I wouldn't wind up looking like most of the girls do when they reach my age. I wandered around, seeking the right opportunity; I passed through Del Rio and I saw . . . a certain potential here. So I bought this place, the Cattleman's Rest, and I run it like a man would, not flat on my back. I've been here a year now, and it's been a good investment."

"Seems to be," said Sundance. "Town looks like it's booming."

"That's right. With the kind of people who put money in my till. Cattle, Jim. More cattle going up the trail from Texas every year."

Sundance said, "There aren't *that* many cattle in Val Verde county."

Kate laughed. "No. But there are plenty in Old Mexico."

"Oh," said Sundance, and now he understood.

"Their backs dry off quick once they're across the Rio," Kate said. "It's a good business, Jim, and it's drawn a lot of people here. Rustle a herd down in Coahuila or Nuevo Leon, bring 'em across the Rio, sell 'em to the drovers headed north. That's where this tough element you see came from and how they live. Fifteen a head on the hoof, and they'll bring over two, three hundred in a night. Live high until the money runs out and then go back for more. The Rangers don't give a damn, and the Mexicans can't stop 'em. But—" She spread her hands once more. "So much for that. How's it been with you? You and your precious Indians—"

"I—" Sundance began, and then he bit off the words.

Calder had taken a long drink directly from the bottle. Now, he shoved back his chair, swaggered across the room, came up to Sundance's table, towering between Kate and the halfbreed. He swayed slightly.

"Kate," he said. "God damn it? You know somethin'? That's a God damn Injun you're sittin' with."

Kate Danton drew in a long breath. "Billy, please. I know who this man is. Now, be a good boy and run along and you and I'll have a drink later tonight."

"That's what you told me last night," Calder rasped. "Only you got hung up with some other joker." His voice rose. "Kate, I won't be thrown over for no stinkin' Injun!"

"Thrown over? Since when were we ever close enough for me to throw you over?"

Calder's eyes flared. "Kate, you know how I feel about you! And—" He reached down, seized her arm, and she gave a cry of pain as he jerked her to her feet. "Not with a stinkin' Injun!" he snarled again and slung her across

247

the room. She cried out and brought up hard against a table, and then Sundance was on his feet and stepping out into the clear.

"Friend," he said, in a voice like ice on steel.

Calder swung to face him, hands dropping low. "I ain't no damn' gut-eater's friend!" And then his right hand moved and he was fast, very fast.

Sundance's right hand did not seem to move. But the gun was in it, pointed at Calder's belly before the other's Colt cleared leather. "Hold it!" Sundance snapped.

Calder froze, staring at the muzzle of Sundance's gun. His face went pale. He let his Colt slide back in leather, raised both hands higher. He swallowed hard.

"You've got an apology to make to the lady," Sundance said.

"I got—" Calder looked into Sundance's eyes. Then, slowly, he nodded. "Yeah," he said weakly. "I got an apology to make—All right, Mister. Put up that gun."

"No," Sundance said. "But you go make your manners. And then you get out."

Calder hesitated. Sundance roared: "Move!"

Then, slowly, Calder turned. He faced

Kate, standing by a table. He took a few steps that brought him toward her. "Kate, I was outa line. I'm sorry."

Her breasts rose and fell beneath the satin. "All right, Calder. Forget it. Just leave, that's all. Leave and don't you come back in here again."

"But, Kate . . ." He put out a hand. Her mouth twisted in distaste and she stepped aside to avoid it and then she was in Sundance's line of fire, which was what Calder had wanted. He dropped into a crouch, and his right hand swooped, and he yelled, "Now, you red sonbitch!" and the roar of his Colt shook the room.

Kate screamed and pitched sideways and landed on the floor, and the slug, a fraction of a second too hasty, chugged into the wall so close to Sundance he felt its passage, and Sundance took better aim and fired. His own bullet smashed into Calder's shoulder joint, and Calder howled and dropped his gun, twisted, falling across the table from the impact. But, already he was reaching with his left hand. Sundance dared not fire again, as Kate sat up. He was across the room in two quick bounds, leaping over her, and as

249

Calder's left hand gun came clear of leather, Sundance swung his own Colt.

Its long barrel smashed with terrific force into Calder's wrist. Sundance felt bone yield beneath the steel. Calder bellowed and the Colt dropped to the floor. Then Sundance had Calder's shirt-slack gathered up, jerked the man to his feet. He swung the gun barrel again. Once, twice, three, four times. It whipped back and forth across Calder's face, smashing one ear, Calder's nose, the sight tearing Calder's cheek. Then Sundance let Calder go. The man, his face a parody of what it had been before, his right shoulder scarlet, his broken left wrist dangling, made a mewing noise in his throat.

"Out," Sundance roared. "Out, damn you, or I'll kill you!"

Calder stared at him with awed, wide, fear-filled eyes, in the bloody mask of his face. He muttered something, turned and staggered toward the doors. Sundance stood there tensely with the Colt ready, but Calder disappeared between the batwings without looking back. Sundance slowly lowered the gun. With his right shoulder smashed and his left wrist broken, it would be a long time before Calder would use a Colt again, if ever. Sundance did not think he had to worry about Calder any more.

But maybe Calder had friends. He whirled to face the room. Then he relaxed. If there were friends of Calder's here, they had seen enough to quench any thoughts of taking up the quarrel. Under his cold gaze, they turned their faces away and kept their hands well away from iron.

"Kate," he said. "Are you all right?"

She was on her feet now. "I'm fine. That wasn't very smart of me, was it, Jim? You'd think I'd know better by now—"

"Never mind," Sundance said. "Let's finish our drink."

"I think we'd better have it upstairs," Kate said. "In my apartment. I'm a little shaky."

"Why," Sundance said, "sure. That suits me fine."

His eyes shuttled to the bar. The bartender had produced a sawed-off shotgun and held it ready for any emergency. Kate said, "That's right, Grover. You watch us. We're going upstairs. And we don't want to be disturbed. Not tonight, you understand?"

"Yes, ma'am, Miss Danton."

Coolly, as if she were at a cotillion, Kate Danton turned then, and for a moment Sundance remembered the Palmer House and the way she had been six years before, as she said, "Well, Mr. Sundance. Will you join me?"

There was a sitting room, a bedroom, a kitchen and a bath with a big iron tub. Jim Sundance, sipping his second drink, soaked in the hot water Kate had had sent up, while she was busy in the kitchen. Even here, he kept his Colt within easy reach.

For more reasons than one, he was glad he had run into Kate. She had kindled that hunger in him, and he knew the same hunger was in her, but beyond that, there could be no better source of information. She was bound to know everything that went on in Del Rio. Those eight men had been cut from the same cloth as Calder; she would know them, too, and maybe who had hired them. Meanwhile, he held the questions in abeyance in his mind and savored his bath. He had been trained in the Cheyenne way to like being clean, and, as Indians did, bathed every time he got the opportunity. He wondered if white men knew how foul they sometimes smelled to Indians with their rank body odors and the bay rum and grease they sometimes used to disguise them.

When he was finished, he dried with a soft towel, slipped into a dressing gown Kate had laid out for him. He had no idea who its original owner had been, but it fitted him well. He buckled his gun belt on and went into the kitchen.

She had just put a huge plate of steak, eggs, and potatoes on the table and a cup of steaming coffee. Her eyes went to the gun. "Don't you ever go without that thing?"

Sundance said, "You've been around long enough to know better than that." He sat down at the table and began to eat. She sat opposite him with a cup of coffee.

"Jim," she asked presently, "where have you been and what *have* you been doing since we last were together? I've heard all sorts of stories. Some of them are so wild—"

"I've been a lot of places," Sundance said. "And I've done a lot of things."

"Working for the Indians."

"Mostly."

"They say, too, you hire out your gun . . . Not on the easy jobs. On the high-priced ones."

"I do," Sundance said. "There's plenty of work for a man like me. I know all the tricks, Indian and white, and I guarantee results.

253

For what I usually undertake to do, the price isn't cheap."

"What do you do with the money? Is what I've heard true? That you send it all back east? To Washington?"

Sundance sipped coffee and leaned back in his chair. "That's where the real fight is, Kate."

"I don't understand."

"In the Interior Department, the War Department, the Bureau of Indian Affairs. And most of all, in Congress. That's where the decisions are made that really affect the Indians. Whether there'll be peace or war. Whether the treaties will be kept, abrogated, or just plain ignored. A lot of people want Indian land, Kate—railroad people, bankers, miners. They've got money to spend, and they spend it buying Congressmen."

"I see. So you buy Congressmen, too? On behalf of the Indians?"

"When I have to. I've got a lawyer working for them there, a good man, the best. He's lost some battles, but he's won some, too. He believes in what he's doing, and he himself doesn't charge too much, but his activities take a lot of financing. I only know one way to earn the money—with my gun."

"I see. And so you go on fighting and fighting—for a lost cause."

"It's not lost yet. If I can save anything at all for them, it's worth it; to me, anyhow." He had cleaned his plate and now he rolled a cigarette. "But I've made some enemies, some powerful ones, rich ones. They'd love to see me out of the way." He let her light the cigarette for him, and then he said, "That's why I'm in Del Rio."

"I don't understand. There are no Indians here."

"No," Sundance said. "All the same—" Then, matter-of-factly, he told her what had happened in Big Bend. She listened closely, eyes widening.

"Jim, you killed *eight* of them?"

"Well," he smiled, "I didn't want them to kill me. Anyhow, that was all I learned. That somebody here had hired Bascomb and his crew to bushwhack me. If there's a price on my head, I want to know about it, how much and who put it there. I aim to find out about it in Del Rio. I hope you can help me."

"I'll do my best," she said. "I know almost everything that happens here. I knew Bascomb, of course, Dan Bascomb, and his bunch. They were running wet cattle across the border like the others. But I don't know who hired them to get you. But I'll surely check every source I've got to find out." She paused, looking at him with magnificent eyes in which something seemed to swirl and flare. "I didn't come this far and look for you this long to have somebody kill you just when I've found you."

"Kate—" Sundance began.

"Oh, I know," she said almost wearily. "You can't promise me anything. Maybe you've even got another woman. If you have, I don't want to know about her. I just want to be with you and pretend it's . . . the Palmer House." She looked at his plate. "Are you through?"

Sundance smiled at her. "I'm through."

Kate stood up, smoothing the satin over her breasts. "I thought we might have your second drink in the bedroom."

Jim Sundance arose. "Do you know," he said, "I think that sounds like a good idea."

Sated as he was with food and drink and the woman, Sundance, as always, slept lightly, the gunbelt with its Colt and Bowie coiled beneath the pillow.

When something awakened him, he had no

idea what it was. He lay for a moment in a half drowse, remembering, placing himself. Then it came back. Kate. Kate, her body surging beneath his, her mouth hungry on him, Kate, crying out the first time and the second . . . His leg moved across the bed, and then he knew why he was awake. Kate was no longer there. Almost instinctively, then, his hand slid beneath the pillow and closed around the Colt's grip. He did not move, but his eyes were half-slitted and gradually accustomed to the dimness of the room.

She was out of bed and moving around.

In the darkness, her naked body gleamed, easily visible. She was at the dresser, quietly opening a drawer. Sundance lay motionless, watching her carefully.

She turned from the dresser, and she had something in her hand, now, and she halted at the foot of the bed and the Colt made no whisper of sound as Sundance drew it from leather. Once his eyes were adjusted, he could see in the dark like a cat. The hammer coming back on the big .44 made a loud click.

"Kate," he said harshly, "don't move and don't try it."

The white body in the darkness went rigid. "Jim—"

"You're covered," he said. "If you don't drop that Deringer, I'll kill you."

For a moment, she made no sound. Then, hopelessly, she said, "All right." He heard the light thud as the little gun landed on the floor.

"Kick it under the bed."

He heard it skid when she did that, and he sat up.

"Now," he said, "light the lamp there."

"I should have remembered," she said bitterly, "that you sleep like a goddamned cat."

"You should have remembered that, yes," Sundance said, gently. He heard a match strike and the lamp flared and she stood there naked before him, light playing on breasts and belly and loins and long, fine legs. She stood naked without shame, for she had stood naked like that before so many men . . . Her red hair was down and tousled, her face slightly puffy with sleep, her mouth and throat and breasts showing faint bruises.

Sundance said, "You aimed to kill me."

"Yes," said Kate wearily. "I thought I would."

He eased the hammer of the Colt down.

"Sit on the foot of the bed. Were you the one who hired Bascomb and his crew?"

"I did that, yes."

"I began to wonder, just a little, when you stepped in front of Calder. A girl like you, who's been around, should have known a lot better. You were giving him a chance at me, eh?"

"It was just something I did on impulse."

"You hired Bascomb on impulse, too, I guess." The earlier whiskey had long since worn off and he felt old and tired and, naked, he swung out of bed and went to a bottle on the table, still keeping the Colt centered on Kate Danton. He poured drinks into two glasses and handed her one. "I expect you need this."

"God, do I," she said, and tossed it off.

Sundance said, "Now. Suppose you tell me. Did you put the price on my head? Your ten thousand? Or whatever? Did you hate me that much?"

"I hated you," Kate said thickly. "I hated you and loved you both. Damn you, if you had never existed, do you know where I would be now? Or . . . if you had just taken me with you. Don't you understand? I would have lived in one of those Indian tents with

259

you. I would have been your squaw. I would have chopped your wood and brought your water and cooked your meals and borne your children. But you just went off and left me."

Sundance said, "I was a lot younger and so were you. But you haven't answered my question."

"No," Kate said. "I didn't put up the ten thousand. I only passed it on."

"From who?"

She did not answer.

"Kate," Sundance said gently.

She turned on him. "Damn you," she said savagely, "if you had just slept a minute longer. Then I would have been even with you. For all those years, for everything I lost on your account, for everything I suffered—"

"Who gave you the ten thousand to hire Bascomb with? Kate, you'd better tell me."

She sucked in a long breath. "I'll fry in hell first. Jim, it was so good tonight. And yet . . . I knew you would leave me again, for those damned Indians of yours. And I would rather see you dead than have you leave me again . . ." She raised her head. "Yes, I took his ten thousand and made a deal with Bascomb."

"Whose ten thousand?"

"I won't tell you. He still wants you. As

long as you don't know who he is, he might get you. Right now, that's all I want, since I failed myself." She put her head in her hands.

Sundance stood there looking at her for a moment. Then he said, still gently, "Kate, I've got to know. You don't understand. There's still so much work I've got to do. The lives of hundreds of thousands of people, men, women, children, depend on what I do. I've stayed clear of the law very carefully. But if somebody rich and powerful enough to make me an outlaw in all but name exists, I've got to know who that somebody is and deal with him. Not out of fear for my own hide. But because I know how much will go undone if I die."

"Go to hell," Kate said hoarsely, face still in her hands.

Sundance went to the bed, slipped his hand beneath the pillow. When he straightened up, he said, "Kate, look at me."

She raised her head, and her eyes widened as she saw the Bowie with the footlong blade in his hand.

"Kate, you're to tell me the name of the man you dealt with."

"I said you can go to hell. Kill me, if you've got the guts."

Sundance said, "You know I won't kill you. But I'll do worse than that if you don't tell me. I've got to know; my life depends on it, and I don't give a damn about that, but too many lives depend on mine."

Kate stared at the great blade, uplifted, gleaming in the lantern light.

Sundance said, "I won't kill you, Kate. But you saw what I did to Calder tonight. He'll never fast-draw a gun again. I want that name or— Do you get my drift?"

She licked her lips. "You wouldn't."

"You just tried to shoot me while I slept."

"Jim—"

"Two or three times forward, two or three times back. You'll live, but no man will ever look at you again. You won't even be able to bear looking at yourself in the mirror."

"Jim, you don't mean it."

"You tried to kill me, twice. I mean it," he said, and his eyes glittered in the lamplight. "Kate, you've got about five seconds . . ." He thrust out the blade and it was very near her face.

Her eyes were fixed on it.

"Jim—"

"About two seconds left."

"Jim, for God's sake, wait! I'll tell you what you want to know!" She fell back across the bed. Sundance did not lower the knife.

"Go ahead," he said.

"All right." She covered her face with her hands. "He was a man I knew in Abilene. That was his robe you wore tonight. He came down here from Kansas and looked me up and said he needed men to do a job. My cut was two thousand, but I would have done it for nothing when I heard it was to be you. I hired Bascomb and the others, paid them five thousand down, another five due when they brought in your scalp . . . !"

"My scalp?"

"That blond hair with enough red skin attached . . . There can't be but one scalp like that! That was what he wanted! Bascomb was to bring it to me and I was to deliver it to him!"

"And who is he?"

She did not answer.

Sundance laid the knife point on her belly, just below the navel. "Kate—"

"His name is Abel Jeffers!"

"What does he do in Abilene?"

"He's a cattle buyer!"

"Who hired him to contact you?"

"Jim—"

"*Who hired him?*" Sundance roared.

"I don't know," she sobbed. "He wouldn't tell me. Only that it was somebody big with lots of money. Prepared to spend a hundred thousand if that's what it took to bring you down!"

Sundance said, incredulously, "A hundred thousand?"

"That's what he said," Kate husked. "His rake-off was five."

"That's seventeen thousand somebody has laid out already." Sundance pulled the knife away. "You've got the other five around here?"

She did not even more. "In the dresser."

Sundance went to it, as she lay sprawled naked on the bed. He opened the drawer, fished beneath lace and silk, drew out packets of greenbacks.

"Yes," he said, the word a sibilant gust.

"Take it," she said. "Just take it and go, please."

"I aim to," Sundance said. "But first I've got to tie you up and gag you."

"I don't care. I don't care what you do."

Sundance pulled stockings from the

264

drawer. They worked well, and in a moment her hands and feet were tied. He wadded a stocking and held another ready as he looked down into her eyes. His hand shook slightly.

"Kate," he said quietly, "I'm sorry."

She met his gaze directly. "So am I," she said harshly. "Now I'll never know whether or not I would have pulled that trigger. I hope he gets you, Jim, I really hope he does. You and your damned Indians—"

Then Sundance rammed in the gag.

She writhed helplessly on the bed as he dressed, put on his weapons belt, gathered up his gear, and went to the window.

"Goodbye, Kate," he said. "I wish it had worked out better for both of us." Then he was gone, down the wall like a fly, dropping the last twenty feet to the alley and landing lightly. As he ran through the darkened town toward the livery where she had had a man take Eagle, he felt no triumph despite the five thousand dollars in his pocket. He only felt ashamed and dirty.

4

WHEN, ten days later, Sundance halted the stallion on a height of ground, a river of cattle flowed across the prairie below him.

The trail herd could be heard—and smelled—from a long way off, three thousand head of steers pointed north, bound for Abilene. And this was only one of many. Another of equal size was twenty miles ahead, and yet another, not much smaller, a day's journey behind. It was as if a great chain of longhorns stretched from Texas to Kansas. Sundance's mouth thinned. Not all those cattle would go to the slaughterhouses of the East. Many were being bought to stock ranges in Nebraska, Wyoming, Montana—Indian country. As the ranchers moved in, the Indians fought back. The ranchers yelled for the Army, and the soldiers came and there was war, on the claim that the tribes had broken their treaties of peace.

That herd down there, Sundance knew, represented a fortune to its owners. Easily, as the market now was, they could clear a hundred thousand dollars on it. The northern ranchers were tired of letting Texas reap such profits, they wanted in. And the stakes they played for in crowding out the Indians amounted to many millions. Again, he wondered if it were cattle money on his head.

He had come hard and fast from Del Rio, pushing the stallion, yet taking time to cover his tracks, knowing that when Kate got free, she would send men after him and also send the word on ahead that Jim Sundance was alive and on the loose. So he had traveled like a hunted wolf, sometimes doubling back, riding in the water when he found a stream, keeping off the skyline, avoiding all contact with humans. He knew where he stood, now. If the word was around that somebody would pay a hundred thousand for his scalp, he was the most hunted man in the West, fair game for any ambitious fellow with a gun. He was, in fact, a walking gold strike. Let the word spread: *get Sundance and get rich!* Cowpunchers would leave their thirty a month and found to look for him, unsuccessful miners their disappointing claims. Professional gunmen would oil their Colts and Winchesters and private detectives, bounty hunters, gamblers down on their luck, even big-dreaming ranch and farm kids with rabbit rifles—all would have their eyes peeled for Jim Sundance. From now on, he could trust no one whose skin was not red. Even old friends might be tempted; among white men, a hundred thousand in gold could cancel out a lot of friendship. He could not even walk into a store to buy a sack of tobacco . . . He was out of tobacco now, but red willow bark or marijuana would have to do until he reached the Cherokee country and could get in touch with John Canoe.

Shielded by an outcrop of a butte, he watched the trail herd for a few moments longer. The smile that touched his face was grim. If those Texans knew how much money on the hoof was up here on this rise, they'd leave that herd, one and all, and come after him. After all, he was worth as much as three thousand head of longhorns delivered to the pens in Abilene.

Presently he swung the horse and rode on, putting a ridge between himself and what men now called the Chisholm Trail, which, ironically, had first been marked out by a halfbreed like himself. Old Jesse Chisholm had been half Cherokee. And his people lived not far from here, in the northern part of what was known now as Indian Territory.

The country was rolling, well-watered, with occasional timber. It had been set aside as a reserve into which various tribes were to be moved as their power was broken. But, barren as some parts were, much was good rangeland, and Sundance wondered how much longer the whites would let the Indians keep it.

By coming nightfall, he was in sparsely settled country and extra wary. A few roads crisscrossed the plains, and here and there were little clusters of rude cabins, and a few better houses, even an occasional store. He did not dare let anyone get a glimpse of him; even at a distance, the Appaloosa was like a signboard proclaiming his identity. He had got it from the Nez Perce of Idaho and there was not another stud like it south of the Platte. He kept to the timbered creekbottoms, and at twilight, he holed up. Not long before midnight, he resaddled the spotted stallion and rode on, emerging from the timber into hilly terrain. There was almost no moon, but he needed none to find the single cabin he sought.

It was in a little valley between two scrub-clad ridges. As he struck the wagon track leading toward it, a razorback hog scuttled into the brush. Somewhere ahead, a hound caught his scent and bayed. Then he saw the little two-room structure of chinked logs, with its shed and barn and pens, only a cube of blackness in a grove of walnuts. Sundance pulled his rifle from its scabbard and laid it across his saddle-horn.

Suddenly the dog, a big bluetick hound, was in the path, baying thunderously. It circled the big stallion, keeping out of reach of the horse's heels, and up ahead, as its belling shattered the silence of the night, a terrier yapped, too; and then, inside the cabin, a lamp was lit.

Sundance reined in, giving John Canoe and his wife a chance to get dressed. Then he put the stallion forward at a walk, as the door swung open, silhouetting a stocky figure against the lamplight. It was a man who held a shotgun.

His voice rang out in challenge. "Who's out yonder?" He saw the rider, raised his weapon.

Sundance halted again, calling out softly: "John. It's Jim Sundance."

"Who?"

"Jim Sundance."

"Jim— Well, I be damned." John Canoe lowered the shotgun, took a few steps forward, stared. "It sure is, I'd know that big spotted stud anywhere." He laughed delightedly. "Hell's fire, Jim, come in the house."

"First, let me put this horse out of sight."

John Canoe's stocky figure stiffened. "You wanted?"

"You could say that."

"Well, that makes no difference. There's an empty stall in the barn." He came forward, as Sundance sheathed the rifle and swung down, a man not much over five feet five, wearing a nightshirt tucked into pants, his feet bare. Tucking the shotgun under his arm, he put out a hard, rough hand. "Jim, it's good to see you."

Sundance shook his hand. "Likewise, John."

"Go in the house. Wilma's dressed. I'll take care of the stud. He knows me, don't he?"

"He knows you," Sundance said, and he passed over the reins. Canoe led the horse away and Sundance went into the cabin.

It had two rooms, and a single lamp burned

on its rough table, filling the air with a rancid stench of what people called rock oil. It came up in a spring on John Canoe's place, and he skimmed it off and burned it, cursing it for contaminating good water. The odor reminded Sundance that he had something to tell Canoe about the rock oil.

As Sundance closed the door behind him, a slight, frail woman in her late forties came toward him, light from the lamp shining on her copper skin, her face deeply wrinkled. She put out both hands. "Welcome, Jim Sundance," she said in Cherokee.

"Thank you, woman of John Canoe," he answered formally, then smiled. "Wilma, how are you?"

"Pleasured by the sight of you." She lapsed into English. "It's been too long. You'll eat with us? I've got fresh deer liver."

"Fine," Sundance said. "How are the children?"

"Almost grown. Asleep in there." She pointed to the other room.

"Don't wake 'em," Sundance said.

"No." She went to the fire, stirred it up, took down an iron skillet from a hook by the mantel. She moved slowly, awkwardly, as if she had rheumatism or arthritis. This was not

272

a country that agreed with mountain Indians.

John Canoe came back in, closing the door, sliding its wooden bar. He put the shotgun on pegs over the mantel, turned. He was in his early sixties, built like a bear, his hair cut fairly short and its raven black threaded now with silver. His eyes were like two jet beads, and his teeth were still good, white, when he grinned. "Damn, Jim, it's been a long time since Pea Ridge." He went to a cabinet, took out a fruitjar and two tin cups. "A drink?"

"Would be good," Sundance said and sat down on the split log bench by the table and watched John Canoe as he poured.

Small and shabby as the man was, he came from noble ancestors. His great-grandfather had been Dragging Canoe, famous war chief of the Cherokees.

Once the Cherokees had held all of eastern Tennessee and western North Carolina, the fastnesses of the Smoky Mountains studded with their villages. Among the most highly civilized of all the eastern tribes, they had lived by farming as much as hunting and had built log cabins long before the first white settlers learned the art. The great Sequoya had given them an alphabet and they could read and write their own language. But they

273

had been among the first casualties of the westward thrust of white men.

Treaty after treaty they had made had been broken. Time and again they were pushed deeper into their mountains. Then the arch-enemy of all Indians, Andrew Jackson, had become President, and he had decided to remove the Cherokees as an obstacle to westward expansion once and for all. He had sent the Army, and they had rounded up the tribe like cattle and, in the dead of winter, had marched them across the Smoky Mountains and out to Indian Territory. It had been a brutal march, a death-march, with men, women, children perishing on the way, from cold and starvation. A small remnant of the tribe, the Quallas, had managed to break away, and they remained in their ancestral home in the North Carolina mountains now, but most of the Cherokees had been settled in the west. Here, malaria and other low-land diseases had taken a dreadful toll. Still, they had survived, on land deemed worthless because even its water was polluted with the stuff called rock oil. There was so much rock-oil, or petroleum as it was now beginning to be called, that crops would not grow on the soil allotted to them.

John Canoe had been a child on that Trail of Tears, as the Cherokees still called it. He had made the long march over the mountains, had lost his mother and his younger brother. Yet, somehow, he had survived. But the memories of that ordeal were deeply engraved in his mind. He was known as a good Cherokee, he farmed well and traded with the white man and was always respectful. But, as Sundance well knew, he hated the whites with a passion he kept well concealed.

Now he tossed off half the cup of whiskey and sighed. Sundance drank, too; it was corn, and very powerful. "So you're wanted," John Canoe said. "I figured you would be, sooner or later. You've been in their way too much, Jim. What kind of price they put on your head? Two thousand, three?"

"A hundred," Jim Sundance said.

"A hundred dollars?"

"No," Sundance answered. "A hundred thousand."

John Canoe stared at him and his wife turned from the fire. For a moment, the room was silent. Then John Canoe laughed sharply, explosively. "You've been hurtin' 'em!"

"I guess I have."

"What'd you do and who—?" John Canoe leaned forward. He listened intently as Sundance told him all he knew. Then he sipped whiskey and shook his head. "Wild," he said. "Plumb wild. And so you got to go to Abilene, eh?"

"Yes."

"Damn, you know they'll burn you down the minute you ride in on that spotted stallion and with that blond hair and blue eyes and skin your color—"

"I know," Sundance said. "That's why I'm here, John. I need help."

"Well, hell, yes. I'll be glad to flank you!"

"Appreciate it, but not that kind."

John Canoe met his eyes. "Then you name it," he said harshly. "Jim, you and me fought together at Pea Ridge under Stand Watie, with his Cherokee battalion, and we whipped the Yankees. You pulled me out of a tight spot then, when you coulda got your head blown off helpin' me. There's been more times than one since that you've pulled me out of a bad hole with a few dollars when I needed it. But it ain't me that counts. It's what you've done for the Indians, all the Indians, and what you can keep on doin' for

276

'em. To me, that's the most important thing."

He stood up, went to the fire, looked down into the coals. "You know," he said, "I remember what it used to be like up in the Smoky Mountains. Big hills, big timber, clean and sweet and lots of game . . . We coulda held that land, Jim. If we'd united with the Creeks and the Shawnees and the Tuscaroras, and we'd made one common cause, we coulda run the white men clean outa Carolina. But we didn't. We fought each other, insteada fightin' the real enemy. And, because we wouldn't unite, the real enemy whipped us and took our land. Well . . . it's gone, now."

He turned. "And the same thing is happenin' all over again out here. The Cheyennes fight the Crows and the Crows fight the Sioux and the Sioux fight the Blackfeet and none of 'em'll git together. And so they let the white men pick 'em off one by one. But, if instead of fightin', all the Indians would unite—"

He came back to the table. "I've often thought about it. And when I do, I think about you, too. Your daddy was a white man, but he traded with all the tribes, they knew and liked him, from the Canadian border clean down into Mexico. You grew up among all of 'em, the Sioux, the Cheyenne, the Apaches, God knows how many others. You speak all their languages, you know their ways, you've been adopted into most of the bands."

He sat down again. "There are more Indians than there are white soldiers. I've always figured that if somebody could unite 'em, get 'em to workin' together against the *real* enemy— Then, by God, if they couldn't take their land back by force, they could make one hell of a bargain. I always figured that the one man who could bring 'em together was you. Jim Sundance, if he put his mind to it, could raise an Indian army that would whip the white man's ass and good. Well, you ask me, I think somebody else is figurin' the same way."

"Maybe," Sundance said.

"No maybe about it. That's why they're scared of you. Think what an army that would be—the Sioux and Cheyenne fightin' societies, *and* the Crows and Blackfeet and Piegans! Maybe the Nez Perce, the Comanches, the Arapahoes and Kiowas. The Apaches and the Navajos— A man like you could put together

278

a force of a hundred thousand warriors, three times what there is in the whole United States Army! And they know it, Jim! Don't you think they don't know it!" He gestured. "And what about us, stuck on this damn rock-oil soaked land out here? The Cherokees, the Choctaws, the Osages, the Seminoles, the Delawares . . . You think we've forgot how to fight?"

"You proved at Pea Ridge you haven't forgotten that," Sundance said.

"Sam Houston knew we hadn't! He lived among us, old Sam did, he was a Cherokee, too, before he went on to Texas! But— Anyhow, Jim, that's it. That's why somebody will put up that much money. It's comin' to showdown now, soon, this year, next, the one after. They want you out of the way before it does."

He drained his cup. "Me, I'll stick my hand in the fire to make sure they don't git you, if that'll help. What can I do for you, Jim?"

Sundance grinned. Something in him unknotted. It was good to be with someone he could trust. "Well," he said, "first of all, I want a haircut."

By the time John Canoe came back from the store, his wife, Wilma, had finished cutting Jim Sundance's hair and rubbing into what remained the can of blacking he had produced from his panniers. She held a small, wavy steel mirror up before his face. "There. How's that look? Only, I don't know what we'll do about them blue eyes."

"I'm half Mandan," Sundance said. "From up on the Missouri River, understand? Lots of the Mandans have blue eyes. There ain't many left, but enough so the story'll hold water."

"I never heard of that."

"Well, it's true. Some of 'em even had light hair. There's an old story that they mixed in with a bunch of Welshmen or Norwegians that came here long before Columbus found this country."

"You know I never been to no white man's school, Jim, I don't know nothin' about that. I only read the Bible in the Cherokee language. But if you like the hair, good. I—" She broke off as the buckboard pulled up out front.

John Canoe came in, lugging a big bundle. "Jim, I bought everything you said. I hope it all fits."

"A halfbreed's clothes hardly ever do," Sundance answered. He ripped open the bundle. "Let's see."

He took out a black, high-crowned hat, settled it on his head. Next came the flannel shirt, the denim jeans, the black boots, with their low stockman's heels, Then the coat . . . "Let me use the other room," Sundance said. When he came out of it, John Canoe grinned.

"By God, you look like an agency Injun if I ever seen one!"

"Half Mandan, half Santee Sioux," Sundance answered. "Right common combination up in the Dakotas. I can't speak Mandan, but I know the Santee dialect well enough. I'll swing around and come into Abilene from the north. That'll make the story look even better. But if I meet somebody on the way, maybe I won't have to duck."

Gone was the long yellow hair, gone the buckskin shirt with the Cheyenne beadwork and the Cheyenne moccasins. The big, cheaply dressed man in the wrinkled clothes bore little resemblance to Jim Sundance as he had appeared the day before, especially with the yellow hair closecropped and blackened. "What about the horse?" he asked.

"You ride my personal mount, Deerchaser.

Half mustang, half Morgan, not as big as your stud, and a geldin', but he'll go like hell in a short sprint and he's got the bottom to carry a man your size all day long. We'll keep the stallion until you come back for him, plus all your gear. You sure you don't want to take that bow?"

"I can't afford to," Sundance said. "I'll wear my Colt, tote that old shotgun of yours, nothing else."

"It's a muzzleloader."

"That's all right, I know how to handle 'em."

"Well, I got plenty powder and lots of caps and buckshot. We'll fix you up good. You sure you got to ride on today?"

"I got to," Sundance said.

"And how you gonna call yourself if somebody spots you and asks?"

"Why," Sundance said, "the white folks call me Charlie. And the Santee call me *Mewahtahne* That's Santee for 'The Mandan'."

" 'Mewahtahne'," John Canoe repeated. "If anybody asks, I'll say it was my old friend the Mandan."

"And keep my Appaloosa under cover in the barn. He'll get rank when he's been shut up a while, but you can handle him if you wear my buckskin shirt."

"Right. My oldest boy has your horse saddled."

"Thanks, John." Sundance walked with him to the door. There, Billy Canoe stood at the head of a horse Sundance immediately appraised as small, but excellent. Sundance said, "Well, John—"

"Jim, before you ride, there's something I want to ask you. You know a lot more than I do, you got an eddication. A feller, a white man in store clothes, come through here last week. Said he wanted to buy my land."

Sundance turned on Canoe, looked at him sharply. "Did he say why?"

"No, but he offered a dollar an acre. Jim, I own two hundred acres. That's a powerful lot of money. And, like he said, it ain't fit to raise a fuss on because the ground's full of rock oil."

Sundance let out a long breath. "Don't sell."

"But, Jim—"

"The rock oil, don't you see? John, up in Pennsylvania and out in Ohio, they're taking that stuff out of the ground and selling it. Where do you think what they call coal oil

283

comes from? It used to be that the only oil in this country came from whales, now the coal oil, the rock oil, is a lot better and cheaper for burning. People are making fortunes on it in the East."

"They are? It stinks like hell when you burn it in a lamp."

"Not if you distill it the way you would whiskey. John, that lousy rock oil of yours may make you rich someday, or Billy, here, anyhow. Someday, maybe, they'll run trains on it instead of coal or wood. You hang on to this land."

"But, Jim . . . I'm hard up. I could use the cash."

Sundance smiled. "That bed I slept on last night, look under the pillow."

"Jim, I can't take money from you.'"

Sundance looked down at him. "John, that three hundred ain't my money. It's blood money. My blood. Indian blood. You're entitled to it. I'll see you, maybe, in a week or in a month. But thanks for everything and whatever you do, don't sell your land and tell your friends not to sell theirs. They're sittin' on a fortune in oil."

"I'll tell 'em, Jim." Sundance and John Canoe shook hands. Sundance swung up into the saddle, then, and shook hands with Billy Canoe as well.

"All right," he said. "I'm bound for Abilene."

As he reined the horse around, John Canoe raised his hand. "Jim," he called, "I'll pray for you to the Little Red Men of the Thunder!"

5

ABILENE was dying.

Once it had been the wildest hell-town of the West. But now track's end had moved on, and Newton and Ellsworth had begun to steal its thunder. Still, there was plenty of life in the old girl yet, and the stock pens by the railroad, Sundance saw, were crammed with cattle. So many longhorns were coming north nowadays that it took three towns to handle them.

The compact little gelding moved smartly under him as he followed the glittering railroad tracks. When a switch engine came down the line, the horse laid back its ears and snorted, but it was obedient to Sundance's strong hands on the reins and his strong legs. He made it trot alongside the locomotive until it was reassured that this monster meant no harm. Then he turned it again and rode on.

Cattle cars were lined up at the chutes from the pens and in the jammed corrals, men ran across the backs of cattle as loggers might scamper across a jam of logs. They punched and prodded and fought the wild longhorns into the cars, the cowpunchers who had given the name of their trade to cattlemen who had never even seen a railroad.

By one of the main loading chutes, a trail-boss in range clothes sat with a buyer. The buyer, in store clothes, mounted on a spotted gelding, made notations in a book. The trailboss had a string across his saddle cantle, and from time to time he made a knot in it.

Sundance knew better than to disturb them now. He waited until the car was full, and while another was being shunted into place rode up alongside.

Becoming aware of his presence, the two men turned and looked at him coldly. Sundance gave them a foolish grin and lifted his hand. "How," he said.

"What the hell you want, Injun?" the Texas trailboss snapped.

"Me name-um Charlie. Me Mandan and Santee Sioux. Me wantum job." Sundance kept his voice slow and guttural, the way most Indians coped with the English language, so totally unlike Indian dialects in grammar.

"Well, goddammit, I don't hire no gut-eatin' cowboys," the trailboss said.

The cattle buyer touched his small, black mustache. "The Santee Sioux ain't too bad, Josh. They been tame a long time."

"A damn Injun's a Injun where I come from. Like a greaser."

Sundance gave no indication that he understood. He said, "Me look for boss man. Boss man named . . ." He seemed to grope. "Boss man Jeffers."

The buyer's eyes lit. "Abel Jeffers?"

Sundance shrugged.

"Who told you to see Abel Jeffers?"

Sundance said, "Me scout for long-knives. Big chief long-knives, he named Custer, give me letter." He pulled out a paper which he had written himself in a fine copperplate hand with perfect grammar in the military way, passed it to the buyer. It was, he knew, absolutely authentic. It said, only: "The bearer has rendered me excellent service as a scout and is now desirous of working for wages in the cattle business. He is steady, reliable, and does not drink, and his ability at handling horses and running buffalo makes me certain that he will be of great value to anyone dealing with longhorned cattle. He

288

has a desire to learn this trade, and any consideration given to him will be appreciated by the undersigned. George Armstrong Custer, Lt. Col., USA, Commanding, Seventh Cavalry."

Respect gleamed in the buyer's eyes as he passed back the paper. "That's pretty damned good, Injun."

"You know Mr. Jeffers?"

"I know him, but I can tell you, he ain't gonna hire no Injuns, either. But likely you'll find him uptown in the Alamo Saloon. If I was you, though, I wouldn't count on him givin' me the time of day. And don't try to sit down in there. They don't sell no whiskey to Injuns or halfbreeds."

"Sure, man," Sundance said, grinning vacantly. "Charlie no sit down. Muchum thanks." He wheeled the horse.

The Alamo Saloon was a big building with glass doors, one of the fancier in Abilene, and Sundance hesitated at the entrance, a little ashamed of the strange embarrassment that filled him. His yellow hair and blue eyes had always bought him entrance to any place he wanted to go, but in this instant he knew how an ordinary fullblood must feel when he had business in such a place. Angry with himself, he shoved open the door and entered.

Although Abilene was fading, there were still plenty of customers in the room, and automatically they looked to size up the newcomer. Sundance dropped his head, and, with shoulders slumped, moved with shuffling gait towards the bar. Immediately the barkeep came from behind it with a bungstarter in his hand. "All right, Injun. On your way—"

Sundance looked at him vacantly. He held out the paper. "Readum. Me lookin' for Mr. Jeffers."

The man glanced at the paper. He frowned, then jerked his head. "Wait over yonder in the corner."

Sundance moved obediently aside, watching as the bartender went to a table against the far wall. It was occupied by four men, and, covertly, Sundance sized them up. He knew almost immediately which one was Jeffers. That could only be the big, florid man in the gray business suit. His hair was coalblack, thinning; a diamond ring glittered on the third finger of his right hand; there was the beginning of a paunch beneath his vest. And yet, he radiated strength, physical strength, and a sure, confident power.

Another of the men sitting with him was

cut from the same cloth, also dressed for business, tall, lean, middle-aged, with an indoor pallor. The other pair at the table were something very different indeed.

One was an absolute giant of a grizzled cattleman, vastly wide across the shoulders, deep in the chest, long in the leg, and perhaps fifty years of age, with graying cowhorn mustaches hanging down around a tight mouth, emphasizing one of the harshest, craggiest, and most arrogant faces Sundance had ever seen. He wore a pearlgray Stetson, from beneath which long graying-brown hair shagged down to the collar of a clean flannel shirt; a calfskin vest; leather chaps over levis, and big silver spurs on his bench-made boots. Everything was custom-made, expensive, including the carved-leather holster that sheathed an ivory-butted Colt.

The fourth man had a face like a skull. He, too, wore range clothes, he was tall, very thin and loosejointed, with black eyes seeming to smoulder in his narrow face, the nostrils of his short nose turned back and up like slits, his mouth thin, his teeth big, protruding. His big hands moved restlessly on the table in front of him, fingers curling and uncurling like snakes. He wore two guns, tied low, and

291

Sundance recognized at once that they were the tools of his trade.

When the bartender appeared beside the table, none of the four looked up immediately, and he waited respectfully until they took notice of him. Then he spoke and handed Jeffers the paper. Jeffers read it, passed it to the others, who read it in turn, and, following the bartender's gesture, they all turned and stared at Sundance. He gave them an idiotic smile, touched his hat, kept his eyes downcast. The four looked at each other and grinned. Then the big cattleman said, in a deep voice, "Well, I reckon that concludes our business anyhow, Jeffers. We'll leave you to your Injun friend. Come on, Denham."

He shoved back his chair, silver spurs jingling. The slender, pallid man in business clothes also stood up. "You'll send a wire up to Cheyenne when you've had some word," the cattleman added. "My people are mighty anxious."

"I'll let you know the minute I hear, Cavanaugh." Jeffers stood up and shook hands with the two of them, and the skull-faced man also arose. Cavanaugh took his hand. "See you, Bisbee."

"Yeah," Bisbee said. "So long." He had a high, thin, spluttering voice, as if his teeth got in the way. But from the way he stood and the way his guns hung, Sundance knew not to underrate him; this man was as dangerous as a rattler in skin-shedding time.

Cavanaugh looked at Sundance again and his mouth quirked under the mustaches, a twist of distaste. His massive weight, apparently without an ounce of fat, shook the room as he went to the door with the slender Denham following. When they had gone, Jeffers said something to Bisbee in a low voice. Then he jerked his head for Sundance to come over.

Sundance went, slowly and timidly, oozing humility. He halted by the table, not looking at either Jeffers or the skull-faced Bisbee directly. Jeffers said, "So, halfbreed. You scouted for Custer, huh? And now you wanta learn the cattle business."

"Yes, sir." Sundance kept his head down.

Jeffers stared at the paper again. "You're damn lucky you had this with you, or I'd have had you pitched outa her on your arse, comin' in and interruptin' an important conference with one of the biggest cattlemen in this country. It's a good thing for you Autie

Custer's a damn close friend of mine. You with him up in Dakota?"

"Yessir, betcha, he say tell you hello."

"Yeah, we played a lot of cards together when he was stationed down here in Kansas. He was a lousy poker player." He handed Sundance the paper. "Damn it, look at me when I talk to you."

Sundance did. Jeffers glanced at him, then away, then raised his head again. "What the hell, a blue-eyed Injun?" He looked at Bisbee, then back at Sundance. Then he grinned. "Yeah, that paper said you were a Mandan. There's a lotta blue-eyed Mandans. For a minute, I thought you might be somebody else, but— Bisbee, you don't reckon—?"

"No," Bisbee said. "I seen him once, in San Antonio. He don't look no more like this one than a wolf looks like a fice dog."

Sundance only looked puzzled. "Me git job?" he asked in apparent uncomprehension.

Jeffers laughed softly. "Yeah, you git job. Start at the bottom of the cattle business. You clean out cattle cars down by the yards, every day but Sunday, four dollars a week. Damn railroads send the cars back filthy, we got to clean 'em ourselves before we can load again, and you can't git nobody in Abilene for that kind of work no more. You can start to work right away. There's a string in down there now." He jerked his head. "Take him down to the yards, Bisbee, and put a shovel in his hand."

Bisbee looked disgusted. "All right. Come on, Mandan Charlie or whatever the hell your name is." He laughed splutteringly. "After tonight, they'll call you Cowshit Charlie."

Jeffers arose, too. "I'll be in my office if you want me," he said. "Drop in about four anyhow. I'll have some telegrams for you to put on the wire to the others."

"Yeah, sure," Bisbee said, and he jerked his head at Sundance to follow and went out.

The cattle cars were on a siding near the yards, a long string of them. When Sundance and Bisbee had dismounted near them, Bisbee went to a tool shed, unlocked it, and took out a flat-bladed, longhandled shovel, which he passed to Sundance. The smell of cow manure was, to Sundance's nostrils, used as they were to the clean air of the open, almost overpowering, but Bisbee appeared not to notice.

"Okay, Charlie, you start at the front car

295

and you don't stop until the back one's clean. Just throw it out on the ground, people are used to walkin' in it around Abilene. And you do a good job, damn your red hide, or you don't git paid come Saddy night."

"I do good job, you betcha," Sundance said. "But maybe you gimme four bits now, huh? Me catchum eat."

Bisbee gave that spluttering laugh. "You catchum eat like hell. We don't advance no money. But don't worry. After an hour's work, you won't have no appetite nohow." He grinned mockingly at Sundance, then strode to his horse and mounted up. "I'll be back to check on you before quittin' time."

Sundance watched him ride away and, after he was gone, rolled a cigarette and smoked it thoughtfully, standing upwind of the cattle cars. He thought about the two men, Cavanaugh and Denham, in the saloon with Jeffers. Likely, it was just a cattle deal: it would be too much to expect, to walk into the middle of the other, cold. And yet, he had a powerful curiosity about the giant cattleman who apparently headquartered in Cheyenne. That city, after all, was, since the coming of the railroad, the gateway to the northern ranges, Wyoming and Montana. Cattle could be driven overland, or they could be purchased here at the Kansas shipping points, loaded on cars, and shunted back and forth, eventually to reach the north. Once the Indians were neutralized, those ranges could fill up in a hurry, and the men on the ground there would make tremendous fortunes. Apparently Cavanaugh was on the ground . . .

Anyhow, Sundance thought, grinding out the butt and climbing into the cattle car, he had to play a waiting game. He dared not tip his hand or be forced into killing Jeffers until he had milked the man of all the information he possessed. It was obvious that Jeffers was the middle man in the plot against him, and likely he knew who the higher ups were—all of them. With that kind of money on his head, Sundance had no time to follow up the chain of conspiracy link by link. He wanted to know who was at the top, so he could go there straight away.

So he would be Mandan Charlie for a while, yet, and he would take whatever Bisbee and Jeffers dealt out to him like a broken-spirited mongrel fullblood from two declining tribes, and only after he had learned all it was possible to know would he think about settling scores . . .

He shoveled hard, industriously, gradually becoming accustomed to the smell. The afternoon was well along, the sun going down, when, as he started on the third car, the drunken cowboy appeared.

Swaying in his saddle, he walked his horse down the spur track, a nearly empty bottle clutched in one hand. He was young, not over twenty-one or twenty-two, with the mark of Texas all over him, a rider who had come up the trail with a herd, had his fling, and was now in the misery of the fag-end of his binge. Likely he was dead broke. Sundance almost hit him with a shovelful of cow manure before he saw him. The wad of dung flew past the young cowpuncher's head, missing him by not more than a foot.

The wiry mustang the man rode snorted, and the puncher reined him around, staring at Sundance with redveined eyes, under which there were dark halfmoons. "Hey," he said thickly. "You, Injun, what the hell you think you doin'? Watch where you throw that stuff."

"Sorry. Me no seeum you."

The cowboy drank. "Well, you damn well better start seein'. You'd hit me with that stuff, I'd a donated you about two ounces

298

of lead, absolutely free." He swallowed, grimaced, fumbled at his shirt, cursed in disappointment. "Tabak. You got any tabak, savvy?"

"Mebbe," Sundance said.

"Trade you a drink for the makin's, okay?"

Sundance's face brightened and he took out a tobacco sack and papers. The puncher rode alongside the door of the cattle car and pulled up. He passed Sundance the bottle and Sundance gave him the tobacco. Sundance took a drink: the whiskey was foul, as bad as the stuff bootleggers sold on the Reservations. He passed back the bottle, and the cowboy lit his cigarette, handed him the tobacco.

"Thass a good job you got," he said thickly, bitterly. "You on the right end of this business. You got to deal with cows, that way beats trailin' their butts a thousand miles for thirty a month and havin' the damned buzzards at trail's end pick you clean in twenty-four hours. Keep on shovelin' and hang on to your money, Injun."

"Um," Sundance grunted.

The puncher drained the bottle, threw it away, staring at it sourly as it bounced along the roadbed. "And that," he said, "is the end of that. Now all I got to do is figure out how to stay alive until next month when Cavanaugh's herd leaves for Wyomin'."

"Cavanaugh," Sundance said. "What Cavanaugh?" He squatted at the edge of the floor, guessing the cowboy was in the mood to talk.

"Lord God, where you been you never heard of Lance Cavanaugh? Used to be one of the biggest ranchers in Texas, then sold out a coupla years ago and went north. Now he's got a big ranch north of Cheyenne, drives herds straight through from Kansas to Wyomin'. Sells 'em in Colorado. Makes twice the money on a longhorn trailed north as us pore bastards do on one brought up from the Neuces and sold here. 'Course, he takes twice the risk, too. That's all Cheyenne and Sioux and Blackfoot country up there . . . Don't make no difference to Lance Cavanaugh. If it was Hell, he'd drive through it jest the same. What he wants, he takes, and God help anybody gits in his way." He rubbed his hand across his sweating face. "He's got a drive leavin' out of here next month. I done signed on. Lord God, now I wish I'd gone back to Texas, though. May still do that. My mama told me, she told me: *Sonny* . . . Thass what they allus called me,

300

Sonny— She said, *Sonny Hamilton, you be a lot better off if you stay away from them cattle and go work with your Uncle Fred on that cotton plantation up near Beaumont* . . . Wish now I'd listened to her."

Sundance said, "This Cavanaugh. He plenty rich white man, huh?"

"He got more money than a coyote got fleas. And one of these days, if the talk's right, he'll have a pot more of it. When they git Powder River opened up as cattle range, all that land east of the Big Horns . . ."

"Powder River," Sundance said. "That Injun country under treaty."

"Thass the redskins' tough luck, ole buddy. That end of Wyomin' and Colorado is jest throbbin' with big ranchers waitin' to pour in there. Cavanaugh ain't the only one . . . much money as he and the others got, the Injuns don't stand a chance. And what about these cattle dealers in the railroad towns all along the line. Don't you think they're in the pot to stay, too? When Wyomin' and Montana open up, they'll make more money than they ever dreamed of. They'll sell the herds that go to fill all that country up there . . ." Sonny Hamilton spat thickly. "Again' all the pressure they can put on the Army, them Injuns ain't got a prayer. They'd better be learnin' a white man's trade, the way you are." He grinned crookedly, and Sundance found himself liking the young man. "I mean—"

He broke off as there was the sound of another horse coming down the track. Sundance jerked his head around, saw Bisbee riding toward them. The man's skeletal face frowned, and he reined in close to Hamilton.

"Cowboy," he said, "we're payin' this gut-eater good money to clean out these cars. Appreciate it if you didn't interfere with his work."

"Well, hell, I just bummed a cigarette . . ."

"Okay. Now, ride on and let him get back to doin' what he's paid for."

Sonny Hamilton blinked and pulled his horse around so he was facing Bisbee. His expression had changed, all good humor gone from his face now. "Who the hell you think you are to tell me when I can ride and when I can't, Big Ugly?"

Bisbee straightened in the saddle. "What did you call me?"

"I'll swear," Hamilton said thickly, "if you ain't the ugliest man I ever seen. That face of yours. It looks like somethin' they buried last year and dug up yesterday."

And suddenly Bisbee's face looked exactly like that, the skin taut over its bony structure, his complexion greenish in the dying sun. His dark eyes, however, were alive and smouldering. Sundance held his breath, but this was not his fight.

"Cowboy," Bisbee said harshly, "I don't let anybody bad mouth me like that."

"Why," said Sonny Hamilton. "I ain't just anybody—" And he made a reach for his gun, surprisingly fast in view of how drunk he was.

But he never had a chance. Sundance was startled at Bisbee's speed. Watching closely, he still never saw Bisbee draw, but suddenly a gun roared and powdersmoke bloomed over Bisbee's saddle horn and Sonny Hamilton cried out and nearly fell from the saddle, his shoulder smashed by Bisbee's slug, and when the smoke cleared, a Colt glinted in Bisbee's hand.

"Christ," Hamilton moaned, pulled up straight with his good hand, then bent over in agony, shirt sodden with blood.

"I ought to of killed you," Bisbee said, thin lips peeled back from big teeth. "I coulda done it, but I done killed too many here and Abilene's closin' down a little. Now, God damn your soul, ride!"

Hamilton moaned, dug in spurs. The mustang galloped off, with its rider lurching in the saddle. Bisbee watched for a moment, Colt raised, and then with speed equal to his draw returned it to its holster. Sundance's eyes narrowed. He had just seen a fine and thoroughly professional gunman at work: now, at least, he would not misjudge the man. Bisbee was as fast—and just as cold—as the rattler he had reminded Sundance of earlier.

The skullfaced man turned in the saddle. "Awright, Charlie. You get back to work. Another hour. And when you git through here, you come uptown to Mr. Jeffers' office, near the Alamo. *Jeffers Cattle Company*, there's a sign if you can read. The nigger that was supposed to swamp it out didn't show. Mr. Jeffers said you clean it, you can have your four bits, Savvy?"

"Savvy!" Sundance gave him a delighted smile. "Me come, catchum four bits damn fast, you betcha."

"Right. Now git back on the end of that shovel."

Bisbee sat there a moment longer, until

304

Sundance was at work again, and then he turned and rode away. Watching him go, Sundance felt a throb of excitement. This was luck: maybe the payoff for shoveling manure would come quicker than he'd dared hope. But in case it didn't— He went back to work with energy, determined to cover his bets, to keep this job as long as he might need it.

6

JEFFERS' office was a small, neatly painted frame building a few doors north of the Alamo Saloon. With his hat in hand, Sundance mounted the sidewalk and knocked on the glass panel of the door. The shade was up, and, inside, he saw a front office where two clerks were just preparing to leave, and, behind a rail, a single desk occupied by Jeffers. Bisbee was lounging in a chair nearby, and at Sundance's knock he arose.

"Here he is, boss. And don't worry, I see he's had sense enough to clean his boots."

"Good." Jeffers hardly glanced at Sundance, arose, took his hat from a tree as the clerks went out and Sundance came to the rail. "When you're through with him, meet me at the Alamo. We've got some things to talk about. I may have to send you down to Del Rio. We're long overdue in hearin' from my friend down there and Cavanaugh wants to know what the hell's goin' on."

"Well, I ain't been south in a long time,"

Bisbee said. "Okay, Injun. Yonder's the broom closet. You sweep and mop the floor and clean out the spittoons real good and I'll be back in an hour to check on you. You do a good job, you git your four bits."

"Me do good job, you damn well betcha," Sundance said, with his vacant grin.

At the door, Jeffers halted. "And tell him not to touch any of the papers on these desks."

"Don't worry," Bisbee said. "He can't read. You heard that, Injun?"

"Me hear."

"Well, git on the bit, then." Jeffers left, and Bisbee stood there a moment more with thumbs hooked in gun belts as Sundance got out broom and mop. Then Bisbee followed, closing the door behind him.

Sundance swept industriously by lamplight for a full ten minutes, until he was sure Bisbee or Jeffers would not come back for something forgotten. Then, in two pantherish strides, he was at Jeffers' desk, which was piled high with papers. Eyes flicking from time to time to the windows, holding the broom in one hand to explain his presence to any passerby, he carefully, covertly thumbed through the stacks of invoices, bills of lading,

307

and correspondence. But he found nothing.

The drawers were next, and he grinned tightly when he discovered that they were not locked. Whatever valuables there were must be in the big safe in the corner. But maybe Jeffers did not count what he sought as that much of a valuable.

Two drawers, three, and then he found it, in the center drawer, a big brown envelope with the scrawled words on its cover: WYOMING DEAL. Sundance unwrapped the twine that closed it, fished out the first paper among many, glanced at it, saw that it was a copy of a letter. Addressed to Lance Cavanaugh, Cheyenne, Wyoming, the first line of the first paragraph seemed to leap out at him. *Have just returned from Del Rio Texas and have procured services to accomplish what we discussed* . . . Sundance read no more, but rifled hastily through the packet. He saw names, brands, amounts . . .

He resealed the envelope, stuffed it in a trash basket. This he carried out the back door. There a barrel held waste paper and the sludge from spittoons. Sundance dumped the contents of the basket, envelope and all, into the barrel, covering the envelope with rubbish.

So, he thought, returning to the office, making sure no sign of his rifling of Jeffers' desk remained. So he had been right. The trail led from Jeffers to Cavanaugh and probably a lot of other people. The hundred thousand on his head had not come from one man, in all likelihood. Bits and pieces of it had been subscribed by a lot of people. Well, later he would read the file at his leisure, but for now—

He did a good job on the office, and the spittoons gleamed when Bisbee returned. The tall, skullfaced gunman looked around, keen eyes raking over the desks, then nodded his approval. "Okay, Injun. You done good. Here's your four bits." He flipped a half dollar to Sundance, who caught it nimbly. "Now, go have your spree, while I lock up. But you be at them cattle cars come seven in the morning, you understand?"

"Me savvy," Sundance said. "Thanks." He grinned at the half dollar, pocketed it, and shambled out, mounting his horse. As he rode away, Bisbee was locking the office door. Sundance watched and saw that when he was through Bisbee went back to the Alamo. Once he had disappeared through the glass doors, Sundance turned the Cherokee horse down an alley.

There was nothing unusual about an Indian poking around in a garbage barrel, and even if someone had noticed him behind Jeffers' office, it would have excited no comment. He retrieved the envelope, slid it under his coat, mounted, and rode at a walk out of town.

Once clear, he galloped for a while, circling cow outfit after cow outfit, traveling a long way until he found a lonesome place to camp in the willows by a little stream. Even its waters were polluted by the droppings of the vast herds upstream, but he dug a hole in a sandbar close to the bank and the water welling up in it was clear and sweet. He built a small fire, put on a pot of coffee, and while he chewed jerky from his saddlebags went through the contents of the envelope.

It took him a long time to read everything it contained. When he had finished, even he was shaken.

Drinking coffee, he read parts of it again. Finally, when he put everything away for good, his face was grim.

The names: the names were all there.

The names of cattlemen, of ranchers from

Texas to Wyoming, men who had made fortunes in the longhorn boom after 1866. The names of buyers, too, wealthy dealers from the Kansas towns all along the track. A web of names and a web of wealth spreading across the entire West from the Rio to the Yellowstone, a syndicate, a company, formed by those rich men who hungered for even greater riches.

And what they wanted, what they were after, was everything the Cheyenne and the Sioux Indians—and, for that matter, all the other tribes—had, west of the Black Hills and east of the Rocky Mountains. The great buffalo ranges, the traditional hunting grounds of the Plains Indians—these were to be turned into grazing land for cattle, no matter what it cost or how many lives it claimed, and the whole vast windfall was to be paid for not only by the Indians but by the white taxpayers of the entire United States.

The letters in the file were vivid in Sundance's mind, and so was the whole enormous, ugly scheme. Most of those letters were signed by Lance Cavanaugh, who was obviously its leader, originator, foremost promoter, the brains behind it. Cavanaugh had crisscrossed the West in person and by mail, recruiting the cream of the cattle barons and the dealers. And the rewards he promised for their participation were staggering, in the tens and maybe hundreds of millions.

The words of one of those letters rang again in Sundance's mind. *"We are talking about doubling the size of the American cattle ranges. Right now, Montana and Wyoming Territories, the best rangeland any of us have ever seen, are going completely to waste, left to Blanket Indians and Buffalo. Ever since Red Cloud burned Fort Phil Kearney and closed the Bozeman Trail, the 'tarnal redskins' as they are called with good reason have ruled like little dictators over the country north of the Platte. The Powder River Range alone, which they hold, is worth millions. How much longer will we stand idly by and watch the Indians thumb their noses at us while the buffalo devour the good grama and blue-joint that would feed our herds?*

"But, you say, what about the Treaties? Well, I say, to hell with the Treaties! And I say if we move swiftly and decisively, those Treaties won't amount to a hill of beans! What I think we should do is this, and I can assure you of the full backing of what I can only refer to in writing as the S & S Concern. They are behind

it one hundred per cent and are prepared to underwrite some of the cost and take the necessary action when the time is ripe.

"Anyhow, if we move and move fast and hard with a hundred thousand head at the very minimum and the necessary fighting men, all the rest will follow in due course. We ram a hundred thousand up Powder River—to be sure the Indians will make war on us. It will be a big war, too, no penny-ante dust-up. And once it starts, the country won't stand idly by and let the Indians win. The Army will be forced to move with all its strength, and the stage set for a final battle . . . No matter how much the Indian Lovers in Washington protest, the matter will be out of their hands. . . ."

Jim Sundance arose and began restlessly to pace around the fire. And there it was: Cavanaugh and all the other cattle interests, busy even now stockpiling the small tag end of southern Wyoming range they held with Texas longhorns. By the thousands they would cram cattle south of the Platte, with tough gun-wise Texas cowhands to herd them, fighting men as well as cowpunchers. Then, when the time was ripe, the whole vast herd would move into the Powder River country, the Indians would fight back on an enormous scale, and the Army would be forced by public opinion to go in and eradicate them once and for all. Probably, Sundance guessed, next spring, when the cattle would be in place for the big push, the grass was up, and the Army could march and fight.

He went back to the envelope and his mouth twisted as he sought and found another letter, squatting on his haunches, re-reading it by flickering light.

"The S & S Concern has made the following urgent recommendation. It believes our tactics can be successful provided the Indians can be fought and beaten in detail. But if they unite against us, they may be too strong even for the Army. There are maybe twenty thousand warriors in that country, if the Crows and Blackfeet join in, and if they come together under one command they will far outnumber any force of soldiers that can be sent against them.

"Fortunately, they hate each other almost as much as they hate us. The Crows fight the Cheyennes and the Sioux fight the Blackfeet, etc., etc. The S & S Concern says it knows of only one man who could overcome their distrust of each other and lead them as a united fighting

force. His name is Jim Sundance, and before we can move, he must be eliminated. The S & S Concern is insistent upon this before joining with us in our enterprise. It suggests putting a reward on Sundance's head large enough to make good and sure that someone delivers his scalp to us by next Spring. In fact, the S & S Concern has subscribed ten thousand dollars of its own funds to such a reward, and suggests that the total go as high as a hundred thousand if that is what it takes. I am in complete agreement, as this man Sundance is the greatest danger to all our plans, and if it takes a hundred thousand, that's chicken feed compared to the payoff. I'll subscribe ten thousand on my own and am asking all others to guarantee at least five. Once we get Sundance, S & S Concern assures us the coast is clear . . ."

Then followed a description and biography of Jim Sundance. It was clear and accurate, and, reading it, Sundance knew that it had been furnished by someone well acquainted personally with him. Kate Danton? It didn't matter: what did was that if it were widely circulated, anybody could recognize him, any stranger pick him off . . . He spat into the fire and pushed the letter back into the envelope. Cavanaugh was a thorough planner and a

315

good letter writer. Like an experienced general, he laid out grand strategy, detailed tactics, overlooked nothing. And, Sundance knew, the scheme as he had outlined it would work.

What Cavanaugh and the mysterious advisers he called "the S & S Concern" didn't know was that they were wasting their money. There was a possibility, Sundance thought, of uniting the Sioux and Cheyennes and Arapahoes, but the Crows and Blackfeet would never join with their hated enemies, even against a threat like this. Probably the Shoshones on Wind River would stay neutral, too. No, it was impossible for Sundance or any single man to block such an invasion by uniting the tribes against it. As Cavanaugh hoped, they would inevitably be beaten tribe by tribe, whipped in detail. But before that happened, a lot of people would die, red and white, men, women, children . . .

Sundance stood up, and the firelight shone on features like something cast from bronze. His eyes, in that red background, were like chips of ice. But there was another way of stopping this invasion.

Cavanagh and the mysterious S & S Concern were the brains and driving force behind the whole scheme.

So, Sundance thought, drawing in a long breath, it was very simple when you came down to it.

Whatever the S & S Concern might be—and he would find out somehow—maybe it was beyond his reach.

But Lance Cavanaugh was not.

And Lance Cavanaugh, in due time, had to die.

Usually Sundance put the day from him completely and slept like an animal at night, unworried, though alert and ready to come awake and into action at the slightest alarm. But tonight he hardly slept at all. As he lay in his blankets with John Canoe's old shotgun cradled in his arm and his pistol within easy reach, he felt the hatred growing in him—hatred of Cavanaugh and the S & S Concern, hatred of every man whose name was on that roster. The men who not only wanted to steal two entire territories from their rightful owners, but to kill them like so many cattle in a Chicago slaughterhouse, using the United States Army as its executioner. That they wanted him dead too hardly counted at all in the hatred: a lot of people had wanted him dead, but he was still alive.

He lay there, nursing the hatred and making his plans. When morning came, he packed his gear and rode back to Abilene, and by full light he was below the cattle pens, in one of the cars on the lonely siding far from town. This time, he did not go to work, but he leaned on the shovel, waited, the horse tethered nearby and John Canoe's caplock shotgun leaning against a wall inside, close to the door. He was fully alert, watching with the relaxed, ready patience of a big hunting cat, his Colt belted around his waist and its holster tied down now, his jacket rolled up behind the horse's saddle, so it would not interfere.

Presently he saw Bisbee.

The skullfaced man came riding down the track, a sour look on his countenance, as if he had caroused too late and had a hangover. On another siding, a locomotive puffed and snorted, shunting cars, making a loud racket. That was good, Sundance thought.

As Bisbee approached, Sundance dug the shovel deep into crusted dung and straw, wrenched off a bladeful. Bisbee reined in before the opened door, tipped back his hat, glaring at Sundance. "Well, Injun, I see you did show up. What the hell you waitin' for, damn your red hide! Git on that shovel."

"You damn betcha," Sundance said, and he threw the dung straight in Bisbee's face. Almost brick hard, it hit Bisbee squarely and rocked him in the saddle. He cursed in rage, instinctively reaching for his right hand gun, pawing at his eyes with his left. "Hold it," Sundance snapped. "Touch it and you're dead."

Bisbee stared at Sundance's Colt lined squarely on his chest, and he froze, his own gun half drawn. "What the hell?"

"Explanations later. Hands up, and step out of the saddle into this car."

Bisbee blinked. "I'll be damned if—"

"Your choice," Sundance said. "I can kill you right there." He lifted the gun barrel slightly and Bisbee stared into those cool eyes and something clicked in his brain then. "Wait," he said. "Wait a damn minute. You ain't— I mean, you're—'"

"Let's say I ain't Mandan Charlie. In this car, Bisbee."

Slowly, the man raised his hands, a strange expression on the bony ugliness of his face. He kneed the horse closer, stepped from the saddle to the car door, pulling himself in by the slats as Sundance backed away a few paces. "Over in the corner," Sundance said.

Bisbee stared at him, then obeyed. Sundance watched him closely. For the moment, the banging of the boxcars on the adjacent siding had ceased but the chuffing of the locomotive was louder. "Now," Sundance said, "you take off those guns—"

At that moment a trainman yelled something. Suddenly the whole string of cattle cars was slammed backwards as a locomotive backed and coupled. Sundance went off balance, to one knee. Bisbee, back braced against the wall, drew then, with the same blinding speed he had used against the drunken cowboy the day before. His gun roared as the car lurched again, and the bullet snapped by Sundance's ear at no more than an inch's distance, and then Sundance's own Colt was lined and he pulled the trigger.

The smash of lead into his chest seemed to to pin Bisbee against the wall of the car. He hung there for a moment while the life went out of him and then he fell forward on his face into the cattle dung.

Sundance quickly reloaded the Colt to replace the used round. As the cars rolled down the track, he picked up the shovel. He knew they were only being shunted, would not go far. Carefully, methodically, he completely buried Bisbee's body in cattle dung. By then the cars had halted, a quarter of a mile from where they had started, and he heard the locomotive pulling away. It went on about its work on an adjoining track.

Sundance leaned on the shovel and waited. He was pretty sure the shots had not been heard. He waited a long time, all through the morning and well into the afternoon. Once in a while a trainman passed, and when he did, Sundance nodded, said, "How," and pretended to be working.

After a while, as Sundance had known he must, Abel Jeffers came.

Even before Sundance saw the driver of the buggy wheeling toward the string of cattle cars, he knew who it was, who it had to be. In his gray business suit, Jeffers came down the track in his rig, looking into each car as he passed it. Sundance's Colt was holstered, he squatted by the door, his left hand out of sight inside. It could have been on the shovel lying partially hidden beside him, but actually it held John Canoe's old shotgun. Hitting a man inside a buggy could be tricky with a Colt, but a double-barreled twelve could hardly miss. And just the sight of it made a powerful impression on a man.

Jeffers pulled up the rig as he saw Sundance hunkered there like something carved from wood. His florid face was pursed with impatience. "Hey, you, there, Charlie, whatever the hell your name is. Mr. Bisbee. You seeum Mr. Bisbee?"

"Me seeum," Sundance said.

"Then where the devil is he?"

"Why," Sundance said, pulling out the shotgun and aiming it, "you might say he's plumb buried himself in the cattle business." And then he snapped, "Don't whip up that horse. Get out of that rig and climb up here and don't try any tricks. You know damn well I can't miss you with two loads of buck."

Jeffers only stared, mouth gaping, red face paling. For a full ten seconds, he sat there thunderstruck. "Come on," Sundance said.

For an instant, he thought he'd have to go down there and drag Jeffers out. Then, slowly, face gone paper white now, the man got out of the buggy.

"Up here in the cattle car," Sundance ordered.

Jeffers looked into the bores of the shotgun and, as if he were in a daze, climbed the embankment. Sundance stepped back and watched as he struggled awkwardly into the car, finally making it on hands and knees, panting. "Stand up and move out of the door," Sundance told him.

Jeffers did, hands high. "I don't understand this," he wheezed. "But if you're out to rob me, my wallet's in the inside coat pocket. You can have this diamond ring, too. And my watch. Only, for God's sake—" He was looking into Sundance's hawklike face, and his voice trailed off. After a moment, he said weakly, "You ain't a Mandan . . ."

"No," Sundance said, smiling thinly. "Only half Cheyenne."

"Oh, my God," Jeffers said, and, as if his knees had failed him, leaned slumping against the latticed wall of the car. "Oh, my God, to think I could have been that big a fool."

"You were a bigger one to leave a certain envelope in an unlocked drawer."

As comprehension of that seeped into Jeffers, he swallowed convulsively. "You—" He let out a long breath. "Last night, when you swamped out the office . . ."

323

"I took it and read it all," Sundance said. "Now, I'll tell you a few things. What you'll hear from Kate Danton is this. She sent eight men against me, and I killed them all. I got your name from her, but she's still alive. That's more than I can say you'll be unless you answer some questions."

Jeffers licked his lips. "I'll tell you anything I can. This wasn't my idea, it was Cavanaugh's. He moved up to Wyoming from Texas two years ago to git into position when the Indians were taken care of, but the Army didn't move fast enough for him, you see—"

"I know all that," Sundance said. "So he wrote a lot of letters, did a lot of organizing . . ."

"That's right. And others have moved in, to join him, and we, not just here in Abilene but all along the line, we've already sold fifty thousand head to be trailed or shipped up there and another twenty thousand more due to go before the end of fall . . . He and the other ranchers were gonna hold 'em over the winter to get 'em used to the climate, then shove 'em all up the Powder River in the biggest cattle drive anybody ever saw. It'll be just like a flood, a . . . a avalanche. Nothin' can stand before that many longhorns and Texas riders. Before anybody knows what's happened, there'll *be* a cattle business north of the Platte, not just a few shirt-tail ranchers, but a business so big the whole country will have a stake in it. Then, when the Indians fight back, the Army'll *have* to move and take care of 'em once for all . . . That'll open up all Wyoming and Montana and it'll generate the biggest beef boom in the history of this country. There ain't enough cattle in the Southwest to stock all those ranges and feed the country, too. Cow prices will shoot sky high and—"

"And everybody on the inside'll get rich while the poor hungry bastards in the east see the price of beef go out of reach. They pay for that and they pay for the Army opening up the range; they pay, the Indians pay, and you and Cavanaugh and the rest reap the profits."

"About like that," Jeffers said weakly.

"Where does the Army stand in this?"

"I don't know. That's Cavanaugh's business. He don't give out no more information than he can help. He just says he's sure they'll move."

"Some outfit called the S & S Concern put

up ten thousand dollars of the money on my head. What's the S & S Concern?"

"I don't know that, either. I know it's a damn big company Cavanaugh's been dealin' with, one with inside connections back East and in Washington. But he won't tell anybody what company it really is."

Sundance shifted the muzzles of the double-barrel a little. "You'd better not lie to me, Jeffers."

"So help me, Sundance, I'm not lying. I don't know who or what the S & S Concern is. There ain't but one man that knows that, and that's Lance Cavanaugh."

Sundance stared at him a moment, guessed he told the truth. "All right," he said. "I guess that's information I'll have to get from Cavanaugh."

"From Cavanaugh?" Jeffers blinked, then laughed nervously. "You'll never git near Lance Cavanaugh."

"And why?"

"Hell, Sundance, I just told you." Jeffers was talking quickly now, wanting to be helpful, buying his life with words. He had to raise his voice. On the other track, parallel with this, the switch engine was banging cars again. "There's fifty thousand cattle massed south of the Platte waiting to move, five or six big outfits, and they all got plenty of riders, and those riders are fightin' men, too; it's an army of Texas gunmen. And Cavanaugh sits right in the center, and he don't take no chances. He's got his own gunslingers, and he's a fast man with an iron himself, he used to be a Texas Ranger and then he was in Hood's Cavalry, and he's hard as nails. He knows every trick in the book. You go up against him, you might as well turn that shotgun on yourself. It'll be quicker and easier."

Sundance digested this information. He smiled coolly. "That's my worry, Jeffers. Yours is, what do I do with you now? The minute I turn you loose, you'll be on your way to send Cavanaugh a telegram in Cheyenne, warnin' him I'll still alive and out to get him. So that presents me with a problem."

Jeffers licked his lips, and his face was the color of putty. "Sundance, you wouldn't kill me in cold blood . . ."

"Eight gunmen that you indirectly hired tried to do it to me," Sundance said. "I don't see where you're due any special consideration. All the same, you're pretty small

327

potatoes. No, I'm not gonna kill you, Jeffers. But I'm sure as hell gonna send you on a train ride."

"Send me on—"

"I've been watchin' those cars on the other track. They're loadin' buffalo hides to ship back East. Well, you're goin' along with 'em. I'm gonna tie you good and gag you and load you in a car of hides. If you're lucky, they'll find you before they git to Omaha or Chicago or wherever they're bound."

Jeffers' lips moved soundlessly, and then words finally came. "Sundance, you wouldn't— That's five, ten days. Tied up, gagged, I'll die of thirst, starvation . . ."

"Maybe you can get loose before then," Sundance said. "Maybe you'll be lucky. Anyhow, you'll have a chance. That's more than you aimed to give me, settin' a price on my head that'll put every gunman in the West after me without my knowin' it."

"They ain't after you yet," Jeffers said desperately. "Kate Danton was to try first, her men to git you when you came back from Mexico. The word hasn't gone out all over yet."

"Another reason for me to shut you up," Sundance said coolly. "The longer you're

quiet, the safer I'll ride. All right, Jeffers—"
He stepped forward with the shotgun raised,
ready to bring its barrels down on Jeffers'
head.

He had not expected Jeffers, after all his
effort to climb into the car, to move so fast.
But fear made Jeffers like a streak. He
jumped sideways, fell backwards through the
door of the cattle car, shrieking with fear like
a hurt rabbit. He landed on his back, and
before Sundance could line the shotgun, he
had recovered, scrambled up the fill, was
underneath the car. Sundance cursed,
dropped the shotgun, drew his Colt, leaped
out. He landed like a cat, whirled and
crouched just in time to see Jeffers scramble
to his feet on the other side of the string of
cars.

Sundance went after him, crawling under
the car between the wheel trucks, emerging
on the other side in time to see Jeffers running toward a string of boxcars full of buffalo
hides on the other track, five yards away. Up
the line, a switch engine whistled. Sundance
aimed the Colt.

He was too late. Like a hare heading for its
burrow, Jeffers dived beneath a boxcar. Sun-

dance took two fast steps after him, then halted cold, just in time.

He saw it happen, but there was nothing he could do. Jeffers in his business suit was a gray blob on hands and knees beneath the boxcar as the switch engine hit the string. The cars rolled back with sudden, savage force.

Sundance heard above the clang of iron and the panting of the locomotive a high, thin scream cut off short. The cars rolled a hundred feet down the line, then halted, started forward as Sundance stood motionless. The string rolled with increasing swiftness as the engine pulled it toward the main track. Sundance holstered his Colt, for which there was no longer any need, and simply waited until the last car passed. Then he turned away, a little sickly.

He had, in his time, seen many men die, but never a death like this. The great iron wheels had passed directly over Jeffers' waist, and they had simply cut his body cleanly in two. One segment of it lay spilling down the far embankment, the other, mostly his legs, lay motionless on the red track.

"Christ," Sundance said, and he turned away, spitting thin, green bile.

Well, he thought, that took care of Jeffers and this part of it was over. What remained now was Cavanaugh and the S & S Concern. And there was no time to lose. Sooner or later, Cavanaugh would hear from Kate Danton that Sundance was still alive, and then the big reward would be publicly posted, and he could not fight every gunman in the West.

Sundance carefully climbed back through the cattle car, not under it. Far down the line, now, the switch engine gave its mournful hoot, like a requiem, again. Sundance jumped out of the other side of the car, with the shotgun, went quickly to where he had tied his horse, and rode.

7

FOR three days the Cherokee horse carried him northwest toward the Platte, and it was good to be out of the cattle stink, away from the choking railroad smoke. In the first creek unpolluted by cow manure, Sundance washed himself and his clothes and renewed the blacking in his hair. John Canoe's shotgun was tied behind the cantle of his saddle; he had caught up Bisbee's horse and robbed it of its Winchester and saddle scabbard before circling wide down the tracks and getting out of Abilene. A rifle was needed on these high plains, for there were Pawnees out here, allies of the white man, and one tribe that would lift Sundance's hair on sight, do Cavanaugh's work for him without Cavanaugh ever knowing it.

Coming out of a coulee at midday, miles north of the Kansas line, he smelled it, a rankness harsh in his nostrils after the clean air. He scouted, and he found a big trail herd moving north, out of Ellsworth, probably, or Wichita. Normally its three thousand cattle might have required twenty riders: he counted thirty, and all were fighting men. Cavanaugh was importing professional killers as well as range stock.

Sundance rode wide of the herd, but he knew there would be more behind it, a river of longhorns flowing to the corners of three territories, Wyoming, Nebraska, Colorado. There, along the railroad, they would form a mighty pool until the signal was given, the dam of restraint broken, and they flooded out into the country of the Indians.

He pushed John Canoe's horse with greater urgency, and by twilight that evening re-read the contents of Jeffers' envelope. It seemed to him that the whole conspiracy was built on two vital cornerstones: one was Lance Cavanaugh, the other the mysterious S & S Concern. They were the force behind it all; maybe, just maybe, if he could eliminate both of them, everything would collapse.

It had to be that way, or otherwise he was faced with an impossible task. There were a lot of names on Cavanaugh's list. He could not go down the roster one by one, killing each man in turn.

So he would concentrate on Cavanaugh and the S & S Concern, and somehow he would have to learn from Cavanaugh—before Cavanaugh died—what that was.

And yet, he wondered, would even the destruction of those cornerstones do it? Maybe it was too late. The cattle were there, a force in being, like an avalanche about to slide. Maybe nothing he could do would stop them; maybe, sooner or later, it was inevitable that they break out into the Indian lands and there be war, and maybe no one man on earth could prevent that.

All he knew was that he had to try.

The plume of smoke, thick and fat, moved from east to west along the green valley of the Platte, a train roaring over the lines of the Pacific Railroad, and Sundance knew that he was not far from Oglalla, Nebraska, one of the two gateways into Wyoming.

He would have known that anyhow by the cattle, the vast herds grazing all along the valley, where, a year before, buffalo had roamed. The longhorns were closely guarded against any possible Indian attack by a lot of Texans, an army of them, and Sundance let none of them see him. He emerged from cover only when he reached Oglalla.

Except that it was in a greener, prettier

334

setting, it could have been one of the Kansas trail towns. It had the same sordid cluster of bars and brothels along Front Street. Sundance slumped in his saddle, pulled his hat over his eyes; his whole bearing listless, sleepy, he once again was Mandan Charlie.

Lance Cavanaugh would be well known here, and Sundance intended to gather as much information as possible about him. He could not question white men, but there would be halfbreeds and Indians here; there always were in such a place, people suspended between two worlds to be close to a source of whiskey, bartering their wild freedom—and often their women—for the next jug of firewater. White men spoke in their presence as if they did not exist, but they heard, understood, and remembered. They had to, in order to survive.

He had no trouble finding them; on a mudflat in the willows by the river there was a kind of shanty town stuffed with them, a ghastly litter of shacks made from discarded lumber, tattered teepees, and brush wikiups, the whole area strewn with rubbish and prowled by naked, spindly children and starving, ferocious looking dogs who were themselves eaten from time to time. Sundance's stomach clenched. If he lost his fight, someday all the proud tribes would come to this.

There were Sioux here now, and Cheyennes, a few Blackfeet and Crows, some stray Kaws up from Kansas, degraded Pawnees, even a Delaware or two from Indian Territory. All the tribes were represented by full, half and quarter bloods, all living in an armistice imposed by poverty and necessity.

Sundance spent two days getting acquainted here, something like a sharp knife twisting in him when he saw these men renting out their women to the Texas cowboys who took them into the willow thickets. He slept in his bedroll at night, but even more lightly than as if on the open plains, for unlike a real Indian camp, theft was possible here, and murder for a few pennies, and besides, a starving dog might bite your face off. The people accepted him as Mandan Charlie, which was what he wanted, and he sized them up in turn.

On the third day, he bought an extra horse for three dollars and crossed the Platte. There was plenty of game out here, but the Indians in the shanty town had lost the initiative even to go hunting. Without trouble, he killed two fat, tender does, brought them back to the mudflat by the river, built a huge fire, let it burn to a bed of coals, and cooked both animals. Then he went through the quarter and told everyone, "I've had good hunting. Come and eat."

They swarmed, stripping the skeletons, cracking the bones, leaving nothing even for the dogs. By the time the feast was over, Sundance had found the two men he wanted. One was a halfbreed white-Cheyenne whose father, a mountain man, had deserted his Indian wife when the son was three years old. Tall Tree was about Sundance's age, his skin the same coppery color, and, surprisingly, his eyes just as blue. But his long fell of hair was a strange, dark red, proof that his father, too, had been blonde. He spoke and understood fair English and would not have been here if his wife had not become a drunkard. But he loved her deeply and had condemned himself to this living hell so she could have the whiskey without which she could not live.

The other was a fullblood Arapaho of the Baáchineña, or Northern, band. Horse Running would sell his soul for whiskey and often sold his two wives, and yet Sundance sensed in him something of honor yet unsoiled; in his day, this man had been a mighty warrior. Moreover, he had a quick, penetrating intelligence, though the snakehead whiskey would one day erase it.

Sundance killed another deer and invited the two to come and eat alone at a wikiup he built. For a long time, they talked generalities and sang: the beautiful song about the Turtle River, ancestral home of the Cheyennes, and the touching buffalo hunting chant of the Arapaho:

How bright is the moonlight!
How bright is the moonlight!
As I ride home tonight with my buffalo kill!
As I ride home tonight with my buffalo kill!

Finally, subtly, Sundance began his questioning. When he judged the time right, he revealed that he was no Mandan-Sioux, but a member of the *Hmisis,* the most important division of the Northern Cheyennes, and a *Hotamitaniuw,* or Dog Soldier. But he lied about his name. He told them to call him Man Hunting, which was also a name he had had among the Cheyenne, and then he told them that he had a feud with Lance Cavanaugh and had been instructed in a dream to kill the man and must know everything about him that they could tell him.

He saw at once the surprise and fear that came into their eyes. It was Tall Tree, the halfbreed, who said it. "You cannot kill that man. Nobody can kill him. He's a devil."

"Perhaps I am, too." Sundance smiled faintly.

"Even a devil could not get to him to hurt him," Horse Running said. "Look. He came here two years ago with many fighting men, bringing a huge herd of cattle. He spread them out along Lodge Pole Creek up above Cheyenne, and he sells some to the mines in Colorado, but he brings more in all the time, and so now do his friends. You have seen the herds." He gestured. "And once," he said, "I thought I would kill him, too. But I found out it is impossible."

"Why did you want to kill him?"

"Because he hangs men," Horse Running said. "He hangs Indians. Last year my brother was here in this place with us. We were very hungry, it was winter and we had to have some meat, my brother's children were starving. We took our last cartridges and we went hunting, and we rode west and saw no buffalo, for Cavanaugh's cattle had taken their range, and we found no deer. All we saw everywhere was wohaws, the white man's beef. At last, we knew what we must do. We found an old cow with a leg the wolves had hamstrung; she would die soon anyhow. So we shot and butchered it, but we had bad luck. The sound of the shot brought Cavanaugh's riders. They were on us before we knew what was happening, and he was with them, a big man with long hair on his face; I will never forget him. They chased us and they killed my brother's horse, and I would have stayed with him and fought, but we had no more cartridges and he made me go on to protect his wife and children. And so Cavanaugh and his men took him."

Horse Running stared into the fire. "I circled back, saw it all, but there was nothing I could do. They had seen the butchered cow and they had my brother and I heard Cavanaugh say, 'Hell, string him up and leave him hanging for a lesson to the others.' They did not even give him time to pray or sing a death song. They threw a rope around his neck, over a cottonwood limb, and they pulled him up. He died bravely, but very slowly. He choked to death; it took a long time. While he kicked, the white men laughed and passed around a whiskey bottle. Then they rode off and left him there."

"You cut him down and took him home—"

"No," Horse Running said, not looking at Sundance. "My heart was no longer strong. I was afraid. I did not dare go near him for fear they would hang me too. He dangled there all winter until the crows and ravens had picked him clean."

"He was not the only one," Tall Tree added. "Cavanaugh hangs any Indian he finds on his range. Last spring, there were five bodies swinging at one time that I know of." He shrugged. "And who can stop him? Who cares about an Indian from the river bottoms of Oglalla or Cheyenne? Not even our own tribes care any more."

Horse Running drew in a long breath. "All the same, my heart grew strong again. It seemed I could not live without taking my revenge. I went after Cavanaugh. I scouted his ranch, I trailed him like a wolf for days. I never had a chance at him. It was impossible."

"In what way?"

"You must see his home," Tall Tree said. "It is like a white man's fort—a strong log palisade all around his headquarters, the big buildings inside with loopholes for fighting, that is what he has built, a white man's fort, in case the tribes came and tried to push him off. But they have not come; they know if they did, the railroad would bring more soldiers to help him than they could fight."

"You cannot get to him in that place," Horse Running put in. "No Indian could. They would kill an Indian before he had got to the big gates of it. And when he comes out, it is just as bad. Always, he rides with many men. Two go in front, and one of them is the man they call Rockford, that everybody around here knows. He has killed more men, white and red, than any other white man in this country. He is one of eight who ride with Cavanaugh everywhere he goes. The two in front, two on each flank, two behind, and he with his own guns, too. He always travels with such an army."

"Still, my dream says that I must kill him," Sundance answered. "I must find a way."

"There is no way." Horse Running's voice was harsh. "Not for one man alone. Believe me, I have tried and I know. And in my time, before I came here, I was a warrior. I have counted my share of coups. I could not get him and not even you, a Dog Soldier, can do it. Not without a big war party of your own." He paused. "Maybe you could go north, raise the Cheyennes, and come against him."

Before Sundance could speak, Tall Tree said sharply, "That's impossible. It would be murder. We would have to go against all these cowboys and all the soldiers from Fort Russell would be there in an hour. Besides, a big war party of Northern Cheyenne would never get close through all the patrols from the Fort and through those cowboys."

"Then maybe I must do it alone," Sundance said.

"Maybe. I don't think you'll have much luck."

"My dream tells me what to do."

Horse Running spat into the fire. "I think you had better have another dream," he said.

That ended the discussion. They sang the dying-fire-song taught to the Cheyennes by their legendary hero, Sweet Medicine, and the Arapaho going-to-sleep song and the two men left. Sundance smoked a marijuana cigarette, rolled up in his blankets, did some hard thinking, and went to sleep.

Two days later, he was lying on his belly in some willow brush along a branch of Lodge Pole Creek, looking at Cavanaugh's fort and realizing that everything the Indians had told him was true.

Here, in the valley of the Lodgepole, not far from the railroad, a large knoll reared up, commanding the lowground all around, and on top it the peeled logs of the great palisade of Cavanaugh's headquarters ranch were silver gray in first light. There was only one entrance, and that through two huge wooden gates made of thick squarehewn logs, and on either side of this were watch towers, small block-houses, with men in them; and Sundance saw the flash of binocular lenses as they scanned the surrounding land at regular intervals. Occasionally he caught glimpses of the interior as the gates opened and closed: solid houses of thick logs, loopholed as the Indians had said.

In addition, the land for miles around was crammed with cattle and gunmen, brought up from Texas for the big push to the Powder. Once, sifting through them, came a cavalry patrol from Fort D. A. Russell, not far away on the west side of Cheyenne. Horse Running and Tall Tree were right. Cavanaugh was as safe in there as a grizzly in its den. His position was impregnable.

Nevertheless, Sundance waited. Cavanaugh could not stay inside forever. He was a man of affairs, with things to do in Cheyenne and

Oglalla and elsewhere. Sooner or later he must come out.

Sundance was lucky. He waited only four hours there in the willows, patient as a stalking cougar, before the big gates opened again and Cavanaugh appeared.

But when he came, it was as the men in Oglalla had said: he rode surrounded by an Army.

First, on the point, a pair of riders, and one of them Sundance recognized immediately as Rockford. It had to be, for he'd had a description of the man's bulldog face with its smeared-back pug of nose, the deepset, slightly slanted eyes, the long black hair that fell in a thick shag to the shoulders of his flannel shirt. Rockford rode with a rifle across his saddle, and there was a holstered Smith & Wesson on each hip, and he made Bisbee, in Abilene, look like a Sunday School teacher, for Cavanaugh could afford the best. Rockford was the best, and Sundance knew it immediately, with the instant recognition of one thorough professional for another. Rockford, he thought, would be something to take, something to go up against, and despite himself, he felt a little surge of eagerness, the curiosity of the gunman, a fatal competitiveness that even Jim Sundance had never quite been able to shake completely.

But Rockford was only one. The man beside him was hardly lesser stuff, nor were the four men on the flanks or the two in the rearguard. And yet, hard as they were, riding in the center under their protection, Lance Cavanaugh seemed to dominate them all. Whatever else he might be, he was all man, all six-feet-four of him, with the great sloping shoulders and the heavy chest beneath the flannel shirt, the long lean legs encased in fringed leather chaps, big cowhorn mustaches curling in the breeze, his rifle also across his saddle, his craggy face turning this way and that as he scanned the terrain. Once he looked directly toward where Sundance lay, and Sundance tensed: it seemed as if those eyes could pierce the brush and find his hiding place. But then Cavanaugh's head turned and the men rode on, bound toward Cheyenne.

When they were out of sight, Sundance scuttled back to his tethered horse unobserved and slowly and carefully followed them.

They did not know it, but he flanked and trailed them all the way, as they jingled toward Cheyenne at a high lope along a well-cut wagon road. And, despite what Tall Tree and Running Horse had told him, there were a half dozen times when a good marksman at long range could have blasted Lance Cavanaugh's tall, arrogant form from the saddle; and Sundance was a good marksman. But, always, the question was in the back of his head: what was the S & S Concern? Apparently Cavanaugh was the only one who knew, and it would do him no good to kill Cavanaugh and leave that question unanswered. No. Somehow he had to get Cavanaugh alone, and he had to make him talk, and there was not going to be anything easy about that.

He was behind them when they reached the town, a clutter of buildings and railroad yards spread out on a dusty flat with mountains in the distance: the real gateway to Wyoming. He could remember, when, in his youth, the Cheyennes had hunted here. Now there were five thousand people swarming through the dusty streets, the railroad yards and smoking locomotives, soldiers, bullwhackers with their big freight wagons, and an added influx of Texas cowboys. The place boomed, with its deadfalls and brothels running around the clock, and nobody paid any attention to the shabby halfbreed who followed Cavanaugh's outfit into town.

They were as careful here as out on the plains. A man like Cavanaugh made a lot of enemies, and he was not going to give any of them the edge. At no time, when the whole crew entered the big hotel across from the depot, was there an opening of any kind, nor when, two hours later, they emerged and mounted and rode out of town. Sundance remained behind, having seen all he needed to. For once, he was baffled, his mind wholly empty of ideas and a deep bitterness within him. But there was more than that, too; within him still flamed the hatred of Cavanaugh that had leaped up that night on the Kansas prairie after he had read the contents of the file. It was deeper now, since he had heard the stories of halfbreeds and Indians hanged on sight for trespassing on what had once been Indian land and to which, even now, Cavanaugh could hold no formal title. Walking the streets of Cheyenne aimlessly, Sundance vowed that he would not give up. He would take Cavanaugh—and alive—and make him talk, and then he would know what to do about the S & S Concern. If he could only get Cavanaugh alone somehow, in his power, Cavanaugh would talk all right. Sundance had no doubt of that. He knew ways.

Night fell, and Cheyenne really came alive, the streets resounding with the tinny rattle of honkytonk music, piano and hurdy-gurdy, the deepvoiced curses and laughter of drunken men, the shrill natter of the dance-hall and whorehouse harpies who preyed on them. Still Sundance had no answer, and, sickening of the noise and glaring light, he left the main street and wandered down a dark alley behind a row of saloons. Presently, finding an upended keg, he sat down and rolled a cigarette, its tip a winking glow in the almost total blackness.

Just as he tossed the butt away, he stiffened and his hand dropped instinctively to his gun. Somebody else was in this alley, somebody coming toward him soft-footed, if not quite soundlessly. Sundance was about to pull the Colt free of leather, and then, when she passed between two buildings, a random ray of light from the street in front showed her to him and he relaxed.

She moved toward him unsteadily, as if very drunk, walking slowly as if quite tired, gingerly as if her feet hurt. Then she stopped and he realized that she had seen him.

Now she moved toward him again. Her voice was coarse, roughened by cigarettes and whiskey, but she tried to make it seductive. "Hey, honey. You there, sweetheart. You want a little fun? Hey?"

Sundance did not answer. She came on a little faster now, only a shape in blackness, and he knew she could not see more of him, but that did not matter. He was a man, a prospect, she knew that much, and she did not care about anything else. "A little fun, sweetie," she went on thickly. "I'll make you real happy. You ask 'em, Gloria knows all the tricks. Only four bits, anything you want."

She was so close he caught the foulness of her breath. Then a match flared, and he saw her, a woman too old and ugly to work the brothels and the dance halls, reduced to roaming back alleys and taking on anything to stay alive. With pity and revulsion, he said gruffly, "Me Injun."

She hesitated, then laughed brassily. "Okay, I like Injuns. Come on, Injun, four bits, I make you happier'n any squaw ever did."

He looked at her in the matchglow. In

350

her forties at the least, face webbed with wrinkles, mouth gap-toothed, body shapeless as a sack of turnips. And, above it all, startlingly, a mass of fine, silky hair as yellow as his own before the blacking. Sundance stared at that hair, incredible on a woman of such age and mileage. And that was when the idea hit him and he knew how he would try to take Lance Cavanaugh.

He stood up. "You got a place?"

"A sort of one." Relief was in her voice.

"Then let's go."

"Yeah," she said. "It ain't far. Come on." And together they went down the alley.

It was an abandoned cabin on the edge of town, dirt-floored, the chinking falling out from between the logs. It held only a rickety table with a chair and a filthy straw mattress in a corner, plus a window of empty bottles and a few cooking utensils. The smell made Sundance's stomach roil as she lit a candle.

In its light, she stared at him. "By God, even if you are an Injun, you're some good-lookin' man!" Coquettishly she touched that mass of yellow hair.

Sundance reached in his pocket, took out a

351

twenty-dollar gold piece and laid it beside the candle. "There you are, Gloria."

She gaped at it, eyes widening. "God Almighty, I ain't got no change for that."

"It doesn't matter," Sundance said. "It's all yours. And another like it if you give me what I want."

Caught by the way his voice had changed, she blinked. "Forty dollars? Man, you can have anything—"

Sundance picked up the candle. "Just stand still. I won't burn you or hurt you in any way." He held it close to her head, touched the hair. It was not as silky as it looked, felt brittle, but it was undeniably exactly the shade of his own without the disguise.

She giggled nervously. "You like my hair? It's my best feature, the boys always—"

"What color was it in the beginning. Brown? Black?"

"Why, I'm a natural blonde."

"Don't lie to me if you want that other forty."

She looked into his eyes, and the simper vanished. "You got blue eyes," she whispered. "I never seen an Injun with blue eyes before."

"The hair—"

"It was black," she said, with fear suddenly in her voice. She backed away a step. "Before the gray come, it was black as your'n."

"How'd you get it that color? That's what I want to know for the other twenty."

Gloria blinked. Afraid, she sat down suddenly on the bed. "I—I learned how to do it years ago in a whorehouse in New Orleans. They like blondes down there and the madam made me change it. I mean, a henna rinse jest turns it orange, but peroxide—"

"What?"

"Peroxide, doctors use it to clean wounds with and you can git it at any drugstore or a sawbones'll sell it to you. That stuff, yonder," and she pointed to a nearly full quart bottle on a shelf. "You put it on and lay out in the sun all day and it turns red, and then you do it one more time and it turns yeller. But you got to stay out in bright sun . . ."

"I'm buying that bottle," Sundance said and took it from the shelf. He threw another twenty into her lap. She picked it up, stared at it wonderingly. "You mean—"

"This is all I want," Sundance said, and before she could speak again, he turned away with the bottle and went out the door.

"Hey," she called behind him, "you can't drink that stuff—" But he was already running toward where he had left his horse.

Although it was not far from Oglalla, they were safe here, the thirty men who sat around the big beds of coals still glowing and pungent with the smell of the venison roasted over them and the fat which had dripped and sizzled on them. Hills enfolded them, hills made barren, bleak, by alkali and erosion, a miniature badlands in the bluffs along the Platte, and there was no grass here for cattle.

They had eaten well, all of them, and were full of meat, and they had drunk coffee and tea, but there had been no whiskey for them. When they had come to this place, one by one or two by two from Oglalla on their dilapidated ponies, some of them had been drunk. The worst ones had been sent back or dragged out into the hills to sleep it off. These men here, Sundance saw, were miserable enough, but they were the cream of the crop of that terrible jammed quarter of Oglalla along the river on the mudflat. They were not too far gone to understand what he had told them, but whether they believed him, or, if they did, perceived the

354

significance of what he said, he could not tell.

He stood there before the fire, letting his eyes range over their faces, coppery in the flickering light. Scars and pockmarks, eyes dulled with despair and malnutrition, some with open running sores and others with the hacking cough of lung disease—they seemed unlikely material for an army, in their tattered, cast-off white man's clothing mixed with a few pathetic remnants of fringed buckskin and high plains ornaments. But they were all he had.

"And so there it is," he finished in the English that all of them, no matter what their tribes, understood, supplemented with sign language. "That's what the man, Cavanaugh, aims to do, he and all these other Texans. That's why these cattle are all here. And if he carries out his plans, by the next winter-count, it will all be over. Then everything will belong to them, to Cavanaugh and the other whites, and the Long Knives. The Powder River Valley, the Yellowstone, the Judith Basin, the Black Hills, the Tongue, the Rosebud, the Big Horn and Little Big Horn, all the rivers, all the mountains, all the hunting grounds, Sioux, Cheyenne, Blackfeet, Crow, and all the rest—Your people will

355

have lost them all. And there is no one to stop them—except you."

He broke off, and for a moment no one stirred, none of the thirty spoke, there was only the crackling of the embers. Then a tall form arose, Horse Running, the Arapaho.

"The tribes will stop them," he said. "If what you tell us is true, every tribe will rise up against them. The Cheyennes, the Lakotahs, all— They will chop the Long Knives down. They will not let the white ranchers take their land."

"They will try to stop them," Sundance said. "But it will be the same old story. The Blackfeet will fight alone, and the Cheyennes and the others, they won't join together, and the Long Knives will take each tribe one by one and outnumber and whip them separately. You, Horse Running. Your people would join with the Cheyennes. But you think they'd help the Blackfeet save their territory?"

Horse Running shook his head. "You know better than that. The Arapaho would die before they'd help the Blackfeet. But the Cheyennes and Arapaho together are powerful enough to whip any army."

"If they can't, the Lakotahs will," a pock-marked Oglalla cut in.

"Listen," Sundance said, "and think. You aren't buffalo Indians any more, you've been here at Oglalla and at Cheyenne and you've seen the soldiers at Fort Russell. You've seen their cannon and their Gatling guns and the repeating rifles they're getting now. And the railroad can bring the troops in by thousands from back east. I would expect such talk from buffalo Indians who didn't know the white man, but not from you." He paused. "If there is war, the tribes will win some battles, yes. But the way the white men make war, it will cost the lives not only of the braves who fight them, women and little children will die, too. When the tribes make war, they kill the men and adopt the women and the children they take prisoner. But the white men kill both, their cannons and their Gatling guns can't tell the difference, even if they didn't have orders to wipe out all the Indians, as if they were wolves." His voice rose, "That's what I'm trying to keep from happening, don't you see? And the only way to do it is to get Cavanaugh, and the only way to do that is for you to help me."

He paused. "And that's why I asked you to

come and eat with me and hear what I have to say. I need fighting men. I need you."

Tall Tree arose, his eyes, as blue as Sundance's own, glinting in the firelight. "Maybe we were fighting men once," he said. "But look at us now." His voice crackled with self-contempt. "Look at me, and at the others. You are wrong, Sundance. We're not men at all. We're dogs, crawling on our bellies to the white men for whiskey, letting them kick us and take our women in return. If we were fighting men, we'd have been dead long ago. The first white man who kicked us, the first who lay with our women—we would have taken their scalps and paid the price." He spat into the fire. "You're too late. We have lost our manhood. If you need help, go north to the buffalo range, where our brothers still have theirs."

"No," Sundance said. "There isn't time, and that would start the war I don't want to happen." He put his hands on his hips, raked his eyes over their faces. "Besides, I think you're still men. I think that with guns in your hands and horses under you, you're men enough to pay off those debts of kicks and abuse of your women. I think maybe you only need the chance."

358

His voice hardened. "I know there are some who're hopeless, whom whiskey has made into old women. But I don't think you're old women. I think you're still braves, Sioux, Cheyenne, Arapaho or Blackfoot or whatever tribe you came from. And I'm asking you to follow me like warriors."

Nobody spoke, and his heart sank. Maybe he had missed his guess. Maybe Tall Tree was right, and there was no more manhood left in them. Then Tall Tree broke the silence.

"And if we do, even if we win—what then? We will have to run, or else they'll hang us and what will happen to our families then?"

Sundance said, "Going home isn't running."

"Going home?" a Blackfoot echoed.

"To your tribes." Sundance's voice rang like steel on steel. "I know, you say you are ashamed to face them. But if you fight this battle for them, you have back your manhood and no longer need be ashamed to face anyone. If we lose, you die like a brave—some of you will, anyhow. If we win, you can go home again to the buffalo range with your heads up and let the strong wind and clean water wash that mudflat stink off of you."

Again that silence. Then Horse Running said quietly, "That might be worth fighting for."

"If it isn't," Sundance said, "your sons and women are. Do you want your sons to grow up with the same stink? Do you want to see them kicked by white men? Do you want to sell your daughters to the cowboys to take into the bushes for a bottle?" His voice rose. "Fight with me, save the buffalo range, the hunting grounds where you belong. And when the fight is over, take your families there and join your tribes again."

As his words died, the wind freshened, blowing clean and cool down through the ravine in which they sat. The embers flared, sparks swirled upward, and somehow it was almost like a sign. In the firelight, Tall Tree's eyes shone like a wolf's. "Feel the wind!" he cried. "Draw it in your lungs! It comes from the north, from the buffalo range. It smells like grass and buffalo and lodge fire smoke! It does something to my heart, and it brings back dreams!" He raised his head. "Sundance! I don't know about the others. But I want to go north again, I want to go home, with my woman and my son! Show me

360

how to do it as a man and I will ride with you!"

The sparks swirled higher in a spiral of thousands of tiny jewel like flecks of red. Horse Running's voice was deep. "I still have a gun and remember how to use it. Where you ride, Sundance, this Arapaho will ride, too, and then go home to his own people—or to the Shadow Land!"

The Blackfoot got up. "If it will save the hunting grounds," he said, "then I will join even with the Cheyenne and the Arapaho. For if we lose them, then we will never have a place to go. Sundance, I'm with you . . ." And then his words were drowned in other voices as men got to their feet. Someone had brought a drum, and suddenly it began to beat, deep and throaty. And now they were all up, that ragtag army of the damned and crowding in on Sundance, and something leaped within him. The greatest risk of all was his, but now at least there was a chance.

He let the turmoil wear itself out, and then, long into the night he drilled them on what they were to do and how they were to do it when he sent them word. Before he was through, he was certain that Tall Tree and Horse Running understood, anyhow, and

Kills-Easy, the Blackfoot. And they could lead the others.

After he was finished, the drum sounded long into the night, and they danced, and then, near dawn, they rode back to Oglalla. But Jim Sundance headed up Lodgepole Creek, to stalk the most dangerous game he had ever hunted.

8

FOR three days he ranged Lance Cavanaugh's land like a great lobo wolf, keeping always to cover, traveling constantly, leaving no tracks, questing, stalking, waiting for a chance at his quarry. So far, he'd had none, but he was not discouraged. Any kind of hunting took a lot of patience, and hunting man the most of all. Rockford was a range boss, and sooner or later he would have to ride out alone; and that was when Jim Sundance intended to take him.

It was on the morning of the fourth day as he put the Cherokee horse along a thickly forested ridge above Lodgepole Creek that he heard the shots. Four or five deep coughs, they came from a good distance down the creek, and rising above them faintly was the sound of whooping, shouting, laughter, the noise of white men enjoying good sport. Sundance frowned and turned the horse. Not letting curiosity overpower his caution, he went carefully, with his own rifle ready, and after a half mile he tied the animal and scouted ahead on foot through the pines. Crawling on his belly to the grove's edge, he stared into the creekbottom below.

What was happening there was laid out like an open book, and as easy to read. Across the creek, on the flat, the carcass of a dead longhorn made a brindle blot. Not far from it, four men on horseback were gathered around something on the ground. Only when one of them moved could Sundance see that it was the body of a man, crippled, but still alive. In terror, it dragged itself over the grass like an injured insect, and Sundance fished in his pocket for a small brass telescope. Unfolded, it brought the crawling man into sharp focus as he put it to his eye, and he saw that this was an Indian dressed in tatters of white man's clothing, a man with hair turned to silver. As he crawled, he left a trail of blood; he had been shot through both legs.

And even as Sundance watched, the black haired man with the bulldog face turned his horse slightly so that Sundance could see his twisted grin. He said something to the men around him, lined a Smith & Wesson and pulled the trigger. The crippled Indian's body jerked, one arm went slack, turning scarlet. Rockford laughed. Indomitably, the old Indian crawled on. The bow and arrows he had used to kill the cow in silence lay far behind him on the grass. He had been unwise to kill so openly, but likely he'd been desperate, starving. There was a quarter in Cheyenne like the one in Oglalla and he must be from there. Anyhow, he had been caught cold, and now Rockford was taking taking his time about shooting him to pieces.

Sundance cursed and raised his rifle slightly, but his finger did not touch the trigger. Rockford had just fired again, and now the other arm went limp, and the old Indian lay helpless on the grass that turned red all around him. One of the Texans, as if he could not stomach this, snapped something at Rockford and turned his horse and galloped off. After a moment, another followed. There was nothing Sundance could do, wounded in all four members, blood pouring from him, the old man as good as dead already. And maybe, just maybe, Sundance thought, his death would buy something more important than a short span of living wholly crippled. Maybe, at least, he would be avenged. Sundance waited.

Rockford fired again, emptying that gun, and the body twitched and still the old man was alive. Rockford drew his other pistol. Now, this had become too much for the stomach of the remaining rider. He swung his horse, gestured at the old man, lying there twitching, snapped something at Rockford. Rockford's pugnosed bulldog's face turned even uglier. Whatever he said, it made the Texan furious. He jerked his mount around and spurred it hard, riding off after the others, leaving Rockford alone with his victim.

Hands clenched around his rifle, Sundance waited.

Rockford, grinning, fired two more careful shots. Each made the body jerk, and yet it lived. Then something leaped in Sundance. The old man raised his silvered head, his lips moved as he looked skyward, and Sundance knew that, in defiance, he sang his death song. The distance was too great for Sundance to hear, but he had seen now that the moccasins the old man wore were of Cheyenne design; this was a member of his own tribe. And he was dying like a Cheyenne should, like a Dog Soldier—

Rockford fired a single shot.

The old man's face dissolved in a wash of scarlet. He fell back, mercifully dead at last.

Sundance let out a long breath that was lost in the soughing of wind in pines and watched as Rockford, still grinning with self-satisfaction, jacked the empty shells from his guns and punched in new rounds. He sheathed the Smith & Wesson and spat. He turned in his saddle and looked back in the direction the others riders had taken. He spat again and rode on down the creek, alone.

Sundance leaped up, ran through the pines, hit his saddle without touching stirrup. He put the horse along the ridge, keeping always to the cover of the forest and yet watching Rockford down below.

There was still no chance: all that grazing land was covered with cattle, and there were too many riders. But there were other herds on the far side of this ridge, and maybe, just maybe, Rockford would swing this way sooner or later.

An hour passed, two, and although Rockford was never out of sight, he stayed beyond Sundance's reach. He rode out to the various bands of cattle, talked with the riders, gave his orders, did a range boss's work—which in this case was demanding with more longhorns on this grass than it could properly support—and Sundance's heart sank, but he would not give up. Ahead, the ridge sloped down, making a natural pass from one range to the other, and— He rode to the edge of the pines there and waited, looking down at the folded gap, marked with a dry wash and a trail. If he took Rockford at all, this would have to be the place, and it would have to be quick. Now he had to gamble.

He tied the horse inside the pines, took the rawhide lariat from its saddle, shook out a loop, not a large one. After careful reconnoitering, he left the woods and ran down the slope into the seam between the two hills. There was a shallow sidebranch of the dry wash that would give him cover, screened as it was with low brush, and from there he would have one chance and one chance only, if he were very lucky.

He made it down the hill and into the gully without being seen so far as he knew. There he fell flat on his belly, judged the distance to the trail that ran at right angles to where he lay and not ten yards away. The riata was a sixty-foot Mexican type and should be long enough.

Mercilessly, the sun beat down on him as he lay there behind the shallow cutback and the wall of brush, and flies crawled on him, and yet he did not move, it was as if he were a rock. But every sense was alert, tuned to highest pitch, throughout the hour that passed and that seemed a year.

Then he bit his lip: up the trail there was a tick of sound, a steel horseshoe on rock. Someone was coming, and maybe, just maybe . . .

Now he could hear the hoofbeats of the walking horse, feel their vibrations, it seemed to him, in the ground. He raised his head slightly, risked a look, and his heart began to hammer. The long chance had paid off; the man called Rockford came, and he rode alone. Sundance's fingers curled delicately around the rope.

Now Rockford was almost even with him. The complete professional, he rode warily, even on his own range, head swiveling alertly, right hand near his gun. For an instant it seemed to Sundance that Rockford stared directly at him, and he lay motionless, face down, an easy target if Rockford saw him. But the horse moved on past, its pace steady and uninterrupted, and then Sundance acted.

He was on his feet like a panther, loop shaken out. He gave it one spin and threw it straight for Rockford, thirty feet away, his back now toward Sundance. The small rawhide circle spread out beautifully, and it just cleared Rockford's hat, and as it landed on his shoulders, Sundance pulled, hard, risking breaking Rockford's neck.

The man had time for a guttural squawk, and then, like a great cat, as he hit the ground with jarring force, Sundance was on him and Sundance's fist rose and fell. After that, Rockford made no other sound . . . Knowing that every second counted, Sundance ran to catch the riderless horse.

The man was spreadeagled, wrists and ankles lashed to four stout pegs driven deep into hard earth. It was not a comfortable posture, but it was better, Sundance thought, than being shot to pieces bit by bit, but Rockford did not appreciate the contrast. He stared up at the halfbreed towering over him, and his lips curled back in a snarl that made him look more than ever like a bulldog.

"Go ahead, yell if you want to," Sundance said. "Yell your damn lungs out. We're a long way north of Cavanaugh's range. And nobody's gonna hear you, unless maybe an elk or two, or a bear."

Rockford did not yell. He only asked harshly, "How the hell did I git here? Who're you?"

"My name's Jim Sundance."

Rockford's face changed. The snarl left it and suddenly it became very grave. "Sundance," he breathed. Then he was silent, staring despairingly at the blue sky overhead.

After a while, he asked, "You gonna torture me?"

"I'd thought about shooting you to pieces," Sundance said coldly. "Like you did an Indian two days ago."

"Oh, God . . ."

"But I've changed my mind. No, I'm not gonna torture you. Unless you lie to me about the S & S Concern. I want to know what that is."

"I don't know. So help me, I've heard of it, but I don't know."

"Of course," Sundance said, "I could skin you alive. One leg today, another tomorrow maybe. I've seen it done."

Rockford sucked in a sob of a breath. "Sundance, I swear to you. There ain't but one man knows what that is, and that's Cavanaugh."

"Well," Sundance said, "I guess I'll have

371

to ask him, then." He stood there thoughtfully for a moment, looking around this hidden valley in the Medicine Bow mountains. After roping Rockford, Sundance had packed his unconscious body on his horse, bound and gagged him, hidden him in the woods. That night, he rode off of Cavanaugh's range, fast, taking Rockford with him, knocking him out again each time he started to wake up. Another night's hard traveling had taken them out of cattle country, and a half day had brought them to this lonesome place. "I'll need your help, Rockford," he added.

"Oh, God, I'll tell you anything I know, do anything you ask—"

"Fine," Sundance said. "That's just fine." He went to where his saddlebags lay beneath a tree and when he came back, there was a big bottle in his hands.

Rockford stared at it. "What you gonna do with that?" he whispered.

Sundance's grin was more like a snarl. "You'd be surprised," he said. Then, opening it, he knelt by Rockford's head. The sun, at zenith, was as bright as polished brass in the sky above . . .

She had been right, it worked like magic. Two applications were enough, and in forty-eight hours, Rockford was transformed. His long shag of black hair was now as yellow as that of the woman in Cheyenne—or Sundance's own without the blacking. And the rest, Sundance thought, would be no problem. He had already made the dye himself from certain berries and rootbarks.

And so, he thought, this part of it was about to come to an end. Rockford had sung like a bird, and Sundance knew every detail now of the inside of Cavanaugh's fort and its routine. There was only one thing more he needed now from Rockford—and he could not take that while the man was alive and pegged out in such a way.

He felt again that surge of curiosity, that instinctive gunman's challenge that had touched him at first sight of Rockford as he cut loose the man's hands. Then, loosely, he hobbled Rockford's feet and allowed the man to stand. He knew it would take a long time for proper circulation to return, and he wanted no undue advantage.

"You just hang loose," he said. "You try to run, I'll give you what you gave that Indian, only slower."

Rockford stared at him as Sundance loaded Rockford's two Smith & Wessons and checked them out, then slipped them into Rockford's holsters.

"I don't git this," Rockford said. "That stuff you put in my hair; now . . . what you doin' with my guns?"

"Why," Sundance said, "when you're fit to fight again, give 'em to you. So you'll have an even break."

"What?" Rockford's eyes flared. He stared at Sundance incredulously. "You wouldn't be that much fool."

"Any time you're ready," Sundance answered. "Just say the word. I've got to kill you, Rockford. I could do it in cold blood, but I'd rather give you a chance, I got enough things restin' hard on my mind. Besides, I want to try you out."

"You want to try *me* out?" Rockford was rubbing his hands together vigorously now to hasten circulation. "Why, ever since I first heard of you, I been itchin' to git a crack at you. I'll take your carcase in, scalp and all, and collect the old man's reward."

"You do that," Sundance said, "if you're man enough."

He waited a long while. Rockford rubbed

and stamped, and knowing he would not run now, Sundance cut his hobbles. After a couple of hours, during which Rockford had undergone considerable pain from returning circulation, the man looked at Sundance with eyes that gleamed. "Let me have my guns," he said.

"Sure." Sundance drew his own, and, covering Rockford with it, passed over the Smith & Wessons and their belts. "It's gonna be even, Rockford, you and me, straight-up. Don't try anything funny or I'll kill you where you stand. Just put on those guns."

Rockford did not answer. He belted the guns in place, tugged the holsters into adjustment, thonged them around his legs. He let out a sigh of satisfaction and stood spraddle-legged. "All right, Sundance."

Sundance kept him covered for a moment more with the Colt. This hidden valley was very silent, only the wind in some aspen leaves, the bright sun overhead, the blue peaks encircling them. "I'm gonna put my gun up now."

"I'll wait," Rockford said, crouching slightly.

Sundance returned the Colt to holster, stood there with hands at his sides. He felt no fear, only that unholy gunfighter's eagerness. He kept seeing the crippled Indian crawling over the bloody grass as Rockford had fired at him and fired again. And he watched, now, Rockford's eyes, and when they changed, as he had known they would, he drew.

Rockford's right hand gun had cleared leather, was coming into line, hammer back, when Sundance's bullet hit him in the belly. Rockford toppled backwards, firing into space. His eyes were wide, face unbelieving. Shock left him with no pain, but the knowledge that his life was ended struck him. "You—By God, you beat me!"

Sundance fired again.

Rockford landed on his back, arms and legs flung wide, sightless eyes staring at the sky, yellow hair vivid against the grass. Sundance looked down at him a moment, sucked in a long breath, and reached for his knife . . .

What a long, bloody way it had been from Rio, he thought, three days later, as Cavanaugh's fort loomed on the knoll before him as he rode up the valley; and what a trail of corpses he had left behind him. And now, the final gamble, the last risk, and, curiously, he felt neither fear nor anticipation, only a great weariness, a disgust with endless double-dealing, greed, and slaughter, that struck through to his bones. To shake it off, he kindled again the hatred, and it grew once more into a hot, bright flame as he thought of Cavanaugh and all his wealth and power and his senseless lust for more. He straightened in the saddle.

Of course, he knew as he neared the fort, he was under observation from the watch towers, and with Rockford missing, everyone would be alert. What the guards saw was a shabby Indian in drab white man's clothing, well-armed, riding a pretty good horse, and with a small canvas bag slung to the horn. It was growing late, but the fort's gates were still open, and as he approached, Sundance raised his right hand in a gesture of peace.

Somebody in a tower yelled, a rifle barrel thrust out. Sundance drew rein, waited. Then three riders galloped from the fort, Texans cut from Rockford's pattern, if not quite of his caliber. The Indian waited impassively as they surrounded him. One, with a fringe of chestnut beard and sharp black eyes lined a rifle barrel on Sundance's chest. "All right. Stop there. No Injuns inside the fort."

"Got business with Mr. Cavanaugh," Sundance said.

"The hell you have. What business a blanket-head like you got with a man like him?"

"I got to find a letter," Sundance said. "I ain't reachin'." Carefully he felt in his coat, left-handed, brought out a thick envelope with a fine copper-plate script address. The bearded man took it, read aloud: *"Mr. Lance Cavanaugh near Cheyenne, Absolutely personal."*

"Who give you this?" he asked suspiciously.

"Man named Jeffers, Abilene."

The bearded man said, "Hold him, boys, and take his guns. I'll carry this to Mr. Cavanaugh." He whirled his horse and pounded off. The other two kneed their mounts alongside, and Sundance made no protest as they disarmed him, taking his knife as well. One eyed the canvas bag. "What's in there?" He reached out, crushed it, nodded. "Something soft. No hardware. Okay."

They waited for five minutes, with Sundance under their guns and then the bearded man came back, looking puzzled. "Mr. Cavanaugh says to bring him in right away. Under guard. Okay, Injun, move out."

They walked their horses through the gates, and Sundance's eyes shuttled from side to side. This stronghold was everything men had said it was, tight as a prison, swarming with hardbitten cowboys. Getting in, he thought, had been simple; getting out would be something else again. They, the Indians from Oglalla, had damned well better have seen the signal fires he had lit three nights before and which had blazed briefly on a ridge above the Platte. They were supposed to be watching for them, and they were supposed to know what to do now and carry out their orders with precision. His lips curled. It was asking a lot of a bunch of drunks, pimps, and human wrecks. But once they had been warriors. Maybe that would count for something.

Behind him, the gates swung shut; now it was nearly sundown. His guards led Sundance toward the main house, a fortress in itself of cottonwood logs, reined in, dismounted. Sundance followed suit, taking the canvas bag from the saddle horn. The bearded man looked at it narrowly. "What's that?"

"Private for Mr. Cavanaugh," Sundance said.

"It's all right, Chess, there's no hardware in it," the guard who'd squeezed it said.

"Okay." Chess prodded Sundance with his rifle. "Come on, Farley, you help watch him." They entered the living room of the house, long and low and wholly masculine, with guns on the wall, horse gear in the corners. They prodded Sundance across the room toward another door, one of massive oak timbers, not cottonwood, and strapped with heavy iron. It was closed, and Chess pounded on it. A voice within said, "All right," and Sundance heard the sliding of a heavy bar. Then the door swung open on heavy hinges, and Lance Cavanaugh was there.

Up close, face to face, the big Texan was even more impressive than from a distance. Tall as Sundance was, Cavanaugh topped him by two inches, and his rawboned, erect, slope-shouldered frame was as powerful and muscular as a longhorn bull's. Eyes like two chips of granite raked over Sundance, the mouth beneath the long mustaches was like the joining of a steel trap's jaws. He wore range clothes, a long-barreled Colt on his right hip, holster thonged. Sundance felt the power, force, emanating from the man and for a moment almost knew fear. He was in the presence of terrific strength and utter ruthlessness.

"He's got blue eyes," Cavanaugh said harshly.

"Me Mandan-Santee," Sundance said.

"Maybe. Take off that hat."

Sundance did; Cavanaugh ran his gaze over hair black as a crow's quills. For a moment, he said nothing. Then: "Is he slick?"

"Plumb," Chess said. "They frisked him good."

Cavanaugh looked at the canvas bag and something stirred in his eyes. "Then bring him in." He stepped aside.

Sundance was prodded into a small room with a single high, barred window, a huge iron safe in one corner, a desk, a couple of chairs, a cabinet for files and accounts. It was a stronghold within a stronghold, exactly the way Rockford had described it. Cavanaugh, he'd said, distrusted banks, kept a fortune on hand in cash in this room built like a vault. "Now," Cavanaugh said, drawing his Colt, "Chess, you and Farley get out. Wait in the front room. I'll call you if I need you."

"Boss, you sure—?"

Cavanaugh's voice crackled. "I think I can

handle one unarmed Injun! Out! This is private!"

"Yes, sir." They exited and Cavanaugh closed the door and shoved the massive bar through its keepers. Sundance's eyes flicked to the window: dusk out there now. His gut was taut, knotted; if Horse Running and Tall Tree let him down . . .

Cavanaugh gestured to a chair before his desk. "All right, Injun, you can sit. But one fancy move and you're cold meat, you *sabe*?"

"*Sabe.*" Sundance threw the canvas bag on the desk and sat. Cavanaugh went around behind the desk, stood looking down at Sundance. Right hand holding the gun, he fingered the envelope and its sheet of paper with his left. "So Jeffers gave you this letter in Abilene, huh?" He drew in a long breath. "And you claim to be the man who took Jim Sundance, huh?"

"I took him," Sundance said. "Miss Danton down in Del Rio, she sent eight men again' him. He killum all. Finally, she git smart and come to me, Mandan Charlie. See now it take an Injun to catch an Injun. He leave Del Rio, I trail 'im."

"And bushwhacked him, eh? You couldn'ta taken a man like him straight up."

382

Sundance grinned. "Sundance no damned fool, 'cept when it come to Injuns. He find an Injun north of Del Rio on the desert, no horse, no water, look like he near dead, he got to stop and help. He turn me over with canteen in his gun hand—and my own gun underneath and it take jest one bullet." He pointed to the bag. "You no believe, you take a look. Ain't two scalps like that nowhere around."

"We'll git to that in a minute. First, these letters. This one from the Danton woman says she paid you five hundred dollars, told you Jeffers would give you another five hundred when you delivered the scalp to him. This one from Jeffers to me says he paid you five hundred and I'm to give you another five when I'm satisfied."

"That right," Sundance said.

"There's a couple of little hitches." Cavanaugh raised the gun, leveled it at Sundance. "First of all, I told Jeffers to send that scalp to me by sealed express box, not have it delivered by some Injun saddle tramp. Second, Jeffers is dead. He got run over by a train in Abilene." His mouth twisted under his mustaches. "And the whole thing stinks."

Sundance said, "I know Jeffers dead, he

383

killed the day after he wrote that letter. The other, I don't know about express. He say I bring this to you, you give me more money, I want everything I got comin'. That's Sundance's scalp in there, I took it, you look-see, you not believe me."

"I'll damned well look-see," Cavanaugh said, and with his left hand he opened the bag, upended it, shook its contents on the desk. Sundance tensed. *Now,* he thought, *if there's to be a chance at all—*

The thing whispered as it landed on the desk. It was not just a scalp, it was the skin of a head, from forehead to nape. In a last ray of dying light, the yellow hair, long and silky, shone like freshly-minted gold. And the dried skin beneath it was the color of a copper penny.

And so there it was, spread before Lance Cavanaugh, the key to the whole northern ranges, the thing he had waited and lusted for so long, and he stared at it, and his eyes flared, and his whisper was hoarse. "By the old Harry," he breathed. "This is it! By God, this is it!" And for a moment he could not resist. The gun's muzzle slid off line as Cavanaugh ran his left hand through the yellow hair—Rockford's hair, peroxide-dyed—as if it were a stack of double eagles, and then Sundance leaped.

He came out of the chair like a coiled spring exploding, and his left hand seized Cavanaugh's right wrist and jerked, and his right hit Cavanaugh between the eyes. The Colt went off, a single bullet going wild, the noise tremendous in the close confines of the room. Cavanaugh, jarred by that tremendous blow, sagged. Sundance went across the desk, but Cavanaugh was already recovering, struggling. "Damn—" he whispered and they were on the same side of the desk then and wrestling for the gun, two big men, each as strong and hard as tempered steel.

"God damn you!" Cavanaugh husked and he got his clawed left hand in Sundance's face, groping for the eyes as Sundance clamped down harder on his gun-wrist. Sundance felt skin rake away as he twisted his face and hit Cavanaugh hard in the belly. It was like striking a stone wall, but the force knocked Cavanaugh back against the big iron safe, and Sundance shoved up tight to pin him there. He exerted every ounce of strength he owned, focusing it all in his left hand, felt bones slide and grate, and then the gun dropped from Cavanaugh's hand. Sun-

385

dance kicked it, and it slid into the far corner.

Boots pounded outside, someone hammered on the door. "Boss, hey, boss!" Somebody threw himself against the door, but the strong oak and steel held, and at the same instant Cavanaugh braced himself, shoved with terrific force. Sundance was hurled back, fell across the desk. Cavanaugh leaped at him. Sundance raised his boots, kicked Cavanaugh in the belly. Cavanaugh grunted, bounced away. As Sundance came off the desk, Cavanaugh turned toward the gun in the corner.

Sundance was after him like a cat, got Cavanaugh's neckerchief, jerked the man around, hit Cavanaugh in the face with a jarring left. Cavanaugh forgot the gun. His mouth twisted beneath mustaches tinged with blood. "All right, damn you," he hissed. "I'll kill you with my bare hands!" The pounding went on, both ignored it. Because now, like two maddened range bulls, they were fighting at close quarters, giving, taking punishment. The room was loud with the sodden sound of fists on flesh and bone, of grunting, heavy breathing. The desk went over, the golden scalp spilling among papers as Cavanaugh bore Sundance against it:

Sundance dropped, Cavanaugh's fist whistled past his cheek. Sundance came up from under, and his head caught Cavanaugh's jaw from beneath; the rancher's teeth clicked and blood poured from a bitten tongue. Sundance hit Cavanaugh twice, one two, in the belly. Cavanaugh chopped him on the back of the neck and almost broke his spine. Sundance slid free, fell on one knee. Outside, somebody yelled, "The window! Damn it, to the window!"

Cavanaugh kicked at Sundance, knocked him sprawling. He kicked again, but Sundance rolled, and his hand slid through the papers spilled from the desk. It closed on something hard and sharp, a letter-opener. He rolled again and came up, and when Cavanaugh saw the blade in his hand like a dagger, he backed away. Sundance laughed and threw the letter-opener with the gun. He wanted to do this with his fists. Mouth puffed, face cut, ribs bruised, he still felt no pain, only a ferocious hatred and the knowledge that he must take Cavanaugh alive and keep him that way for a while. Fists up, he came in and Cavanaugh was backed into a corner. Showing no fear, the Texan squared himself, brought up his own fists. Sundance took one blow, two, and came in inexorably. Now he had Cavanaugh crowded and he hit the man in the face once, twice, and Cavanaugh groaned and pounded him in the ribs, but Sundance only hit Cavanaugh again, and now Cavanaugh's face was a bloody mask, nose smashed, eyes closing, and Sundance hit him once more and then another time. Cavanaugh made a whistling sound as bone in his jaw yielded. Then he was crumpling. Sundance stepped back, cocked a fist. But now Lance Cavanaugh, Cavanaugh the proud, rich Texan, was on his knees, looking up at Sundance through pouring scarlet. Beneath sodden mustaches his mouth moved. "Don't," he said thickly. "No more. I'm beat."

Gasping for breath, Sundance only whirled away, seized the Colt, spun. Cavanaugh had not moved. but at that instant, a face appeared at the barred window. Sundance raised the gun, fired, and it disappeared in a wash of red. He ducked, sprang to the window, closed the massive inside shutter that matched the door, and whirled. Cavanaugh was getting shakily to his feet.

"All right," Sundance rasped. "They can't

help you now. We're shut up in here just like your money. You know who I am?"

"I . . . know . . ." There was no pride left in Cavanaugh now. "I . . . For God's sake, Sundance . . ." Now he was just a bloody old man, head bowed, legs trembling. "Please don't—"

"The S & S Concern," Sundance snapped. "What is it, who is it? Tell me, Cavanaugh! Tell me, now!"

"I—" Cavanaugh's mouth opened and shut, blood dribbling from his torn tongue. "I—"

There was a pounding at the door, at the shutters. But Sundance remained cool. "If you don't tell me, I'm gonna start shootin' you to pieces. You got ten seconds, Cavanaugh."

The beaten man blinked dazedly. "You'll never git . . . out of here . . . alive . . ." he husked.

"My worry. The S & S Concern—"

"For God's sake. All right." Cavanaugh sagged against the wall, sucked in breath. Then, thickly, he said two names.

Jim Sundance stared, shocked, appalled, and, for a moment disbelieving. "Them?

They put up ten thousand of the money on my head?"

"They did it," Cavanaugh said. "It was their idea in the first place. They said you had to go before the rest would work—"

"All right," Sundance said bitterly. "I should have guessed, I reckon. Well— Open the safe, Cavanaugh."

"Sundance—"

"Open it. I'm due a reward, Cavanaugh. I've taken some of it already off of dead men. I figure I still got ninety thousand comin'. Likely there's that much in there. I want it, I got a use for it. And I want your papers. All of 'em, about the S & S Concern."

"If I give those to you . . . I'm finished."

"And where you think you'll be if you don't?"

"Sundance . . ." Cavanaugh was stiffening now. "We can bargain. I'll pay you a hundred thousand and give you safe conduct outa here—"

"You're damned right you will," Sundance grinned, through blood. "Open it, Cavanaugh." He jerked the gun. "Two seconds left."

"Yes," Cavanaugh breathed. He seemed to crumple, dropped to his knees before it, spun the dial with one hand, mopping blood from his eyes with the other. The door swung wide, Cavanaugh reached inside. Then he rolled, and when he landed on his back, there was a snubnosed Colt in his hand.

Sundance aimed and fired instinctively. Cavanaugh screamed as the bullet smashed his forearm and the pistol dropped. "You don't git off that easy," Sundance grated, and he picked up the gun. "You tough old bastard, you. No, not that easy . . ." As Cavanaugh rolled over, moaning, Sundance went to the safe. He let out a breath of satisfaction. Money, in big bills, stacks of it. And files: right there on top, one marked *S & S Concern.*

There were folded money bags in the bottom of the safe. Sundance crammed in the file, wads of currency. When they were full, he latched two together, slung them over his shoulder and arose. Outside, the turmoil had taken on a different note. All around the fort, now, men were shouting, yelling, and he heard the thud of horses' hooves. Inside Jim Sundance something unknotted. They had kept their word . . .

"Boss!" Chess's voice roared outside the door frantically. "Boss, there's a range fire, a hell of a fire—Boss, damn it! All hell is breakin' loose!"

Cavanaugh raised his head, blinked. Sundance grinned. "He's right, Cavanaugh. All the range from the south bank of Lodgepole on is burnin' now. Good dry, rich grass. Grazed down, yeah, but plenty of fuel to keep it going. That ain't the main thing, though. The main thing is the stampedes, you understand, Cavanaugh? It's a chain, the fire starts the first herd to runnin', it breaks into another, spooks 'em . . . Pretty soon, there's gonna be the damndest mess you've ever seen, all the way from here to the Platte. All those cattle you've brought in here runnin' like hell . . ." He grabbed the rancher by the collar, jerked. "On your feet. We're gonna wait a while until that draws off most of the men in this fort. Then you're gonna escort me out of here, and the first man that snaps a cap at me, you die. You understand that?"

Cavanaugh mumbled something. He leaned against the wall. Sundance waited patiently. The turmoil outside heightened. Most of the men within the fort were cowboys with responsibility to the herds, those of Cavanaugh and of other brands. There would be guards left, yes, but at least not an army of them. And out there in the night there would be fire, stampede, confusion, enough to give him an even chance at getting away.

Now the tumult faded. Most of the riders must have gone. Sundance collared Cavanaugh and jammed the pistol in his back. "Unbar the door."

Tensely, he waited as it swung open. Outside lamps were lit in the front room, and in their light Chess and Farley stood, with guns up. "Boss—" Chess began and broke off, as he saw Cavanaugh's battered face and the battered Indian behind him with the gun.

"Don't shoot," Cavanaugh husked. "He'll kill me if you do. Let . . . let us through."

"Boss—"

"You heard the man," Sundance said. "I want two horses out there and the gates open. Lead the horses outside the gates and hold 'em there. We'll come on foot."

Chess opened his mouth to protest, but Cavanaugh gasped, "Do what he says! Both of you!" He swallowed hard. "This here's—"

"Don't say that name!" Sundance rasped. Cavanaugh bit off the words. "Move," he said weakly. "Dammit, you two move . . ."

They paused only a moment longer. Then

Chess said, "Hell. There ain't no option, Farley. Let's go."

They backed out. Sundance prodded Cavanaugh on, and they passed through the front door. On the porch, they halted, even Sundance awed.

To the north the sky was a blaze of orange light as far as he could see. They had fired the range all right, fired the grass, the knots of timber, all of it. The wind was from the north, and the fire was moving fast, and there was a sound like thunder out there which would be thousands of running cattle, a wild bawling and bellowing, as the jammed herds ran ahead of fire. Horses whinnied, men shouted, and guns went off as riders tried to turn and slow the herds. All at once there was a crash, the stockade trembled, as a panic-stricken bunch of cattle collided with it, sheered off. The gates across the yard were open, in the firelight Chess and Farley stood holding two wild-eyed nervous horses.

Sundance looked at the guard towers. There were men in them, but that was a chance he had to take. "Move, Cavanaugh," he said.

That trip across the yard to the gates was one of the longest journeys he had ever made, but the men in the tower only stared and held their fire. At the gates, Chess and Farley stood tensely, guns holstered, holding the nervous horses. Beyond, on the open range, Sundance saw longhorns running in the hectic glow of firelight. It was like hell out there, an inferno of flame and stampeding cattle.

"Drop your gunbelts," he told Chess and Farley.

They obeyed, one-handed. "Now," Sundance said, swinging lithely into the saddle of one horse, keeping Cavanaugh under the muzzle of his Colt, "mount up."

Cavanaugh did so, stiffly. Sundance crowded up, took his horse's reins with his left hand. "Tell 'em to go in and close the gates."

Cavanaugh's orders were lost in the noise, the turmoil. Sundance did not even wait to see if they were followed. Suddenly he kicked his horse and lashed Cavanaugh's with rein ends, and both animals broke into a gallop. "Hyaaaaaaaiiieee!" he yelled, Cheyenne war-whoop rising above the racket. Then, leading Cavanaugh's horse, he rode straight into the hell of flame and running cattle.

To that hidden place north of the Platte and west of Fort Laramie they came, one by one or in weary, smoke-smudged little groups of two or three; some coughed with tuberculosis, and several had got hold of whiskey and were drunk. But most of them rode tall, straight in their saddles, like the warriors they once had been and had again proved themselves to be tonight. The hills ringed them in, the wind blew fresh and cool from the northern ranges as they dismounted in the first gray light of dawn.

Horse Running was grinning broadly and Tall Tree's eyes shone with a strange light as they faced Sundance. "Good! It worked! You got clear!"

"Thanks to you," Sundance said. "It was beautiful work you did."

"We only followed your orders. We wore no feathers, gave no warwhoops, moved in stealth, shot only in self-defense, rode only shod horses, and as soon as the range was burning, rode out. But it was a beautiful sight to see, all those *wohaws* and white men running . . ." Then Tall Tree's eyes shuttled to the man with the battered face and bandaged arm and hobbled ankles sitting by the fire. "Cavanaugh!" he gasped. "You took him alive!"

Sundance nodded. All the men from Oglalla were in now, and they crowded around, and Cavanaugh raised his head, eyes staring, as a soft, yet terrible murmur, like the first rasp of wind before a storm, went through the gathering. "And what will you do with him?" Horse Running asked softly.

Sundance hesitated. "That's for you to say," he answered finally.

"Sundance—" Cavanaugh levered himself to his feet. His voice shook. "For God's sake, man, you're half white, anyhow. You wouldn't leave me to these . . . these wolves." His licked his battered lips. "Don't you know what they'll do to me?"

"No," Sundance said. "But I know what you've done to them. You've hanged their friends and relatives just for riding on their range, or let men like Rockford shoot them to pieces. And I know what else you aimed to do, Cavanaugh. Sand Creek, the Washita, I know how the Army handles Indians. I've seen the dead women and the little children, Cavanaugh. I've seen babies shot apart by rifle fire or burned in teepees or frozen because their homes were destroyed in the dead of winter. I've seen what's happened to captured women when white soldiers who've been penned up for months without any women of their own got hold of 'em. That's what a full-scale Army campaign against the tribes is like, Cavanaugh, that's what you wanted, worked so damned hard to get." He paused. "It's not a thing that pleasures me. But if a man plays for big stakes like you played for, he's got to be prepared to lose and take big consequences. These men are your consequences, Cavanaugh. They're entitled to their own justice in their own way."

"Sundance," Cavanaugh said and sat down heavily and stared at the dawn with despairing eyes. Again that wolfish murmur went through the crowd, but Sundance's voice rode above it, harsh and clear. "Hear me, warriors!"

There was silence.

Sundance said, "My way lies east, where I have important business. I must ride. I leave Cavanaugh to you. But this I ask. Whatever happens, whatever you decide to do, no one must ever see this man again, dead or alive. Do you understand? It must be as if the earth had swallowed him or the wind had lifted him to the stars."

"If it is important, we'll guarantee that," Horse Running said.

"It is." Sundance paused. "I must go now. But you— When this affair is finished, what will you do?"

Horse Running shrugged. "I know who I am again—a warrior of the Arapaho. I'm heading north to join my people. Tall Tree says he goes again to the Cheyennes. Others—" he swept out his hand "—also seize the chance to go home again in pride. You've given us that much, anyhow, Sundance. Pride enough to return to our own with our heads up." Then he looked at a couple of men lying on the ground nearby, whiskey bottles in their hands, one snoring, the other making gargling sounds. "Some will go back to Oglalla. Some are dead inside already and nothing can be done for them. But the rest of us say our thanks."

"No, I say mine to you. I went into Cavanaugh's fort not knowing whether I'd ever come out again. I had to take whatever chance came along. But none of the chances would have been any good without you." Suddenly he swung up into the saddle. "I've got to ride. Good hunting to you all! Maybe I'll see you in the Fall up north for the last buffalo run!" He could find no other words, pulled the horse around, kicked it almost savagely. It thundered into the night as, behind him, Cavanaugh's voice cried his name one last time, despairingly, and then was cut off short.

9

IN his suite at the Palmer House in Chicago, the tall halfbreed dressed in suit and tie, the gun shoulder-holstered beneath his coat, faced the two men in uniform.

One was short and swarthy, running to plumpness; the other, leaner, with a hard, hickory-wood face and a tuft of beard, towered over the short one. The faces of both were dour, and neither would meet Sundance's eyes.

Sundance's voice was bitter, scathing. "The S & S Concern," he said, lashing them with the words. "I should have guessed. Lieutenant General Philip H. Sheridan, commander of the Division of the Missouri. And General William Tecumseh Sherman, General of the Army of the United States." His mouth curled. "Sheridan and Sherman, S & S. And using ten thousand dollars of Army funds to put a reward on the head of a United States citizen with no charges of any kind against him."

Sheridan, the short one, fingered his dark

mustaches. "Sundance, you can't talk to us like that. We agreed to meet you here, General Sherman came all the way from Washington. But not to—"

"Shut up," Sundance snapped. "Do you hear me? Shut up!" His eyes raked over them. "For God's sake, when I thought it was justified, I scouted for you two and for your Army. I advised you on Indian affairs—not that much of it was ever taken, but you asked my opinion and I gave it. I risked my life on your orders more than once when there were rogue Indians about to break the peace and you asked me to make sure they didn't. And then you connive with Cavanaugh and the other ranchers to put a price on my head big enough to turn the hand of everybody in the West against me. When you did that, you ordered my execution, hell, my murder—"

"Sundance, you don't understand—" Sherman began in his scratchy voice.

"I understand this. I thought you were my friends. And you betrayed me. But I should have known. You said it, didn't you, Sheridan? *The only good Indian's a dead Indian . . .*"

"I was misquoted!" the little cavalry general blurted.

"Well, you're not misquoted in these papers." Sundance strode to a table, slapped a pile of documents. "These, gentlemen, are copies—I trust you read them all in the time I gave you. The originals are in the hands of someone in Washington who has orders to release them if I'm not in touch with him every month one way or the other, for at least the next year. Well, have you read them?"

"We've read them," the lean Sherman said almost wearily. He took out a big black cigar and lit it while Sundance waited. "And—all right. You've got us cold. Those documents would ruin Sheridan, me, and every rancher mentioned in 'em as subscribing to that reward. But the idea didn't come from us, Sundance. It came . . . from higher up."

"I know where it came from," Sundance said. "It came from Cavanaugh through the Indian Ring to the corrupt men around President Grant and got bucked down to you. That makes no difference. You didn't fight it, you went along with it, because you don't want peace, you want war. Without war, you can't get your appropriations and get your pet officers promoted. War's your business, and when business is bad you try to make it better. It's good business for your suppliers and contractors, too. It ain't much business for the poor bastards that take an arrow or a rifle ball in the gut, but it's fine for generals."

He paused. "All right. These prove that you and Grant's administration intended to break the treaties and start a war in cold blood and wipe out all the Indians. If I release 'em to the press, there'll be a public howl you can't handle, and you know what will happen? You'll be the scapegoats. Grant and his people will blame it all on you, and you'll be kicked out in a hurry, maybe even court-martialed. There are enough decent people in this country to make sure of that. The treaties were represented to them as triumphs of fairness. These papers show what you really meant to do all along."

He broke off, and there was silence in the room. Sherman blew a puff of cigar smoke, then went to the window and looked out, the stars on his shoulders glinting in the lamplight. After a moment he said, "Sundance, we'll not argue with what you say. All right. What's your price for silence?"

"I think you know that," Sundance said quietly. "All you have to do is keep the treaties as they're written. The ones guaranteeing Sioux territory—keep the miners out of it, out of the Black Hills. The ones guaranteeing everything north of the Platte to the Cheyennes and the Blackfeet and the others. There'll be no cattle on the Powder River or anywhere else up there—you'll see to that."

Sherman was silent for a moment. "That may not be easy. There's a lot of excitement in Wyoming right now. The disappearance of Lance Cavanaugh, that big prairie fire that stampeded all those cattle . . . There's talk that it was Indian doings and demands for retaliation."

Sundance smiled coldly. "You've got your spies among the treaty tribes, I know. And not one word of evidence have you had that any of those tribes had anything to do with that. They were all north hunting buffalo."

"All the same, it was likely Indians—"

"Cite me one Indian sign that was found. One feather, one unshod pony track, one warwhoop that was heard—"

"I will," Sherman turned. "It was a blue-eyed Indian who took Lance Cavanaugh, abducted him from his home ranch." His eyes bored into Sundance's. "A blue-eyed Indian . . ."

"In white man's clothes and speaking

English," Sundance said coolly. "Not a real Indian, a renegade . . . You can't blame him on the tribes."

"We know who to blame!" Sheridan burst out.

"Do you, now? Maybe you have some proof. All I know is that I have plenty. These documents will break you, gentlemen, and maybe even break the President . . ."

Sherman chewed his cigar. Then he said quietly, "Yes, that's true. All right, Sundance. Your terms are met. We'll protect the treaty lands. We can't keep all the miners out, but they enter at their own risk. As to the cattlemen, no matter how they squawk, we'll turn their herds back. You have our promise—for a while."

Sundance's eyes narrowed. "A while?"

Sherman said, "Sundance, you're no fool. You've won a battle, but you can't win the war. It's not the Army, not the Indian Ring, not even the President. It's the American people. The land is there, Sundance, waiting, and the people want it. Thirty, forty thousand Indians ruling a country bigger than the eastern seaboard, producing nothing, consuming nothing except what they hunt and kill? And in the East, immigrants pouring in, looking for the streets paved with gold. They won't find them, the Irish, the Italians, the Poles and Swedes and Germans and all the rest, but they don't care, as long as they can take some land and hold it. Under the threat you've thrown at us, we can stave them off a while. But nobody can do it forever. It's not us you're fighting, Sundance; it's history."

"Then I'll fight history."

"You can't." Sherman paused. "One man can't hold back the tide. It will have to engulf him sooner or later. Where and when, I can't say, now. But somewhere out there, some-day—who knows? On the Powder River or the Tongue or the Yellowstone; on the Milk or Tres Marias or the Big Horn or the Little Big Horn— Someday the tide will rise, wash over and—"

"Until then," Sundance said harshly, "you keep your miners and your cattle and your God damned soldiers off of treaty lands. If you don't, I'll ruin you."

"We know that," Sherman said. "We're no fools. We'll hold it back as long as possible." He went to the table, ground out his cigar. "General Sheridan? I think we have finished our business."

"Yes," Sheridan said. He and Sherman went to the door. There Sherman turned. "There'll be no campaign this year and none next unless your tribes give us provocation, you have our word on that. Beyond that—who can say? Good day, Sundance." Then they went out, closing the door behind themselves.

Jim Sundance stood there staring at it for a moment. He had won, yes, but it was true that he felt no sense of triumph. This was a battle without end. Still, a year's grace, two, was better than none at all.

He owed himself a drink. Going to the table, he poured it. Tossing it off, he thought that anyhow his man in Washington had enough money to operate on for a while. Cavanaugh's money, the reward for Sundance's scalp.

And that, at least, would buy him some time for something besides the grim and endless warfare. With the northern Cheyennes somewhere along the Yellowstone, a woman waited for him, and guns were being oiled and lances sharpened for the fall buffalo hunt. He poured another drink, went to the window, flung it open.

The reek of stockyards, the stench of cattle,

poured in upon him. Sundance swallowed hard, shut the window again, and had his second drink. Then, hastily, he began to pack his gear, determined to take a train tonight, all at once very hungry for the sight of endless rolling plains, the smell of lodge fires, his woman's body, and the clean wind blowing fresh and free as he rode into it with a good horse under him.

THE END

H